PRAISE FOR PETE KRAMER'S CHESAPEAKE BAY MONSTERS

"You get much more than you realize you're getting."

— Fantasy for the Ages

"The unique storyline was engaging and had me guessing until the end."

— Reader's Choice

"These characters were really good. I really enjoyed our three main characters."

— David's Book Reviews

"A heck of a fun read."

— Talking Story

"Go in blind and tell me this isn't a Banger!"

— Beard of Darkness Book Reviews

"A fantastic mer-beast creature feature that also has twists, turns, and some dark humor to round it all out. Highly recommend!"

— Horror Reads

THE SKYMAN'S LEGACY

Pete Kramer

ISBN: 979-8-9884513-2-7 (Paperback)
ISBN: 979-8-9884513-3-4 (Ebook)
LCCN: 2024926680

Interior Book Design/ Formatting: Tamara Cribley, The Deliberate Page
Cover Design: Eric Labacz, Eric Labacz Design

Any references to historical events, real people, or real places are used fictitiously. All characters, incidents, and dialogue are drawn from the author's imagination and are not to be construed as real.

AK Publishing
23 Leigh Drive
Smyrna, DE 19977

This one is for Leo for giving
away what I value most.

PART ONE

What Goes Up...

Within sight of the Mupai coast in the Bay of Mensai, the Gilded Saaktopas towers three thousand feet above the crashing waves. The infamous *cloud-reacher* is the first, and only, such habitat constructed above water and the smallest known *reacher* at roughly one mile in diameter.

Over three hundred Marabeshi died during its construction…

ONE

CAL BANNON GRIPPED THE ROUGH handrail of the creaking metal bridge and made his way back across towards Raja. His companion had remained on the radio platform, where he stood trading glances between Cal and the distant waves beating against the base of the tower.

"How far down is it?" The Marabeshi's normally tanned knuckles had turned white, his hands clenched around the strap of his patched green backpack.

Cal clanked back the final few steps and grabbed the meaty part of Raja's clublike arm. "Far enough that you don't want to fall off."

Cal shared Raja's trepidation, but a skyman who was afraid of heights was a bit like a doctor who was afraid of blood. He fixated on the adjacent maintenance platform, directing the Marabeshi back across the walkway, and only released his hold on him after they'd stepped onto it.

"Give me the number five." Cal kneeled next to the control panel. His muscles tightened as Raja's shadow fell across him.

"How long will this take?" Raja asked in quivering breaths.

"A moment."

"You're sure the woman procured the correct code?"

Raja laid the rubber handle of the rivet turner on Cal's shoulder, and he took it without answering.

She always does.

Cal removed the outer panel, exposing the mild electrical heat pulsing inside. Mag had given him three codes to try. He slipped in his right hand, stretching his fingers until he found the edge of the combination dials.

They should be set to 0-0-0. If they weren't, this was going to be over before it even started.

"Faster, Sand Face."

First combination: 4-4-9.

Cal turned each dial with the tip of his middle finger, then waited.

Shit.

"It is a trick," Raja said. "They know we're here. Busain cuts heads off, Sand Face."

Intelligence reports indicated Busain tended to reserve that special honor for card cheats, but it wasn't something Cal wanted to find out for sure. "If it was a trap, they wouldn't have let us get this far," he said, rotating the dials for the second code. "Relax."

2-8-5.

Shit. Shit.

Raja rocked on his toes. "We need to go."

Cal shushed him with his free hand and spun the dials again.

Shit… shit…

The door groaned as it lifted off the outer latch.

Cal took a breath. "That's it."

He pushed into the darkened corridor. Raja shimmied inside behind him, grabbing hold of the closing door.

"We should wedge it open."

Cal pulled Mag's handkerchief map from his back pocket and flapped it open. "No need. It's unlocked now."

"But we need the light."

Cal looked up from the diagram. The sunlight from the doorway only stretched a few feet into the narrow hallway before being smothered in blackness. He stepped back and took hold of Raja's wrist. "Watch."

He peeled the Marabeshi's hand away from the heavy door, and it whistled shut. Recessed lights flickered on, illuminating the gritty steel walls.

"Come on." Cal returned his attention to the map and started forward, Raja shuffling behind him.

"How far is it?"

Cal traced his fingers along the diagram. "Should be about fifteen yards past that short flight of stairs ahead. A left at the fork after that."

The door for the Maintenance Section E Machine Room was where Cal was expecting it, marked with blocky, crimson Marabeshi characters.

"We cannot enter here," Raja said, pointing to a blue wire that ran to a small junction box above the frame. "The door is wired. There's no way through."

"That's not where we're going." Cal pointed to the grille next to Raja's sandaled feet. A few wisps of steamy air rose up from the vent in swirling curls.

"You are not serious."

Cal shrugged.

"I will not fit."

Cal looked him up and down. "Sure, you will."

"We cannot remove it." Raja pointed to the dusty, bare frame. "There are no fasteners on this side."

"In your bag, front pocket," Cal held his fingers three inches apart. "This big. Green handle."

Raja fished around in the bag and passed over the tool.

Cal had purchased the inverted magnet at an unlicensed bazaar in Kalbaba two years earlier, and he'd been shocked by how often it had come in handy. He extended its adjustable C-shaped tip and passed it between the thin metal wiring at the grille's top corner. The latch scratched against the inside frame and the corner sprang free.

"I still won't fit in there," Raja said, shaking his head.

Cal set the grille to the side. He had no doubt Raja would fit. Besides, now that they were inside, he had even less doubt Raja would run. There was no place to go. Still the Marabeshi was a variable and Cal hated variables. "Get your flashlight."

Raja crouched next to him and clicked on the tubular light. There was little to see, only slick looking panels extending into darkness.

Cal placed his hand on the damp metal. "Ow!"

"Still hot, Sand Face?" Raja asked.

Cal ignored him and shook out his fingers. He retrieved his gloves from the inside pocket of his leather jacket. "Okay, kill the light for now," he said, pulling off the jacket and tossing it in a heap next to the grille. "We won't need it." He slipped on the gloves and started into the shaft and had slithered a few body lengths before hearing the *kwump, kwump, kwump* of Raja coming down behind him.

Take a right at the first junction, Mag had said the night before. *You should be able to see a light after about ten feet.*

"Is this it?" Raja called.

"Yes, towards the light," Cal whispered, adjusting his chafing shoulder holster. "Keep it down."

Cal pulled himself around the bend and, sure enough, there was light ahead of him, passing through another grille. He slid forward and peered through the lattice of wires.

Three more heating ducts dissipated hot air across stacks of grime coated crates stretched out below him. The towering boxes created a haphazard maze across the gymnasium-sized strongroom.

"Can you see it?" Raja whispered behind him.

"Not from here. Pass up your rope."

Raja *kwumped* onto his side and worked off his backpack. "You're sure no one is down there?"

Cal was rarely *sure* of anything. In his business, it was best to hedge your bets.

He unhooked each fastener with his finger and was setting the grille gently to the side as the thick cords of rope came slithering up alongside him.

Cal stuck his head out into the blissfully cool air. He had a much better angle now. He still couldn't see the shelves or any sort of library area, but he could see the top of the vault door at the opposite side of the room. It was shut.

Regulations are the door remains open when anyone is working in the vault other than Busain or his wife, Mag had told him.

"It's clear," he said, and took hold of the rope, pushing himself further out as Raja traded him more slack.

That's interesting.

Running directly above him was an industrial sanitary pipe more than sturdy enough to hold his weight. He'd expected to need Raja to keep hold of the rope and lower him down, but this would make life much easier.

Cal tossed the end of the rope over the pipe, caught it, and worked to hitch it. "There's a place to tie off the line," he whispered back to Raja. "You can head back. Wait for me by the door and don't move."

"No. We leave together, Sand Face."

Mag had warned him about bringing in the outsider. *If I can find someone to bring in for this, and that's a big if, they're going to want a gun.*

Starting his descent, Cal surveyed more of the vault. Still no shelving to be seen on this side. If there was a library or archive, it had to be on the other side. Unless his intel had been wrong…

Bannon, we shouldn't be doing this, Mag had said. *Busain's out of the game.*

He'd smiled at her. *If he's got anything that improves our research in any way, it'll be worth the risk.*

There were no prizes for second place in the sort of race they were in, and they both knew it.

He touched down and had already started off through the crates before Raja's sandals slapped against the tile floor.

"Everything is going perfectly," the Marabeshi said.

"It always is, until it isn't."

Cal made a path through the boxes. Turning a corner, he stopped short, Raja almost running into his back. Raja gasped at the guillotine towering before them, his eyes fixed on the blade resting through the collar. "You see, Sand Face?"

Cal turned away and pressed on. Two more turns and there it was. His heart skipped at the sight of the steel bookshelf embedded into the wall next to the vault door.

That's more like it.

Raja exhaled loudly. "*Scaap re Daap.*"

Cal glanced over his shoulder to see what his companion had found.

Oh no.

The painting was uninspiring up close, about the size and shape of a berthing compartment porthole. Cal had seen it on display in Pantopolis during a traveling show when he'd been a teenager and wondered why it was so renowned. But for many, particularly the Marabeshi, the image of the god with the playful, yellow eyes spoke directly to their souls.

"*Scarishnu…*" Raja murmured

"Don't touch it," Cal said, turning back to the shelving. "We're not here for that." He scanned the uneven spines of the books. His ability to read Marabeshi was rudimentary, but Mag had burned the proper arrangement of characters into his mind. He soon spotted them, inscribed in pale, flaking gold leaf, on the third shelf from the top.

He extended an index finger, hooked it over the soft spine, and pulled the thin, blue book free.

This is it.

"Alright," Cal said. "let's… *what the hell are you doing?*"

Raja pulled a small silver pistol as he sent the contents of his pack skittering across the smooth floor. "Keep your money," he said, sweat trickling down the lines in his face. "Here is my payment." He positioned himself under the painting, sizing it up.

"Like hell."

Raja steadied his gun arm. "If you would not mind placing your weapon on the floor and kicking it away?"

Cal glanced at the vault door. On the other side no less than four *surukhai* would be standing guard. "You won't risk shooting me in here."

Raja shook his pistol impatiently. "Do not be stupid, Sand Face. I do not wish to kill you. Keep your book and the money, but I am taking this."

Cal stuffed the thin journal into the back of his weathered trousers and eased his revolver free of his shoulder holster.

Raja raised a warning hand. "Slowly."

Cal slid his sidearm across the tiles, and the Marabeshi tapped it away with a leather sandal.

"You'll never be able to sell it," Cal said.

Raja shrugged and looked up at the miniature portrait of the deity. "Maybe I do not wish to sell it."

You will.

"Fine," Cal said, turning back towards the heating duct and his way out. "I don't care. Take it."

"Not so fast, Sand Face." Raja clicked back the pistol's hammer. "You stay right there."

Idiot, Cal thought as Raja angled himself under the frame and placed a hand on its lower right corner.

"At least let me take a look at it," Cal said. "You don't know what it's hooked to."

Raja thought a moment and stepped back.

Cal came forward and slid a thumb around the rounded frame where it met the smooth wall. There was no way to see behind without lifting it away. "This is a bad idea."

"We will see," Raja said, waving him away with his pistol.

Cal winced and took several deliberate steps backwards. The Marabeshi manhandled the artwork off the wall, revealing two thin hooks set into the discolored paneling.

Raja gave a toothy grin and stuffed the painting in his pack, flipping the leather flap over the tarnished frame. "Do you know what this is?"

"Trouble," Cal said. "Would you stop pointing that at me?"

"You godless corporatists are all the same."

Mag was never going to let Cal hear the end of this. It wasn't all bad, though. He had the book, and Raja would need him alive to get out of here. He only hoped the oaf knew it.

Raja lowered the pistol twenty degrees and eased down the hammer. Cal let out his breath and set off back to the rope. Raja set down the misshapen bag and climbed up ahead of him, the cord slithering between his legs. He pulled himself inside and the panels groaned as he jostled himself around and poked his head back into the vault. "Now if you wouldn't mind attaching the bag to the rope."

Cal tied the line around the pack's arm straps. He hadn't served on an airship in years, but if there was one thing every skyman could do, it was tie a strong knot.

Raja hauled up the pack, gripped the straps and pulled it inside the shaft.

Cal glared up at him. "Now drop the rope."

Alarms blared from everywhere around him and Raja's eyes went wild. "Sorry, Sand Face."

The rope fell, coiling snakelike on the floor. Somewhere behind Cal, the vault door banged open.

Cal whipped around, looking for a hiding spot. He gripped the lid of the nearest crate and pulled.

Nailed.

Shit.

Shit… shit… shit…

The steel walls echoed with thundering footsteps and garbled shouts in Marabeshi. Cal jumped away, ducked behind a short stack of crates and peeked over.

Five armed *surukhai* stood under the open duct, pointing up at it and barking at each other in their guttural tongue.

Cal slipped away into the labyrinth, running backwards on the balls of his feet.

"*Scarishnu gala.*"

Cal halted at the sound of the voice up ahead. Peering around a dusty, coffin-shaped box, he saw a *surukhai* standing under the round, faded section of paneling where the portrait had hung. The *surukhai* took off out of sight, and Cal swept his eyes over the ground. He spotted his revolver lying where Raja had kicked it, its wooden grip raised against the rim of a bronze floor drain. If he could…

"*SCARISHNU GALA!*"

There was no time. Cal shoulder-barged the door, crashing through it harder than he'd intended, sliding across the waxy playing cards that had been scattered across the floor of the vault's outer room.

His gaze locked on a sign, printed above the adjacent door in both Marabeshi and Basic: Observation Ring.

Okay. The west corridor is not that far. And the west corridor has elevators.

I can make it.

Cal half-tripped into the door's panic bar and spilled out into blinding white light. He blinked up at the reflective dome overhead, eyes struggling to adjust. A black-and-white blur was coming at him, and Cal grabbed hold of a wad of a dinner jacket to keep from falling.

"Kwan ape!" The bells dangling from the four corners of the man's flat-topped *barishe* jangled wildly as he ripped his dinner jacket away.

Cal held up his hands in apology, then raced off down the bright, window-lined corridor.

Hundreds of dark carpet tiles stretched ahead of him, at the center of each a familiar golden eye.

As if there weren't enough people looking at him, without the gaze of Scarishnu.

The whole passageway was littered with suspicious and alarmed tourists, diverting from the picturesque views of the pleasure airships sailing in from the arid Mupai coast.

"Bow baha!" came a distant shout behind him.

Cal slid to a stop at a pair of majestic red-leather doors at the end of the walkway. His heart was hammering in rhythmic counterpoint to the jazzy beat thrumming on the other side.

Where the hell are the elevators?

This wasn't the West Corridor.

I'm on the wrong side of the casino.

"Bow baha!"

Cal burst through the doors, into a smoky gaming room. A few players looked up from their cards and may have started shouting. It was hard to hear anything over the small band playing ahead of him on a sparkling stage. An expansive window behind it looked out on the open sky beyond.

da... na

do... dee... do... dee

Cal recognized the tune as *The Stranger Named Saint Podlick*, but the singer—a woman with towering golden hair who moved between the players as flames erupted from strategic points around the stage—had substituted exotic Marabeshi lyrics over the melody.

Whatever.

Cal ran past and the eyes of the saxophone players followed him as they blew out blustery notes.

His focus was more on the stitch growing under his ribcage and metastasizing as he sprinted across the lounge's blood-red carpeting.

His hip banged the edge of a card table, and he stumbled, crashing into a stiff cigarette girl. Her tray tipped over, and cartons of smokes scattered everywhere.

"*Boorkh*," Cal sputtered, hoping it sounded like the Marabeshi word for *sorry*, but the blank look in the girl's eyes told him it didn't matter. Like all *gulars,* she was someplace else entirely.

He staggered towards a set of saloon doors, slamming through them into a clattering kitchen heavy with pepper and garlic fumes. He slid around a pair of *gulars* meticulously slicing thick cuts of lamb. Neither paused to look up as he burst out onto the Saaktopas' adjacent observation ring.

Ahead of him, a shiny bronze blur materialized into a bank of lift doors.

Not far now.

His side was screaming from the stitch now, and he collapsed against the wall and punched the 'up' button.

The only sounds were his pounding heart, ragged breathing, and the distant thrum of guitars. He looked back the way he'd come. Except for a distant couple taking in the Bay of Mupai at the far side of the walkway, he was alone.

The indicator above the lift doors showed the car was descending towards him.

Let this thing be empty.

The doors rattled apart, and a gentle melody of jingling bells spilled out. The yellow eyes stitched into the lift's carpet had been worn to the shade of overripe bananas.

Now we're talking.

Cal stepped aboard and thumbed the top button on the gold-trimmed panel. The doors closed and he rested his cheek against the cool glass of the elevator's wall, watching the casino level fall away.

Nugging Marabeshi.

Outside the lift, a triple-decker yacht was making its final approach towards the docking platforms, its ballooned green and gold sail, releasing a long trail of pinkish lift gas.

The lift shuddered to a stop, the doors clunking open. Cal checked the sign facing him as he stepped off the lift.

Docking Platforms 11-20 →

He was going to make it.

He imagined the sideways smirk Mag would have waiting for him when he stepped aboard the *Equinox*, notebook full of formulas in hand. She would no doubt be on deck now, hand wrapped around the blast valve of the brassite burner, ready to fill the sail and lift off.

He jogged onto the upper deck, the wind whipping at his loose-fitting shirt. Most newer cloud-reachers were fitted with a dome, but these original designs were different. Despite the wind-break walls built along the perimeter, the gales on the deck were strong enough to toss a man over the side… and sometimes did exactly that. He had no desire to linger.

The approaching yacht still floated twenty feet off the platform, its sail rippling above a chrome-plated pilothouse.

The reacher's deck was deserted.

Where is everyone?

Inside the airship's pilothouse, Cal could make out its two occupants watching him wide-eyed and slack-jawed.

"Where you going, Sandy?"

Shit.

Name: Aruhla Busain

Aliases: Multiple. Most are variations
                         of the Marabeshi words for
                         'chemist' or 'apothecary'.

Age/Description: Marabeshi male, approx. 40 years old.
                         Brown skin. Expensive false teeth.

Comment: For many years, Busain was an
                         instrumental scientist of the UMT.
                         He is widely assumed to have fallen
                         out of favor with current leadership.
                         Purchased the Saaktopas cloud-
                         reacher approximately four years
                         ago through the Marabeshi state
                         bazaar. Source of funds unknown.

Charlton Pond,

Head of Mupai Division, Sky Fleet Special Section

TWO

CAL WAS TAKING SHUFFLING STEPS towards something he vaguely recognized.

A stage.

The blissful darkness surrounding him seemed to bleed away as he focused on the blinding spotlight, trained on… a blonde. She wore a shimmering gold dress, tight over her hips. He remembered her voice: a husky Smithon accent, peculiarly mixed with exotic Marabeshi lyrics.

Sausage-sized fingers dug into Cal's upper arms.

"Hold it, Sandy. She's almost done."

Where the hell am I?

They'd dosed him with something—some kind of mutated *altim*. If he hadn't been treated with the inhibitor for the drug, he'd be as docile as the *gular*. Luckily, he still had control, but that hadn't stopped his growing headache from stretching down to his shoulders.

He opened his eyes and found his vision had mostly cleared save for the occasional explosion of reddish, purple spots.

The woman reared back her head and finished the catchy number with an excruciating, eternal note that her Marabeshi backing band matched and held. Each of them wore a *barishe* with bells hanging from its short brim that rang when they moved.

Cal's pulsing headache stretched down to his lower back. *How could they stand wearing those bells all the time?*

The singer made a deep bow and sashayed off the stage, making her way into the cluster of warmly lit tables. Through the wide window behind her, Cal could see the twinkling red and white navigational lights of passing ships in the twilight.

The heavy behind Cal punched him forward. "Keep moving. Follow the girl."

They slid through the gaming room towards an elevated VIP area. The woman hiked up her lounge dress and climbed the short flight to the central platform.

Cal found his eyes level with her smooth legs and allowed himself to dwell on them until she stopped at one of the tables. The Marabeshi sitting behind it looked familiar, and when the singer lifted the corner of his *barishe* and whispered into his ear, Cal foggily recognized him as Aruhla Busain.

Busain permitted the singer to plant a light kiss on his cheek before turning his attention to Cal. Lowering the cigarette he was smoking, he smiled a too-white, too-perfect smile. The gorilla-shaped man seated to his left leaned back in his chair and unfastened the top button of his dinner jacket.

"I hope you enjoyed the show," Busain said, knocking some ash into a shallow crystal bowl. "Miss Thomas, this is Callum Bannon. Have you heard of him? One of your countrymen. He's becoming quite the celebrity."

The singer tucked a strand of hair behind her ear and smiled. "Allie Thomas."

Another thrust shoved Cal into the back of the chair opposite Busain.

"Is he alright?" Allie said, pulling her hand back. "A bit underdressed, isn't he?"

Cal looked down at his attire. His shoulder holster was gone, leaving him with only his sweat-stained, ivory-colored shirt and tan work pants. "Forgot my suit."

Busain gave a smoky, coughing laugh. "Mister Bannon forgot to come through customs as well, it seems." He reached around Allie's hips and tugged her close. "I assume he's here to beg my forgiveness."

Allie's brow creased in confusion. "What's wrong with him?"

Cal straightened his back, pulled the chair out from the table, and planted himself in it as casually as he could. "That's a good question," he said. "It's nice to see another friendly face at a flathead bar."

Busain flicked his cigarette into the flame burning low at the center of the table, his perfect smile retreating. "Now that's not very nice. Perhaps you've had a bit too much to drink?"

Cal shook his head.

Settling himself deeper into his chrome chair, Busain picked up a two-pronged roasting fork with an extended neck. He rotated it gently with his fingers and clicked the back of his teeth with his tongue, before waving the fork like a baton to one of the dozen *gular* waiters standing like statues along the edge of the platform. There were always plenty of them around in these types of places. In Marabesh, you were either rich or *gular.*

"I left instructions that you receive a *welcome cocktail,*" Busain said. "Did it not agree with you?"

Whatever they'd given him, Cal couldn't remember much past reaching the deck, but the sky through the window wasn't too dark yet, so he couldn't have been out long.

A dead-eyed *gular* waiter, his white robe secured with three black fasteners the size of fists, slid forward. He was holding a gold-rimmed flat dish loaded with glistening pinkish cube. He placed it under Busain's chin, bowing low before scurrying away.

Busain speared one of the wet chunks of meat. "No thoughts, Mister Bannon? Tell me, what did you think of it?" He extended his fork into the flame in the center of the table, and a thick dollop of fat sizzled off the lamb.

The savory aroma brought Cal back to his senses a little. "I think… it's giving me a headache."

"That is troubling to hear," Busain said. He looked over Cal's shoulder at his escort. "How long has it been in his system?"

The tree-like man hovering over Cal said, "A few minutes."

"It seems like you're busy," Allie said, stepping away from the table. "I should go."

"Don't move," Busain said, lifting his charred chunk of flesh from the flame. He popped it into his mouth. "What did he have on him?" he asked between chews.

"He had this when we picked him up" the thug said, sliding the thin journal across the cream tablecloth, "and a hand-drawn map of the maintenance section. We also found a gun in the vault. An Enforcer P.90. Sky Fleet standard issue."

Busain set aside his fork and picked up the book. He fanned through its pages. "I see," he said, still chewing. "This makes better sense. I'm a great fan of yours, Mister Bannon. I was disappointed at the idea you were a petty thief." He returned the book to the table and retrieved his fork before stabbing another slick cube.

Cal's hearing was settling into something close to normal, the tinkling bells and clinking dinnerware below the elevated VIP area seeming loud and clear now.

"Who is he?" Allie said.

Busain ignored her and his bushy eyebrows narrowed on Cal. "The man who smuggled out Doctor Sushain would not stoop so low as to try to steal Scarishnu."

Cal held up his hands in a pose of ignorance. "Who's Doctor Sushain?" His palms felt damp, but the fact that he could feel anything was good. He stretched his fingers, testing their dexterity.

"I wouldn't want to claim credit for that one if I were you either. Quite a *messy* operation that turned out to be."

Cal had done what he had to do. It was a war.

"Play games if you like, it will make little difference. But I would like to know if it was your intention to rob me of my artwork."

"It wasn't."

"Good. I wouldn't want to lose faith in the supposed nobility of the Confederacy. And I do not like the thought of dining with thieves. It is not civilized." Busain put the tip of the fork to his lips and pulled off the final blackened hunk of meat. "Would you have guessed that my wife didn't want me to install a transmitter into Scarishnu's frame? She told me it was a waste of credits."

"Who's Scarishnu?" Allie asked.

Busain turned towards her. "Strange that anyone should visit my lovely country and not have heard of Scarishnu, my dear. Some would say such ignorance should be punishable." He held up the book, waved it at Cal. "So, this is why you came?"

"Yes."

Allie craned her neck to see the slim volume. "What is it?"

"I think you know, my dear." Busain placed his fork neatly across his plate and drew a satin napkin, cleaning each greasy finger down to the knuckle. "It's one of my old journals. A *very old* one."

So you say, Cal thought. Even if Busain had hit a wall with the formulas, any research could help. It was a race to stay ahead of the *altim* variations. One the Confederacy couldn't afford to lose.

"I keep it for… *sentimental* reasons," Busain said. "I hadn't realized intelligence gathering at Special Section had degraded to this level of desperation. I'm *retired* from my government, Mister Bannon. Have been for some time."

"Seems like that's going well for you," Cal said. "Real nice place…"

Allie put a slender hand to her mouth. "This really doesn't sound like any of my business."

Busain leaned forward. "Is it any of her business, Mister Bannon?"

"No."

"Why don't you tell me how many accomplices are here with you?"

"Just me and the jackal who took your pretty painting."

Busain looked at the enforcer over Cal's shoulder. "What dose did you give him? It does not seem to be working."

"We didn't want him to lose consciousness."

Busain nodded. "I see. Bring him a bit more. Some for Miss Thomas as well."

"You can't be serious," Allie said, tripping over her feet in her hurry to back away. "I don't know this guy."

"Mister Singh."

A thick arm shot out from the table and the gorilla-shaped man locked his hand around the singer's wrist.

Busain indicated the chair next to Cal. "Please sit down, Miss Thomas."

"But I don't know him!"

"We'll soon find out if that's true."

"It is," Cal said. "I don't know her."

Busain wagged a finger at him. "Now, now, Mister Bannon. A little mouse told me you worked with a woman. A very pretty woman. My squeaking friend also shared a rumor that she's even smarter than you."

"But I'm not smart!" Allie screamed.

Busain coughed with laughter. "That's true, you don't seem to be… but you *are* the only Smithon woman here. And I am afraid you are lovely, my dear."

Cal focused on turning his head. It still felt heavy, but his neck had loosened a little. He forced himself to focus on the wide window behind the stage. What looked like the top of an inflated sail was passing nearly close enough to brush the glass.

Focus.

"Now, Miss Thomas," Busain said as his simian bodyguard forced her into the chair beside Cal, "it will make this much easier if we can remain civilized. May I offer you something to eat?" He waved over another *gular*. "We have spiced cake. It's quite delicious."

Allie licked her red lips and shook her head.

"Let me at least show you what your options are," Busain said, as the *gular* scurried forward.

The servant carried a flat tray domed with an ornate metal cloche and placed it in front of Cal without bowing. Busain leaned forward, and his shadow stretched across the table. "How many are here with you at the Saaktopas?"

"One," Cal said.

Busain lifted the dome.

Allie screamed as Busain gave Raja's mop of soiled hair a squishy tap. The thief's head had been placed neatly on his dismembered hands.

Cal straightened his back. "Is it too late for the cake?"

Busain chortled and knocked on the table. "We picked him up inside one of the maintenance sections. It seems he had locked himself inside."

Cal shrugged. "Sounds like he should have kept the door wedged open."

"I think he would agree."

"Would you mind putting the lid back, please?"

"Squeamish?"

Cal forced a smile and shook his head. It was easier to move now. "No, it's just that Marabeshi cuisine has never agreed with me."

Busain laughed freely and settled back into his chair. "I like you, Mister Bannon," he said. "You're a good sport. It will be a shame to kill you if it comes to it."

Cal's temples pulsed. "I don't know this woman." His hand slipped under the table, and he cupped the outer edge with his fingertips.

Now or never, Mag.

Another *gular* was clambering up the stairs, this one holding a tray with a mound of powder at its center.

Altim.

Busain waved the *gular* forward. "Mister Singh, start with Miss Thomas."

The back window exploded; shards of glass blown in on the screaming wind.

With one hand, Cal snatched Busain's fork and stabbed blindly over his shoulder, feeling the prongs sink into the thug behind him. With the other hand, he flipped the table onto Busain's lap.

Cal spun and pulled the fork from the screaming man's stomach before turning towards Busain. The Marabeshi's dinner jacket had caught fire on the table's burning centerpiece. Singh leapt onto his howling master, attempting to smother the flames.

Cal pivoted towards the stairs down from the VIP level. Beyond the screaming mob of guests, the hull of a ship filled the frame of the shattered window before sinking out of view.

He clamped onto Allie's bony upper arm and dragged her down the stairs after him.

"Where are we going?" she yelled over the howling wind. Her feet began to lock up as she realized Cal was pulling her up onto the stage, toward the window. The rushing air tugged at them as they closed the distance to the opening.

"Are you nuts!"

He shrugged, let go of her arm, and pushed her out.

Allie hit the deck of the *Equinox* a second before him, rolling heavily into a bulkhead.

Mag glanced down at her as she pulled the chrome-plated wheel to the left. "Who's she?"

"Who am I!?" Allie screamed. "Who am I!?"

"Does she have any other volume?" Mag said, leaning between the rims of the wheel.

"I'm sure she does," Cal said. The heat of the lift gas inflating the sail above him warmed his skin as he pulled himself to his feet. "She's a singer."

"Of course she is."

Allie crawled across the deck and grabbed a wad of Cal's pant-leg. "Who the hell are you people?"

"Didn't anyone tell her this is a rough part of town?" Mag asked. She pressed the elevator lever forward and the airship dropped, leaving behind a trail of red mist.

Cal couldn't help noticing the singer's pale cheeks had turned an enticing shade of pink. "It's okay, you're safe now. We're heading—"

"Bannon!" Mag shouted distantly. "Get down."

Something punched into him. Hard.

The wind whistled in his ears as the ship's polished wooden gunwale rushed up to meet him.

Cal's eyes flickered open.

The gentle rocking might have sent him back to sleep, but his shoulder was on fire. He reached up and touched it, his fingertips brushing coarse bandages.

As his vision adjusted, he realized he was in a berth on the *Equinox*. The bulkheads were rumbling in the wind, and faint light was coming down the bronze spiral stairs that corkscrewed up to the deck.

He'd made it.

Never a doubt.

He shimmied himself into a sitting position and pushed aside a bowl of towels on the bedside table. The clock that usually sat there was missing; Mag had likely moved it while she stitched him up.

Someone was snoring rhythmically. He peered across to the opposite side of the cabin and saw a woman lying on a low cot. Allie was asleep, her slender arm draped across her forehead.

Cal eased himself out of bed and padded to the connected washroom. He relieved himself, then shuffled up the spiral stairs to the deck. The cold air sent his injured shoulder into a tantrum.

"How are you feeling?" Mag said, the breeze whipping at her strawberry-colored hair. She locked off the wheel and bent down to pick up a checkered blanket that had been folded near her feet.

Cal indicated his shoulder. "I think someone shot me."

"Someone did." She moved in close and looked up at him with pale blue eyes as she flipped the scratchy blanket around his neck. "Right after you jumped out the window with the blonde lounge singer in the tight dress."

"What was I supposed to do?"

She touched his forehead with the back of her hand. "You hit your head too."

"And they gave me one of their *altim* variations."

Mag's eyebrow's arched upward.

"I'm fine. Whatever it was didn't work."

"We'll run some blood tests. You might not remember if it worked or not."

"Trust me, it didn't. But maybe we'll be able to learn something from it." He slid beneath the warm inflated sail and leaned against the ship's mast.

They were flying low, no more than thirty feet above a sea of slate roofs. "We're in Sanland," he said. It was thousands of miles from home, but the shared culture and architecture bred warm familiarity. "How long have I been out?"

"Almost nine hours," Mag said. "We'll be in Anchor Bay by the time the sun comes up. They're going to take you as soon as we get there. Get you to a proper hospital."

He'd slept through the night. *It's tomorrow already.*

He turned to Mag and smiled. "Happy birthday."

"Bannon?" Mag's face lit up. "You remembered."

"Of course." Cal said, pushing off the heavy guilt that settled on him. What he hadn't remembered was to buy her a present. He moved to the railing and watched the houses and trees roll below them. "That's Rowertuch Bridge," he said, pointing. "It's huge."

"It's a pretty city," she said. Beyond the bridge, were two shadowy half-constructed cloud-reachers. The new designs wouldn't be solely indoor habitats with limitless wind energy. They would have buildings and structures built directly onto the deck, protected by a dome. True cities in the sky.

But even with the promise of limitless power and a protective dome, Cal couldn't imagine living on one, so high and confined. It was bad enough so many Confederate agencies had transferred their operations to them.

"We should go have a look around Rowertuch before we head home," Cal said. "Pick up some souvenirs."

"There won't be time. I'm shipping out on the *Briar* tomorrow… well today. You are too, if you're cleared to travel." The wind pitched the ship to port and Mag returned to the helm and adjusted the ship's angle. "But that reminds me. I picked something up for you back in Marabesh."

"You found time for shopping?"

"I managed a quick stroll through the bazaar level. I think you'll like it." She dug into her knickerbockers and pulled out a diamond-shaped keychain. She dropped it into his palm.

It was a rendering of an old single-sailed airship floating towards a distant horizon. An inscription was engraved into the thick copper:

Commemorating the Maiden Voyage of the S.S. Secret Dream
15th Rotation, The Rainy Season, 1410 OS

"How much was this?"

"The vendor pretended he didn't speak Basic when we got talking about price, but it wasn't that bad once he saw I had Confederate credits."

Cal admired the tag another moment then tucked it into his pocket. "Well now I feel terrible."

She stepped around the helm and touched his arm. "Then make it up to me."

"Next assignment. No matter what, I'll have something for you. Something special."

She laughed and pushed him away. "We'll be lucky if we get a next assignment. There's going to be hell to pay when we get back." She retook the shaking wheel. "How did we know Busain had a journal?"

Cal looked at her, confused. "You know why."

"I know I know why," she said. "I'm practicing for the questions we're going to get asked at our debriefing."

Cal nodded, understanding. "We had a reliable informant. And there *was* a journal."

"An old one."

Cal's face twisted in annoyance. "She told you about that."

"Oh, yes. Allie the singer was very chatty."

"Well, we didn't know it wasn't important. If Marabesh strikes one of the Prakesh islands, free travel into Mupai will become impossible. That made it a risk worth taking."

"Let's just hope you didn't start a fire we can't put out."

What was wrong with her? "The fire has already started," he said. The Marabeshi population problem was real. Their empire was expanding too fast. Soon they would need to start looking outside of their population for *gulars*. The members of their voting class would demand it.

And even if the Marabeshi didn't invade Prakesha soon, the Heilish likely would. The world was a powder keg ready to explode.

Mag frowned. "Bannon… don't you want to be in one of those houses down there?"

Cal looked over the side. "You want to move to Sanland?"

"No, not Sanland. I mean maybe… but in a house…"

"I live in a house."

"Bannon… come on. I mean a house with kids and pets."

"I have a pet."

"It's a fish." Mag thrust a hand to her hip. "Don't you ever just want to… ?"

She lost the words. Stepping away from the helm, she gripped his wrist. "You were almost killed today. Don't you want to have something that's at least reminiscent of a normal life?"

"This isn't normal?"

"You're crazy if you think what we did here is going to just blow over. If they drum us out of the service, you won't have a choice about settling down."

Cal smiled. "No chance. They need us. We'll be back out there as soon as I'm healed up. Promise."

Patient Information:

Name: Callum Bannon

Age: 32

Sex: Male

Rank: Commander

Assignment: Formally special projects
                   (temporarily assigned to
                   Pantopolis Academy).

Summary Evaluation:

Patient has established himself as a dedicated
defender of corporate values, though it is
my finding that this dedication may border on
obsession. This condition is not uncommon among
veterans of Special Section, as most assets
have, by design, very few social connections.

Despite his background, the patient
displays clear signs of becoming a risk to
himself and/or to the confederacy.

It is my recommendation that the board make his
temporary reassignment from field work permanent.

                    ~ Dr. Myra Tishner, Associate Director
                           of Psychology, Sky Fleet Medical

THREE

"CAL, YOU'VE BEEN IN HERE all day." Allie wandered up to a bolt of elaborately patterned fabric and rubbed the material between her fingers. "I'm bored."

Cal pretended not to hear her, focusing instead on the shirt he was attempting to sew.

Dr. Tishner, the company psychologist, had recommended he take up a hobby—*"It'll take your mind off things"*—and sewing had made sense at the time. Cal's clothes were consistently battered when he was on assignment, and, if he had to select a hobby, it seemed logical to pick one his father wouldn't approve of.

"Come on," Allie said, gripping his shoulders. "I'm more fun than a needle and thread."

While that had been true a few weeks earlier, Cal was beginning to enjoy the quiet solitude of creating—or attempting to create—something resembling a garment. So much so he'd lost track of time: checking the oak-framed clock on his desk, he was alarmed at how long he'd been working. "I have to go to the office."

Allie put her hands on her hips. "The office?"

He sidled around her, and his hip knocked against a low bookcase, dislodging a smattering of books and wobbling an empty fishbowl.

"So, you're just going to leave me here?" she said, following him into his cluttered dining room. She skirted a tower of mismatched journals and manuals, getting ahead of Cal as he made for the back door in the kitchen. She leaned against the baby-blue fridge, blocking his way. "I've been waiting all day, Cal."

Allie was supposed to have left five days earlier—her second planned departure. Today, she really would be going, and Cal didn't want to be here when she found out. Bringing her home with him hadn't been all bad: she had insisted on helping him recuperate, and the first few weeks with her in Pantopolis had been pleasant enough. But she was bored easily, messy, and overly chatty, so while one month was great, two months had been grating. Three months was a nightmare.

She had repeatedly agreed to leave, saying her father would come to collect her, but two nights ago, when he had failed to appear a second time, the truth had come spilling forth.

"I don't know why my father isn't here yet" she had said. "Maybe I could stay a bit longer." That had turned into, "It's for the best. You need me."

Finally, she had admitted, "I haven't called him."

Cal placed a call to her home the next morning from his office at the academy. Her supposedly dead mother answered before putting her irate father on the line. An awkward phone call to be sure, but one he was glad he'd made.

Now Mr. Thomas was due in a couple of hours, and Cal wasn't about to tempt fate by hanging around until he got here.

"Please, Cal," Allie whined. "Just stay home today. We can do whatever you want." She hooked her thumbs under the straps of her nightgown. "We could play, House? You can rip this up and sew it back together for me later."

"I… look… they need me at the academy. I can't just not show up. Those kids depend on me. I'm behind on papers to grade and I left them all at the office. I need to go back."

"I thought you were a substitute?"

"And a damn good one," he said, hopping on one leg as he pulled on one of his loafers. "What do you want me to do? This place isn't free. I have to work."

"Are you coming right back?" Allie stepped closer, whispering in his ear. "I thought we could go out tonight."

Cal took two steps back into the cluttered living room. "You thought that, huh?"

"What's that supposed to mean?" She scowled. He had seen the look before: the displaced singer was already scanning the kitchen crockery for something to throw. She grabbed the thin handle of a cream-colored pot and lifted it over her head.

Cal put up his hands and began circling towards the door. "I'll be home as soon as I can, okay?"

She lowered the pot. "Do you promise?"

I can't be in this house with you anymore.

"Absolutely, I promise."

Allie was presenting herself for a kiss as he stepped outside, the storm door clicking shut behind him.

He set off across the garden, the chirping of insects sang a sweet song before a sharp slap cut through the chilly air.

"Hell of a lot of bugs down here." A tall lanky man, all bones and angles, stood up from his spot on Cal's garden bench. He wore a gray trench coat and matching hat and carried a folded over issue of *Weird Menace Magazine* under his arm. He was rubbing the back of his neck where something had bitten him.

"Patterson?"

"Quite the uhm… *lady* you've got in there," Patterson said, smoothing his bristled mustache.

"You heard some of that?"

"Only a bit, Commander. I didn't want to interrupt. But she's very…"

"Loud," Cal said, extending his hand. "She's very loud. How's your wife?"

"Beth." Patterson forced a smile and took his hand. "She's good, Commander. So's the boy."

Cal didn't know he had any kids. "If you don't mind, could we walk and talk?" he said, taking Patterson's arm. "Why are you here?"

The lanky man slapped away another insect with his magazine. "How can you stand it down here, sir?"

"I'm afraid of heights," Cal said, noting a particularly vicious pink welt forming on Patterson's neck. "I think they like you."

"Since I've had the altim inhibitor, the bugs have been relentless whenever I come down from Brunswick, Commander."

"I take it we're heading up there then?"

"Unfortunately, not, sir. The admiral wants to see you."

"Which one?"

"Well… *your* admiral, Commander."

I knew it. Cal tried to conceal his satisfaction. "Are you sure you've got the right guy?"

"He was very specific, sir."

"You talked to him yourself?"

Patterson's Adam's apple bobbed up and down as he nodded. "Briefly. We're stretched pretty thin at the moment. Most assets above level five are on assignment."

That would explain why Patterson was here at all. He was a cypher analyst, not the sort of man to be sent to pick him up. But still a man with an advanced clearance.

"What's going on?"

Patterson rubbed the back of his neck nervously. "I'm not sure, sir. But the admiral seemed *anxious* to speak with you."

The old man forbade most exterior lights near the manor but there was still a single floodlight allowed near the main gate. The skyman sitting in the gatehouse was using it to read a book. He looked up as the sedan approached and jerked to a halt.

Patterson rolled down the driver's window. "The admiral is expecting us, Lieutenant."

The skyman bent down to look into the car, and Cal recognized him as Lieutenant Hendricks. "Yes, sir, Mister Patterson. He's out back. I'd stay on his good side, sir. He's…" Hendricks' eyes widened as he recognized Cal.

"Thanks," Cal said, trying not to betray too much amusement. "We'll be able to find him, Lieutenant."

"Yes… yes, sir," Hendricks said, making a frantic salute and returning to the gatehouse.

The weathered gates split open, and Patterson accelerated through. He parked at the top of the manor's horseshoe driveway. "I take it you know the way?"

Cal stepped out in front of the darkened mansion, gripping the car door as he leaned back inside. "You're not coming?

Patterson licked his lips, "Is that a joke, Commander?"

Cal smiled and nodded.

"Well, it's not funny, sir. Not funny at all."

"Relax," Cal said. "This shouldn't take long."

He closed the door and followed a sweet, burning scent down the hedge-lined garden path, which twisted away from the mansion before opening up onto an expansive, meticulously maintained lawn.

Alerted by Cal's footsteps crunching on the gravel, Cal's father sat up on his garden lounge. "That you, Cal?"

"Yes, sir."

A low-burning firepit provided some illumination to the darkened lawn, creating dancing shadows against the waist-high hedgerows. Cal stepped past it, and his father indicated the wicker chair opposite.

"Have a seat."

"Yes, Admiral."

Admiral Bannon hunched forward in his seat, hackles raised. "At ease there, *Commander*. Sit down."

Cal sat stiffly at the edge of the damp chair and rubbed his hands together. It was only a few months earlier that his father had ended their argument with: *"That's Admiral to you."*

"Look, I don't want to fight," his father said, pulling out a dented bronze case from inside his dark-blue Sky Fleet windbreaker. "How's the shoulder?"

Cal shrugged. "It's as fine as it's going to be."

"That's good to hear." His father clicked open the case, slipped out a thick cigar and offered another to Cal. "If you want to get back in your father's good graces, you'll have one."

Cal took the fat, flaky cigar and allowed his father to light it. The old man settled back into his chair as Cal puffed the tobacco to smoldering life.

"Do you see that?" his father said, pointing to the left of the glowing half-moon.

A dark shape with flashing red and green navigation lights blotted out the stars behind it. At low altitude, even in moonlight, Cal could see the mast towering above its inflated sails. The huge central column housed the ship's emergency chute, something few ships of the fleet had. "It's Typhon class."

"Very good, Cal," his father said. "You've always had a sharp eye."

Something was wrong. The old man was never this nice.

"Sharp enough to end this punishment?"

"Your sharpness, eyes or otherwise, has never been your problem," his father said, rolling his cigar between thumb and forefinger. "And it is not a *punishment*. Commander Peinwell tells me you're doing well at the academy. The cadets think highly of you."

"They're good kids, Adm… Sir." Cal still wasn't sure enough of the old man's mood to know what to call him. "But there's a time for teaching and a time for doing,"

His father nodded. "That's true… but only The One gets to decide what time it is."

Cal slumped back into his chair. "Well, I suppose it's good I have you to let me know the time, *sir*."

"I suppose it is." His father took another long draw. "Are you aware of the situation in Aruminia?"

Even temporarily reassigned, Cal still received regular intelligence briefings. Aruminia was in open rebellion, particularly outside the capital. "The rebels haven't begun consolidating around a central leader yet. But a band of two or three joining together would be more than enough to take the capital city and the port. If I had to guess, I'd say that's exactly what will happen over the next few months."

His father nodded. "An apt interpretation. Fortunately, at present it seems the rebels are more than happy fighting amongst themselves."

"Am I going to Aruminia?"

His father's lips twisted as if he'd bitten into a rotting fruit. "I suspect you may be." He narrowed his eyes. "Don't look so pleased with yourself."

Cal forced a neutral expression. "I'm going to need Mag."

"We reactivated Doctor Silverfinch last week."

Cal barely stopped his jaw falling open. He hadn't seen Mag in at least a month. How could she have not mentioned she had been reactivated?

"One of our agents has been killed in Aruminia."

Cal's heart skipped a beat. "Not Mag?"

"No… no," his father said, swiftly raising a hand to wave away the notion. "A new agent, Lieutenant Seymour Michaels. His first assignment. We paired him with Commander Hunt. You're famil-iar with her, of course."

Very familiar, Cal thought. "She was the training officer assigned to me when I was sent to Taplawoo five years ago. *My* first assignment."

"Indeed." The admiral took a deep pull on his cigar. "We've a well-placed asset in Cyio De Reyes. They've been making consis-tent contact with a high-placed Marabeshi banker who has been visiting the city regularly for the past year and a half."

"Anyone I know?"

"You know many Marabeshi bankers?"

"The important ones."

"Vihaan Bulkarni."

Cal nodded. Bulkarni was one of the earliest supporters of President Tumar. "He's a high-level secretary at the Marabeshi Ministry of Finance."

"Bulkarni has been visiting the country to pass escalating bribes to a General Dieglo. From what we understand, the general is an instrumental cog in the coast's air-defense systems."

If Bulkarni was involved, Cal knew he had to be bankrolling something important. And this General Dieglo could give him unrestricted access to shipments entering and leaving the country. "Sounds like a Marabeshi smuggling operation in our hemisphere."

His father nodded. "That's our concern as well."

It was impossible to say what was being smuggled, but whatever it was, Marabesh couldn't be allowed to operate this close to the Confederacy. "Has our asset gotten close?"

"Very close. But then we received a message from Commander Hunt this morning that Michaels' body had been found near the club where the asset works, not far from the port: it's called The White Tbizah. Michaels had been taken out, execution style."

Why the hell would they send a new agent on an assignment this important? "This was Michaels first assignment?"

His father sighed. "Yes." The old man crossed and uncrossed his legs. "That's not all, though. We received a coded telegram from Michaels during a regular check in a few days ago. He'd included a personal duress code in the message. We almost missed it."

"A duress code?" Cal said. "Someone close was moving against him?"

"What's more, Commander Hunt tells us that our asset, Nia Santos, is now missing."

"Has Mag been briefed?"

His father shifted uncomfortably. He lowered his eyes so they wouldn't meet Cal's. "Yes."

"Dad… *Where is she?*"

"I'm sorry, Cal. She was scheduled to report in last night. No word yet."

The cigar slipped from Cal's fingers.

His father stood and ground the cigar into the lush grass with the tip of his brown loafer. "We've had almost constant leaks in the last six months. I needed someone capable and vaccinated, on short notice, who speaks the language and *who wasn't suspended.* We sent Doctor Silverfinch in covertly when we uncovered the duress code."

"I can't believe you sent her down there without me," Cal said. Mag had never been on an assignment alone. *She had never been on any assignment without him.* "When am I leaving?"

"We're partnering you with Commander Rian Tomas. He left Sanland this morning, should be here in three days. You'll…"

"Three days!" Cal said, choking on the words. "Then it's another eighteen hours from here to Aruminia. Have him meet me down there."

"Out of the question."

"I'm leaving tonight."

"You are, are you?" his father said, looking down at him. "Do you know what the Judge Advocate's recommendation was, with regard to your *operation* in Mupai?"

"I'm sure you're going to tell me."

"Sufficed to say he didn't want you reassigned. *He wanted your skin.*"

"You want some more apologies you can have them. Take them all," Cal said, standing up. The old man still stood nearly a full two inches above him. "I made a gamble. It didn't work. The formulas—"

"Were not retrieved and were likely worthless anyway. Everyone knows Busain hasn't been a serious player in the Marabeshi government for over two years."

"Even old research could help."

"And you left evidence. Your company-issued sidearm."

"I won't lose my next one," Cal said, barely containing his anger. "We both know the stakes. The Marabeshi are going to make their move soon. If they had enough brassite mines to fuel a fleet, they'd have made it already. And if they don't go it alone, they'll partner with the Heilish. They don't have the harvesting facilities to keep up with *altim* demand. Invading Sanland will get them all the factories they need, plus a big new workforce as a bonus."

His father studied him.

The Marabeshi's greatest weapon—a totally submissive working population—was becoming their chief liability. If Marabesh didn't find a way to produce more of the drug that kept their slave caste docile, the labor population would tear everything apart. They needed to expand. At some point the dam would break.

The old man sighed. "You going back in the field isn't going to win me any new friends in accounting, I can tell you that. They've been gushing since we took you off the board."

"You want to let the Sanlish be turned into zombies because it's not cost-effective to stop it?"

His father grunted. "I'm not unsympathetic to the situation, but the truth is once things became political there was very little I could do, even for you. Blame for the mess in Mupai needed to be assigned somewhere."

"And you wouldn't want to be seen showing any *favoritism*."

"You're damned right." His father snarled, his breath carrying acrid undertones of tobacco smoke. "Don't underestimate what it took to get you pulled back on active duty for this. An Eagle-class yacht, the *Sky Fish*, is docked at Brunswick. Commander Tomas has already been briefed. You can both leave as soon as he's back."

"I don't need a babysitter."

"Tomas is not a babysitter, although I have no doubt you *do* need one. We've lost Michaels. Doctor Silverfinch is missing, and Commander Hunt is potentially compromised. The board will not let you go alone."

Cal licked his lips, his mind racing. "Let me take Patterson."

"Patterson?" His father gave a humorless laugh. "Patterson is allergic to cotton balls."

"You said yourself, I only need him for a few days."

His father thunked back down into his chair, shoulders slumped. "He's not like you, Cal."

"He's been vaccinated with the inhibitor."

"That won't make him into what he is not. This time next year, near everyone in the Confederacy will have been vaccinated—are you telling me they'll all make good field agents?"

"I'm leaving tonight. With or without him."

His father cocked his head, studying him. "I could stop you."

"You could try."

His father looked unsure, before his expression softened. "The *Sky Fish* is docked at slip sixty-two. We'll get a message to Commander Hunt to rendezvous with you at the port in Cyio De Reyes. Your usual codes have been reactivated and assigned. Your cover will be a photographer for the World Press. Relevant files are already in your cabin safe, with a replacement sidearm, thirteen pocket detonators, a new watch, and three thousand credits."

"A watch?"

"New equipment. Got them in a few days ago. Patterson can show you how it works."

"Understood."

"Cal, take care of him. He's not like you."

"I'll bring him back," Cal said, turning away across the darkened gardens. If anything went wrong, it would be the board's fault for forcing this on him, but yes, he'd keep the cypher man safe.

"He's going to hate this," his father muttered to himself, before calling out, "Oh and one more thing." Cal stopped but didn't look back. "Even discounting what you did on the Saaktopas, it's become nearly impossible to find assignments for you after the mess you left getting Sushain out. You've become too well-known to the opposition. No matter how this job works out… *it's your last one.*"

Subject: Operation Black Orchid,
Appendix B: Antonia Jasmine Hunt A.K.A. Ava Lily

Rank: Commander

Phys. Desc.:   Aged 45, 5 feet 8 inches, 135 lbs.

Fair skin, with a small but distinctive birthmark under her left eye. Natural straight blonde hair, brown eyes. No tattoos or other identifying marks.

Background:

Admitted to Sky Fleet twenty-one years ago as part of Chairman Gilpin's female expansion program. Hunt was the only graduate from the program in that iteration—was immediately assigned to Special Section. Notes from Commodore Hester indicate her assignment was primarily due to issues housing her, however Hunt quickly established herself as a high-performing intelligence officer and skilled interrogator.

She has since served as one of the agency's more decorated training officers. Her notoriety has limited her operational use to low-leverage missions supervising new graduates. Her success in this area has led to further high-performing civilians being recruited directly into Special Section without prior academy training.

See Also: Further details available
                       in Appendices C and F.

FOUR

MY LAST MISSION?

Yeah, right.

Cal watched his reluctant partner struggle with the harness of his jump seat, fighting to get the safety belt's locking mechanism to engage.

Why would Special Section need me when they've got fine specimens like Gordon Patterson?

If Cal was uncertain this would be his last mission, he knew for sure it would be for Patterson.

He's not like you, Cal.

Of course, he wasn't… but Mag couldn't wait three days. She needed help now, and bringing Patterson along was the only way Cal could make that happen.

The overhead intercom buzzed to life. *"Twenty seconds to splash down."*

Cal leaned in. "Do you need a hand with that?"

Patterson scowled. "I've got it, sir," he said, yanking on the belt. "Haven't seen one like this before." He finally snapped the leather strap in place around his narrow midsection, before turning his attention towards the window and the fast-approaching land mass.

Cal hadn't seen much of the cypher clerk before being called to landing stations. As soon as they'd boarded the *Sky Fish*, Patterson had shuffled off to his quarters, wheezing and grunting. He had even missed breakfast. Cal had enjoyed his morning meal with Captain

Ramsay and his first officer: the private pilots were usually private chefs too and kept a well-stocked galley.

"Stand by for impact," Captain Ramsay said over the intercom.

The ship splash-landed, spraying blue-green water down the portlight as Patterson's forehead smacked against it

"Gentlemen of the World Press, welcome to Cyio de Reyes. You are free to disembark."

The *whoosh* of lift gas being sucked back through the reserve regulators echoed through the landing cabin. Patterson ripped off his belt and grumbled back to his stateroom.

Cal unbuckled his own harness and started towards the opposite end of the deck. Patterson had very specifically chosen a room as far away from him as possible.

The *Sky Fish* was large for a civilian craft, capable of comfortably carrying as many as six wealthy couples. From the ground, the wide, flat Eagle-class yachts looked like shiny flying nickels.

Cal's cabin still smelled of charred mission files, burned after reading. The night before, he had spent four hours reviewing the documents before giving in to sleep, finding little he could use to help Mag. Most of the company's intel on Aruminia was months out of date.

As was often the case, the only intelligence he could rely on, he'd have to collect.

Cal unstowed his brown valise and made the short trek to the central deck lift. The fresh briny aroma intensified as he ascended. A pair of tropical sea birds glided overhead, squawking.

He hadn't been back to Aruminia since his first shore leave a decade earlier. It had been crowded with tourists then. For every missing rich foreigner, there now seemed to be a suspicious looking Aruminian wearing a blue police sash and carrying a bolt-action rifle.

At the top of the gangway, Captain Ramsay was just finishing bribing one. He turned back to Cal and shook his hand.

"Mister Coleman, good to see you, sir. How's your friend?"

"Mister Poppin is fine," Cal said with a polite smile. As if on cue, Patterson appeared through the ship's entry port, dragging his over-stuffed luggage and visibly repulsed by the dock's fishy aroma.

"Hurry along, Mister Poppin," Cal called over the salty breeze.

"Sorry Mister… Misssster…"

Cal frowned. "Coleman."

"Of course, sir. Mister Coleman."

"Forget it." Cal took the cypher man's stick-thin arm and led him down the gangway. A weather-beaten fishing skiff was descending into the slip, expelling its lift gas in a red plume as its sail furled against the vessel's single short mast. Cal released Patterson's arm and stepped back as the ship splashed down, sending a wave of water over the cypher man's shoulders.

Cal slipped back and took hold of Patterson's pulsing upper arm. "Look, I know you didn't ask for this," Cal said, "and there's no need for you to come along with me. Why don't you get to the hotel and check us in?"

"Where will you be?"

"Waiting for Miss Lily."

"How will you know her?"

"Oh, Mister Coleman and I are old friends."

Cal turned to see Antonia Hunt lounging against a thick wooden rail overlooking Penoa Bay. Keeping one hand on her flapping wide-brimmed hat, she extended the other to Patterson. "You must be Mister Poppin. I'm Miss Lily."

Seven years had not aged her in any meaningful way. Her brown eyes still maintained their hint of mischief and her bare legs were as toned as they ever were.

Patterson slid forward. "Yes. Miss Lily. Yes."

"Mister Coleman and I covered a few stories together. You might say I taught him everything he knows." She regarded Cal with poorly disguised amusement. "I'm surprised he's not here with his usual photographer. I thought they were *inseparable*."

"I've an interesting story about that," Cal said, leading them off the dock and towards the fish markets. "Have you had lunch?"

Antonia shook her head. "There's a café this way," she said, angling her head towards it. "Very nice view of the capitol building. It's also extravagantly priced."

"I'm famished," Patterson said.

Antonia led them down an aisle of tightly packed fish stalls. The most elaborate of them were the size of small houses, made of clay and straw. The most basic were little more than a stiff piece of driftwood laid across two barrels.

The open-air café was a simple roped-off area of the dockside, a few yards past the open market. Wind and rain had eroded most of the flat wooden sign and the area was empty save an Aruminian barking into a steaming shack.

"*Stupideh agrhole cablahs, agbora ista!*"

Patterson whispered, "This is the expensive restaurant?"

Antonia smiled. "It's a bit overpriced, which helps with privacy."

Cal didn't need to know the language to know the shopkeeper was annoyed. "Any idea what *agrhole* means?" he whispered.

"Well, it didn't sound friendly, whatever it was," Patterson said.

"*Agrhole*," Antonia said, rolling her tongue around the word, "… means blue."

"Blue hairs," Cal said, putting it together.

"You think there are Heilish here?" Patterson said, glancing around as if foreign agents might pop out from behind tables at any moment.

"I've seen a few," Antonia said, nodding. "They've all checked out though."

Spotting the trio, the waiter rushed forward to meet them. The top of his shirt was split open past his chest, wiry black hair spilling out like thirsty weeds. "My apologies for the delay, Miss Lily. I see you have brought some new friends, yes?"

"Yes, Maimundo. These are my colleagues from the paper. Mister Coleman and his photographer, Mister Poppin."

"A pleasure to meet you both," Maimundo said, shaking each man's hand vigorously. "You have come to the right place. We have something very special today. Very special. Will Mister Roberts be joining us as well?"

Antonia went pale for a moment. "I'm afraid not."

"That is too bad. Too bad. I'm sure you will let him know what he missed, yes?"

Seeing Antonia lost for words, Cal said, "Can we have that table in the back over there?"

Maimundo looked over his shoulder at the isolated bamboo table overlooking the bay. "Of course, sir. Of course." He led the way and shooed off a seagull that had perched on the back of one of the table's four chairs.

Antonia sat down, removed her hat and shook out her blonde hair, as Cal and Patterson took seats opposite her.

"This is a nice view," Patterson said, setting down his suitcase. Across the shimmering bay, the capitol building loomed oppressively despite a freshly scorched tower. Crowds clustered around its outer walls like hungry mice.

"Can I get you all something to drink?" Maimundo said. "Food today is soup or sandwich. They are both *magnificash*."

"What's in the soup?" Patterson asked.

"*Cranga.* Very good, sir."

Patterson's look of concern brought a smile to Cal's lips. "It's like chicken, Mister Poppin," he said. "We'll have three of them. Do you have whiskey?"

"Oh yes, sir."

"Just water for me," Patterson said.

Cal simply nodded. There was no sense arguing with him. He'd find out soon enough. "Two whiskeys and one water then."

"Absolutely, sir. Absolutely." Maimundo bowed, started away, and immediately began shouting at the shack

"I'm sorry about Lieutenant Michaels," Cal whispered. "What happened to him?"

Antonia lowered her gaze, avoiding eye contact. "He went out to meet our asset for the usual check-in. And he was…" She shook her head. "I should have gone with him."

"He was found near the club, the one where the asset worked. Why would they risk meeting so close and blowing her cover?"

"I… I don't know."

If Antonia was acting, she was putting on a good show. If it hadn't been for the duress code Michaels used, Cal wouldn't doubt her for a minute. But until the code could be explained, she wasn't someone he could trust.

But that level of caution wasn't a hard thing for him. There was only one person he trusted.

"I know this is difficult," he said. "But we don't have a lot of time here."

"I understand."

"Do you have anything that can help us?"

"I think so." She pulled her elongated cotton handbag off her shoulder and placed it on the table. It was lime green and large enough to hold a bowling ball. "I managed to secure this from a local policeman," she said, producing a folded scrap of paper. At some point earlier, it had been wadded into a ball. Cal assumed Antonia had flattened it out. "It was in Michaels' pocket."

Cal craned his neck to read it across the table. The paper was etched with several lines of symbols—a code. "This is Mag's handwriting."

"What does it say?" Antonia asked.

"Could I have a look?" Patterson leaned in closer. It was the most confident Cal had seen the man. Antonia handed the delicate scrap to Patterson and his eyes darted across it. "Do you have any spare paper? Pen?"

"Don't you reporters keep any supplies?" Antonia said. She produced a small flip pad and a black fountain pen from the front pocket of her bag.

Patterson scratched symbols in a silent trance that was only broken by the return of Maimundo. "Here you are, gentlemen and madam. Enjoy. I will return shortly with your drinks. Very good whiskey. I am loathe to share it." He tucked his tray under his arm and skipped back towards the kitchen window.

Antonia slurped a chunk of meat and yellow broth off her spoon as Patterson looked down at the bowl. He moved the thick chunks of meat around with his spoon. Slowly, he lifted a morsel into his mouth.

"Something wrong?" Cal asked as Patterson chewed.

"It's a bit… *gamey*," he said, his mouth still full. He dribbled the mashed-up paste back into the bowl. "What's this sauce on it?"

"*Sucupio*," Cal said. He took a bite of the stringy, pungent meat. "It's good." *At least it's good for Aruminia.* He'd have warned Patterson not to skip breakfast if he'd had more time with him.

Maimundo returned with their drinks. "You'll have to tell me what you think of the whiskey, sir. How does it compare to your blends in New Parkland?"

Patterson snatched up his glass of water, took a sip and spat it into his lap.

Maimundo stood back rigidly, rocking on his heels.

Cal casually sipped his drink. It was much sweeter than anything he preferred, but certainly better than Aruminian water. "It compares very well. Bring one for my friend here as well. He's changed his mind."

Maimundo glared across the table before thrusting his tray back under his arm. "Of course, sir," he said, turning on his heels and striding away.

"*That's the water?*" Patterson gasped.

Antonia smiled. "I should have warned you."

Sanitation in Aruminia was at least thirty years behind the Confederation and the algae from the São Fanco River gave the water an aggressively metallic, bloodlike taste. Cal took another sip of his whiskey and passed over his glass. "Try that."

Patterson studied the brown liquid and took a tiny taste. "The One help me." He took another, larger sip and gargled it.

"So, what have you found out here?" Cal said, taking the notepad and flipping through the pages. Patterson had moved the symbols around, reorganizing them, assigning them to Basic characters and then crossing them out.

Patterson swallowed another gulp of whiskey and coughed. "I might be able to work through it given time."

"How much?"

"A few days," Patterson said. "If it's Doctor Silverfinch's work, her active key will be at Pantopolis. One thing I definitely do not recognize is *this* symbol." The shape had been scrawled at the top corner of the page. "This isn't any part of the company's alphabet that I'm aware of."

Cal recognized the geometric octagon, but wasn't sure what it meant, other than that Mag had definitely left the note. It matched an obscure charm she wore representing The One and his seven companions. "There's no time to puzzle it out," he said. "We'll need to send the note back with Captain Ramsay. Get it translated with Mag's master key."

"Is the captain authorized to handle these materials?" Antonia asked. She knew damn well he wasn't, but this was one of only two leads they had, and Cal wasn't going to let that stop him.

"No, he's not," he said, shaking his head. "But my photographer here is."

Patterson cocked his head. "I was told not to leave you, Commander."

"I'll keep an eye on him for you, Mister Poppin," Antonia said with a grin. "Make sure he stays out of trouble."

"She was my training officer," Cal said as he handed Patterson the crumpled piece of scrap and the notepad. "There's no better babysitter for me."

Patterson traded glances between them. "Well… what are you both going to do?"

Cal turned to Antonia. "Do you have transportation?"

"I have a roadster parked down the street," Antonia said. She rested her chin in the palm of her hand. "Where are we going?"

"I want to see where Michaels was found."

Cal walked in step with Patterson back up the *Sky Fish's* clanking gangway.

"I don't think the Admiral will approve of me leaving you alone so quickly," the cypher man grumbled.

Cal looked over his companion's shoulder to ensure no vendors had followed them and could overhear. "I'll be with Commander Hunt," he said in a low voice.

"We shouldn't trust her."

"Who says I do?"

"I say you do," Patterson said, "because you've *been* with her before." He took Cal's arm and stared him in the eye. "I'm right, aren't I?"

"I'm not going to dignify that with an answer," Cal said. *The best liars don't lie. They deflect.* "You can tell the admiral I ordered you back. I'll take full responsibility." He doubted this was going to be his last assignment, but if it was… well then it didn't much matter what punishment the board cooked up for him, did it?

Patterson shifted his weight from foot to foot. "I don't know…"

"I had cream chipped beef for breakfast."

"Cream chipped beef?"

"And bacon."

"Do you think they have any left?" Patterson said, his eyes already drifting to the *Sky Fish*.

"I'm sure they do. But the captain mentioned he was hoping to pick up some fish from the market. Said he's planning to stuff them with crab meat if he can find any."

"*Karanjeugos?*"

Cal nodded. "*Karanjeugos.*"

Patterson licked his chapped lips. "Okay, Mister Bannon. Just don't lose sight of why we're here."

"I'm here for Doctor Silverfinch."

Patterson studied him with squinting eyes. "That's what I'm afraid of," he said, dryly. "You won't blow anything up, will you?"

"Will you get going? We're running out of time."

"Do you have everything you need from the ship?"

"I do… except," he held up his wrist so Patterson could see the gold-trimmed face of his watch, "before you go, could you show me how to set this?"

Top Secret: Operation Black Orchid

Eyes Only: Chairman Micen Peromay; Chief
of Staff Robinson Gibbs

This memo provides an extensive overview of suspected Marabeshi smuggling operations in Aruminia, and potential Marabeshi alliances with unknown Aruminian rebel forces. Note the emphasis on air traffic lanes in the vicinity of Panoa Bay—these lanes are still policed by the formally recognized government and have been vital to its remaining in command of international trade. By extension, they are essential to maintaining control of the country.

POST UPDATE:

Long-distance radar has picked up two unknown contacts above international skyspace in the area. Speed and altitude are consistent with Sharnmark-class Heilish battleships.

Recommend additional resources be dispatched to the area.

~ Marleen Quinn, Undersecretary
to Admiral Tyson Bannon

23rd Rotation of the Blooming Season

FIVE

AFTER A FEW MILES, THE wide dirt road out of the capital city had shrunk to little more than a single lane, closed in on both sides by thick trees and untamed underbrush. An oncoming horse reared up in fright when it saw the speeding black roadster approaching, nearly unseating its equally terrified rider.

Cal looked over his shoulder as they passed, but his driving goggles had caked over with dirt, and the horseman was obscured by a gritty layer of sand.

"It's just up ahead," Antonia said, turning the wheel.

"Pretty isolated for a club."

"Patrons of the *White Tbizah* value their privacy."

According to the mission briefing, the *Tbizah*—named after the country's monstrous jungle cats—was an invitation-only gentleman's club, and had been a good source of intel over the two years Nia Santos had worked there. He hoped he wouldn't have to access the place himself, because getting in would be next to impossible without raising alarm bells.

He felt so naked without Mag.

They crossed a bridge over a thin creek, the dirt road transitioning to deteriorated gray cobblestones. As the roadster rolled past it, Cal caught sight of a wooden sign bearing the name of the town—Lana—in angular painted letters.

Utilitarian houses and squat buildings dotted the roadside as they approached the more developed, center of town, but there were only a few scattered residents milling about.

Antonia parked along a stone curb outside a newly constructed store. There were still piles of unused building materials outside the building, covered with a white tarp, and largely obscuring a stocky A-frame sign.

"Dentist?" Cal said, nodding at the sign's cartoon-style extracted tooth.

"Doctor Ruiz," Antonia said, lowering her driving goggles and letting them hang around her neck. "He heard the shots and found the body, but not the assailants. It was him who contacted the local police."

"You've spoken to him?"

She shook her head. "He's seventy-five years old and grew up right here in town. Policeman I talked to says he's clean."

"Same policeman who gave you Michaels' message?"

"Yes. And it needed an expensive bribe to persuade him to part with it. I doubt he'll want to speak with you."

Cal pointed at a narrow alley between the dentist's office and the slanted two-story building next door. "Michaels was found down there?"

"That's right."

Cal hopped out of the vehicle and leaned against it, taking in his surroundings. It was the eighth day of the week: The Day of Truth. The shopkeepers at the port hadn't bothered to observe tradition, but things were different further away from the urban zone. The shops in Lana were closed, and it was quiet save for the crack of a nutball bat intermingled with the excited shouts of distant children.

A policeman on horseback turned a corner and trotted up the street towards them. He adjusted his sash and regarded them a moment as he passed, before increasing speed to a full canter.

Antonia popped her door open.

"No, wait here," Cal said.

She frowned. "What's going on with you? Why are you trying to get rid of all your help? I don't need your protection, Cal."

"I know you don't."

"We've watched each other's backs before." Antonia said, moving next to him and putting her hand over his.

"That was a long time ago." He slid his hand away, pulled off his goggles and tossed them to the roadster's mud-caked floormat.

"Well, whatever your reason is," Antonia said, dusting off her pale khakis, "you're not getting rid of me."

She strode off into the alley, and Cal had to jog to catch up, working hard to keep his eyes off her gracefully shifting hips.

It was alarming that Patterson had noted their old connection so easily. *Was it so obvious?* It had been Cal's second—and final—assignment with Antonia when they'd gotten closer than he'd intended.

It had been a mistake.

His father had let a mistake like that happen once, and Cal had been the result. It wasn't something Cal had let happen again, and he wasn't about to start now.

Antonia stepped off the sidewalk and into the darkened alley. Cal unfastened his sports coat and eased his way into the shadows behind her. At the far end, three sheets flapped on a clothesline connecting the two buildings.

"They found him here," Antonia said, pointing to a low stack of crates.

"One shot to the head…" Cal said to himself, examining the tops of the boxes. He traced his eyes along the dried blood splashed across the wood, mapping the bullet's trajectory to a cracked hole in the alley wall. "Shooter would have been about where you're standing."

The sound of clacking hooves made him turn. A tired horse shook its muzzle as it pulled a wagon loaded with hay across the face of the alley.

"What time did the dentist hear the shot?" Cal asked.

"Just before sundown."

The shooter wouldn't go back towards the main drag, Cal mused. *It would have been too crowded.* He slipped past Antonia and swam through the billowing sheets at the end of the alley. Beyond them was an open green field. At its center, a chapel sat in quiet decay. The hole in its roof was an open wound to the heavens.

Cal's heart skipped a beat.

That has to be it.

He turned to Antonia, who was pushing past the sheets behind him. "I want you to find the dentist. Ask him if…"

"What is it? You're trying to get rid of me again, Cal."

He clenched his teeth. "Fine."

"What do you see?"

"Come on," he said, and led her towards the crumbling structure.

They crossed the field to the building, which was surrounded by a broken white fence. On the unkempt lawn, a large, mud-caked bell was embedded in the dirt, partially claimed by the long grass.

"It's a church," Antonia said.

Cal nodded. "Followers of The One." He stepped onto the dilapidated porch and looked around. From his new position, he could see at least fifteen more ramshackle buildings between the church and the coast. A skiff hovered like a kite in the distance, attached by cable to an unseen anchor below the tree line.

"Doesn't look like anyone has prayed here lately," she said, joining him by the door and pushing down on the stiff entry latch. Paint flaked away in razor-thin sheets and drifted to the deck. "Cal. *What is it?*"

"The symbol on the message," he said brushing past her. "It's an obscure symbol from the old texts representing The One and the seven's pilgrimage to Voshby."

"I've never heard of it. How do you know?"

"Mag, Doctor Silverfinch, wears a charm with the same symbol."

Antonia blew out her cheeks. "That's a stretch."

Cal shrugged. Maybe it was, but then again, he knew Mag better than anyone.

Antonia folded her arms under her chest. "So, you saw this church and tried to get rid of me."

Cal hopped off the porch into the weeds, circling round the building to two side windows. They were high in the wall, and he lifted himself up on his tiptoes to reach one. He could just feel the lower frame, but there wasn't enough leverage to pull himself up.

Antonia crunched through the underbrush towards him. "Is there anything else you need to tell me?"

Cal ignored her and kept moving down the side of the church, running his hand along the flaking siding. He turned the corner into the rear yard and skipped onto the back stoop. The door into the rear of the church had several panes of frosted glass, and without hesitating, he knocked one out with his elbow. Even before the sound of breaking glass had died, Cal had pushed his arm through the jagged opening and unlocked the door.

"Mag!" he called out.

No reply.

Antonia opened her handbag and produced a short-barreled pistol, but Cal blocked her way forward with his arm. "Someone should stay here and watch the door."

"Is this how things typically work between you and Doctor Silverfinch?"

"You're not Doctor Silverfinch."

"You've made that quite clear."

"I've been given operational command of the assignment," he said, reaching for the doorknob.

"You have not."

"You can telegram Pantopolis and take it up with them when we get out of here. Now I'm ordering you to stay here and watch the door."

Antonia huffed and leaned her shoulder against the weathered siding. "Yes, *sir*."

Cal pulled his revolver from his shoulder holster and stepped inside.

He was in a kitchen, the air thick with the smell of mildew. A rat the size of a tabby scurried across the tiled floor and vanished into a crack in the moldy cabinets. Cal's eyes were drawn to the butcher block countertop. Two stacks of unlabeled metal cans stood on the surface, almost—but not quite—shielding a woman's handbag from view.

Cal knocked the cans to the side, sending most of them clattering to the ground. One stopped before it could roll off the edge. The word 'BEEF' had been scratched into the metal.

He didn't recognize the purse. It wasn't one he'd seen Mag carry. He ripped out the contents and rifled through them. Beauty products, an unmarked book of matches, and two unopened glass bottles of foggy liquid. Aruminian water.

Antonia's head poked through the door frame. "Have you found anything?" Her eyes locked onto the handbag.

Cal tossed it back onto the counter. "Nothing yet. I'll be another moment. Stay where you are."

There was a door at the opposite side of the room, and he pushed through. The kitchen backed directly onto the nave, which seemed to have been cleaned out, save for bits of shadow-swathed debris. Overhead, through the hole in the roof, thick clouds passed across the scorching sun.

Something stank.

As he approached the front vestibule, the sickly-sweet smell of rotting meat intensified.

Time stopped as he spotted the woman lying in a heap against the front door. Relief—and guilt—flooded over him when he saw the crumpled form had black hair.

Black, not red.

He crunched across broken glass, knelt beside the woman and peeled sticky strands from her face.

It was the asset, Nia Santos. She couldn't have been much older than twenty. Vomit caked her chin and the front of her shirt, a puddle of it splashed onto the floor near her body. Fragments of a broken bottle lay scattered around, the same kind of bottle as Cal had seen in the kitchen.

Cal pieced it together. Aruminian water may taste like blood, but it was relatively safe to drink. Which meant someone had poisoned it.

He scanned the area for anything he'd missed, and soon spotted a small journal splayed open on the ground. He holstered his weapon and picked it up. Some of the water from the broken bottle must have got on it, because it was damp to the touch. He dried it off on his pant leg, making a mental note not to touch his mouth with that hand.

The word 'Gutierro' was printed across the front in gold lettering.

He flipped through the cream-colored pages. They were filled with columns of currency amounts and dates. The first log entry had been made two years prior. He fanned through to the end and found the last entry was the fifteenth rotation of the blooming season. Eight days earlier.

"Have you found something, Commander? Would you mind handing that over."

Cal froze as the owner of the voice stepped in closer behind him.

The accent, all precise consonants… it was Heilish.

Cal turned slowly, keeping his hands visible.

There were three of them, all with tightly trimmed, bruise-colored hair. One had Antonia in a stranglehold, her neck in the crook of his arm, her own pistol pressed to her temple.

"Sorry, Cal," she choked out.

"Would you mind, please?" said the one who'd spoken earlier, indicating Cal's shoulder holster with the tip of his revolver. He was the oldest of the three men, his blue hair receded nearly to the back of his head, and he stood almost a foot shorter than his bullish companions.

Cal pulled his jacket open deliberately and removed his weapon with his thumb and index finger.

The lead blue-hair directed one of his companions. "Hans."

The large man not occupied by restraining Antonia stepped forward and plucked the gun away. He shuffled backwards into place, smiling and showing off a chasm between his two front teeth.

"And that little book, as well."

Cal tossed the journal flat like a saucer, and the leader caught it, cradling it into his chest.

"Much appreciated, Commander." He holstered his weapon inside his jacket and began leafing through the pages.

"Do we know each other?" Cal asked.

"Only by reputation, I'm afraid. I heard you blew up a perfectly good factory in Marabesh."

"Well then, it would seem you have me at a disadvantage."

"In more ways than one, Commander. In more ways than one." He closed the book and nodded to the body. "Friend of yours?"

"Never seen her before."

"I see." He held up the book. "And what is this?"

"Couldn't tell you."

The man treated him to a playfully doubtful smile. "No guess?"

Cal shrugged. "Shopping list?" He relaxed his muscles and focused on not appearing disconcerted, but there was a tingle of sweat forming beneath his arms. They had gotten the drop on him and Antonia so easily… how long had they been following them?

The older blue-hair exaggerated a frown, puffing out his bottom lip. "Yes, of course. I am going to bring my car around to this door. You and the woman will be coming with us. You will not be harmed unless you resist." He turned to Hans. "What happens if they resist?"

"They get the bang-bang in the knee."

The man nodded. "And if they continue resisting after that?"

"They get the bang-bang in the other knee."

"I get the picture," Cal said.

The older man smiled. "Good." He strode back into the nave as Antonia was sent stumbling forward into Cal's arms.

"Good catch," Hans said, chuckling. His partner got busy ripping out the lining of Antonia's purse, sending its contents tumbling across the rough, slimy floor. "Now please, sit on top of your hands."

Cal remained on his haunches. "Is it necessary to sit down? I mean, you've seen the floor."

Hans smiled. "This is good, you resisting. Gives me a reason to give you the bang-bang."

"Pretty confident, aren't you? You sure you can manage it?" Slowly, Cal eased up the right leg of his pants.

Chuckling, Hans pressed his tongue tight through the gap between his teeth. "This is good. The funny ones are always criers. Want their mummies."

Cal whipped up his hand from his ankle and fired.

His first shot blew out the back of Hans' head. The second took his friend in the shoulder, the third catching the wounded man in his midsection as he spun away.

"I was getting tired of losing my gun," Cal said to a shocked Antonia. He scooped up his regular weapon and inserted the smaller gun back into its ankle holster. "Come on." He punched down and the door latch and pushed.

It was still stiff.

Antonia picked up her pistol and her ravaged handbag as Cal smashed the door open with his shoulder, breaking apart the dry, rotted frame. Stumbling out into the sunlight, he barely had time to spot the older blue-hair halfway across the field before the man fired two shots at him. Both went wild, and the Heilish leader sprinted the rest of the way to the alley, disappearing through the flapping sheets.

Cal raced after him, but the older man had too much of a lead. By the time Cal reached the alley and emerged from the far end onto the sidewalk, there was no one in sight.

A distant whistle sounded.

Antonia skidded to a halt behind him, breathing heavily. "Where'd he go?"

There were several buildings he could have gone into, and several more alleys up and down the street.

A second whistle joined the first. Then there were several, weaving and piercing together.

Antonia took Cal's arm. "We have to get out of here."

As Commander Bannon had predicted, Captain Ramsay's dinner had indeed been decadent. *Karanjeugo* meat was sweeter and plumper than the crabs harvested in the Confederacy—or any-where else in the world—and the captain had served the juicy meat slathered in butter and clumped on top of baked, lemony fish.

Now Gordon Patterson lay in his cabin, listening to the water slapping the hull outside his window. It relaxed him in a way that his wife would have found bizarre. Beth's mind wouldn't be on the soothing sounds of the wind and water, but on the flimsy protection the *Sky Fish* provided from Mother Nature's ever fickle mood.

He was drifting in and out of sleep when he heard the thunder. But it wasn't the pleasant, distant sound so often the companion of heavy rain. This thunder came from the corridor outside his room. He bolted upright.

"Mister Patterson," said a high voice on the other side of his cabin door.

Recognizing the co-pilot's voice, Patterson sprang forward and ripped open the door.

Phillips stared at him with baleful eyes. "Captain needs you in the pilothouse," he spat, as if the words had been wound up tight inside him and suddenly released.

"What's going on?"

"Two Heilish heavy cruisers…"

"Where?"

"Right on top of us."

Sky Fleet Special Section
Confidential Report

Heiland Political Landscape and Recent Activities

Since Chancellor Ayon's rise to power in the
Dry Season of 1456, Heiland has undergone
significant transformation. The following
key developments have been observed:

1. **Consolidation of Power:**

   - Chancellor Ayon's 'Fleish Decree'
     has allowed him to restrict civil
     liberties and bypass the Relmslag,
     establishing a totalitarian state.

   - By mid-1457, the regime had purged internal
     dissent among the ranks of the wehrcomache,
     thus consolidating Ayon's control over
     both the parliament and the military.

2. **Propaganda:**

   - Ayon's Ministry of Information, led by
     Anna Gubinette, has been instrumental in
     disseminating propaganda through state-
     controlled media, films, and mass rallies.

3. **Militarization:**

   - Heiland has embarked on a rapid
     rearmament program. The Kiegimmel has
     aggressively expanded its air fleet,
     including at least two new Sharnmark
     battleships, bringing their total to 34
     known warships of various classes.

- The wehrcomache has expanded its ranks by 30 to 40 percent over the last two years.

4. **Territorial Ambitions:**

   - There is increasing evidence of Heiland's ambitions to expand its territory. Chancellor Ayon's economic and military cooperation pact with Gensari has effectively made the country a vassal state under Ayon's direct control.

   - The potential military annexation of Prakesha is of particular concern to Sanlish intelligence officials.

5. **Biological Warfare:**

   - We suspect there has been aggressive expansion of resources in pharmaceutical research, but more information is needed.

   - There is evidence the wehrcomache is responsible for last month's disappearance of the Marabeshi scientist, Aruhla Busain.

SIX

THE SOUND OF WOODEN CHAIR legs scraped across uneven deck plates.

"Alone at last," a voice said. The man's vowels were long and razor-sharp, but he seemed so far away. "I must apologize for… hey…" A rough hand patted Patterson lightly on the side of the cheek. "Wake up."

Patterson looked up from between his knees. "I'm… I'm awake."

Across from him, a middle-aged Heilish man pulled off a blood-red lab coat and hung it on the back of his seat.

"I must apologize for your treatment," the man said. "We have been investigating a smuggling operation. I regret that you have become *entangled* in our investigation."

Patterson couldn't feel his hands. They'd been cuffed tight behind his chair. Everything after the *Sky Fish* had been boarded was a blur. He vaguely remembered being dragged to the cargo hold…

How long had he been here?

He licked his chalky lips. "Apology accepted. Now would you mind getting a message to the nearest Confederate consulate?"

"Of course. In a moment." The man dug a veiny hand into a deep pocket of the draped coat and produced a brown leather sack. "Perhaps if you can help me with our inquiries, we could speed your processing along." He opened the bag, plucked out a brightly colored blue ball and popped it into his mouth, slurping it with his tongue. "I am relieved that you do not appear to have been involved."

"Where are Phillips and Ramsay?"

"You travel with strange company," the man said, retrieving another candy from the bag, this one lemon yellow.

"They're not smugglers."

"I see," the man said, crunching. "Then who are they?"

Patterson tilted his head back and looked up at the gears and pulleys chugging against the roof of the bay. "I need some water. Something to drink."

"In a moment," the man said again. "Perhaps it is good that I introduce myself. My name is Frederick Zolbar. You may call me Doctor Zolbar. What is your name?"

"Poppin. Leon Poppin."

"Yes. A photographer for the World Press." Zolbar shook his head. "We are not off to a good start." He threw another colorful sphere into his mouth, then offered Patterson the bag. A moment's pause, then Zolbar seemed to remember Patterson's hands were cuffed. He shrugged ruefully and withdrew the candies.

"Look, can we just get down to it, please?" Patterson said. "Enough games."

"But I love games," Zolbar said, misshapen bits of wet candy spraying from his mouth. "Are you sure you do not wish for one? It is good."

Patterson stiffened and shook his head, pulling away as far as he was able.

"Nonsense," Dr. Zolbar said, holding up a shiny red sphere. "I insist. Trust your doctor." He held the ball inches from Patterson's chapped lips. "Open, please."

Patterson opened and Zolbar dropped the sweet, berry-flavored morsel onto his tongue. "It is good, yes?"

Patterson chewed and swallowed. "It's okay."

Dr. Zolbar smiled and placed the bag on Patterson's chair, in the space between his shaking, twiglike legs. "Good. Now that we are proper friends let us begin again." He leaned forward, huffing out fruit-scented breath. "What is your name?"

Patterson's mind raced. If they wanted to kill him, they'd have done it already. "I can't say."

"Oh… but sure you can. You remember it, don't you?"

"I am a citizen of the Smithon Confederacy, over international waters."

"In the company of international terrorists."

"What are their crimes?"

Zolbar frowned for the first time. "You seem to misunderstand our current relationship. I ask the questions, and you answer them. Now, *what is your name?*"

"I don't recognize your authority to hold me. This is illegal."

The doctor chewed idly. "You're going to make for an entertaining challenge. Not difficult but *entertaining*. You will wait here a moment." He pushed himself up and walked behind Patterson and out of sight.

It was nothing but scare tactics. The Heilish wouldn't risk an armed conflict over *him*. "You won't kill me," Patterson said.

"Kill you?" Zolbar said with laughter in his voice. "I wouldn't dream of it."

Boots clacked against the steel deck plates and a door groaned open.

"Strip him," Zolbar said. "Oh, but be mindful of my sweets."

The sack disappeared as Patterson was yanked to his feet. A razor edge ran down the length of his back, along his arms and legs, and his clothes fell away in tatters.

"Spin him around." Rough hands turned Patterson to face the door. His manhood shrank to an almost imperceptible nub, and his shaking knees were close to giving out. "Steady him."

Two soldiers clamped onto his arms with vicelike intensity. Each wore the red band of the *wehrcomache,* Chancellor Ayon's political police.

Another naked man stumbled through the open door, two steps ahead of another pair of sour-looking *wehrcomache.*

Ramsay…

"That's far enough," Zolbar retrieved his lab coat and slithered into it as Ramsay dropped to his knees. "Captain," he said, pointing at Patterson. "Who is this man?"

Ramsay glanced up for only a fraction of a moment. "He is Lieutenant Gordon Patterson of the Confederation's Sky Fleet."

"I see," Zolbar said, nodding. "And what is his clearance level?"

"I don't… I don't know. High. He works out of Special Section, reporting directly to Admiral Bannon. I delivered him with the admiral's son to the port of Cyio de Reyes. That's all I know."

"Interesting," the doctor mused. "The hero admiral and the hero son."

Ramsay was shaking uncontrollably. "I… I don't…"

"Never mind," Zolbar said, and the captain sunk into a ball, rubbing his forehead against the deck plates.

How wonderful a thing it would be to melt into that floor.

Dr. Zolbar squatted down on his haunches alongside Ramsay. "Now tell me, why is Commander Bannon not with his usual partner?"

"I… I told you. I drop them off and pick them up."

"I see." Zolbar stalked over to Patterson, his wide grin displaying an array of blue-stained teeth. "I take it we understand each other a bit better now, eh Lieutenant?"

"Yes…" Patterson could barely hear himself speak over the sound of his pumping blood.

"Is your name Gordon Patterson? Are you a member of Sky Fleet's Special Section?"

Patterson nodded.

"Yes or no, please."

His throat was dry as sandpaper. "Ye… yes."

"This is good. And you have received the Confederacy's *altim* inhibitor?"

"Yes."

Dr. Zolbar looked over his shoulder at the *wehrcomache* guards in the doorway. "Go ahead then."

Ramsay looked up. "Go ahead with—"

The front of his head exploded and the guard behind him calmly holstered his pistol.

Zolbar sucked another candy past his lips. "Welcome aboard, Lieutenant."

"Doctor?"

Zolbar let the wind take the last of his cigarette and pushed away from the deck rail. "What is it Theodor?"

"The minister wishes to know if we're ready to get under way. He commands your presence."

He commands scared boys like you. Not me. Zolbar turned his gaze back over the rail to the rolling waves far beneath him. He'd been up on deck earlier to dispose of the *terrorists* earlier, but it was a rare thing to be topside at deck speed in this part of the world. He intended to make the most of the experience. Only at the apex of the dry season was there ever a breeze this warm in Heiland. "Thank you for informing me."

"Well," Theodor said, "have you finished?"

Zolbar allowed himself a smile. The boy was charming in his way, irritating nasal voice notwithstanding.

It was often like this for the doctor aboard airships, this kind of deference from the crew. He was an outsider to these boys. *How could they know who he was?* They only knew he made their *kapitain* nervous.

"I suppose I have," he said. "Where is the good minister?"

"He's in the *kapitain's* study," Theodor said stiffly. "I'll direct you."

"That won't be necessary. I know the way." Zolbar brushed past him, making for the deck lift. He stepped onto the shaking cage and began closing the gate, allowing Theodor barely enough space to shimmy onto the lift after him.

"I was ordered to accompany you, Doctor."

Relax, my boy, Zolbar thought as he threw the brass handle forward and the lift clanked downwards. *Soon I'll be gone.*

They found the minister sitting on a leather couch, chatting idly with Kapitain Holler. "You wanted to see me, Minister?" Zolbar said, cheerfully.

Kapitain Holler's walrus-like face appeared to swell up. "I sure as the devil do. I've given you exceptionally broad latitude, Doctor…"

"That'll be all, Theodor," Minister Lichten said, cleaning his optics with a cotton handkerchief. "You may go."

"Yes, Minister," Theodor said, looking relieved.

The door groaned shut behind him, and Zolbar squished down on the fat arm of the sofa. For a stateroom, the space was expansive, all leather and rich, dark wood, with a wide brass-trimmed window. It was exactly the sort of over-the-top opulence weak men used to project strength.

"I'm afraid disposal of the *Sky Fish's* crew was necessary, Kapitain," Zolbar said.

"How can there be any need to do that? Those men knew nothing. It would have been cleaner to scuttle them with the ship. My men don't fancy mopping up bits of brain and skull."

"Kapitain, I do not presume to instruct you as to your duties on board. I would insist you do me the same courtesy."

Holler growled over his shoulder at Lichten. "Are we finished? Am I clear to return to cruising altitude?"

As Lichten opened his mouth to speak, Zolbar clapped his hands and rubbed them together. "We are, Kapitain. We are," he said. "Set course for Yalespitz at maximum speed."

Minister Lichten waited a moment and nodded. "Proceed, Kapitain."

The beefy man grunted under his breath and left the room.

"He is right," Lichten said as he fitted the adjustable temples of his rimless optics back around his ears. "Tensions are high with the corporatists. The chancellor will not appreciate anything that might instigate a direct conflict with them before he is ready."

The chancellor's only goal is winning prosperity for our people and restoring social order, thought Zolbar. *If my work is successful, there may not be a conflict at all.*

There will be surrender. From everyone. Everywhere.

"I am sorry, Minister," he said, smiling. "The display with the ship's pilot was a necessary part of my work with the subject. But rest assured… *the chancellor trusts my judgement.*"

The minister ground his teeth together. "It would seem he does. For now." Lichten had opposed Zolbar's plan to abduct Aruhla Busain, but the power of the parliament was little more than ceremonial at this point. Still… it was fortuitous that Zolbar had been able to make such excellent use of Busain's old formulas. The chancellor was not a man who handled disappointments well.

Zolbar reached into his coat for his bag of candy. "Would you like one?"

"I don't eat sweets."

"As you wish, Minister." Zolbar tossed a ball into the air and caught it in his mouth. He sucked on the grape-flavored morsel before biting it. "I had hoped we would get Commander Bannon himself," he said as he chewed.

"This man Patterson will do though?"

"Oh yes. He has received the Confederacy's *altim* inhibitor. He'll do nicely."

"What are you going to do to him?"

Zolbar smirked. "I'm afraid that while you may be authorized to hear the information, Minister, explaining the finer points of psychology and brain chemistry to you would be a painful process for both of us."

"Granted. But, how do you know this man will be what you need?"

"I do not *know*. But my most successful subject since acquiring our new research had received the Confederate inhibitor."

The couch squished with the minister's shifting weight. His face contorted as if smelling something foul.

"You do not approve of my work, Minister?" Zolbar asked.

Lichten eyed him carefully. "Your *most successful* subject nearly escaped. And is now dead, unless I am mistaken."

"I see. Perhaps you wish to take up your disapproval of my project with the chancellor?"

Lichten cleared his throat. "Of course not. I approve of any program sanctioned by the chancellor."

"As do I, Minister. As do I. Hail Ayon! My Chancellor and My Guide."

"Hail Ayon! My Chancellor and My Guide," Lichten recited.

"Good," Zolbar said. "Now, since we've established we're all one big happy inner circle, has there been any luck decoding the notepad?"

Lichten shook his head. "Why don't you get your new *subject* to break it?"

Zolbar frowned. "I'm afraid I'll be keeping him far too busy for code breaking, Minister. Was there anything else of interest on board?"

"Not much. A dozen pocket detonators."

"Indeed?"

"Radio controlled," Lichten said. "We have something similar in development. Fairly low yield but we activated them as part of our ruse when we scuttled the ship."

"Is there any chance of securing Bannon?"

Lichten shook his head. "Our men almost had him…"

"Damn."

"Unfortunately, we cannot afford to linger for a second attempt. We were able to recover a journal from him, however. It seems the Marabeshi are shipping *altim* into Aruminia. They're supporting one of the rebel factions."

"The corporatists will not allow that."

"Of course they won't," Lichten scoffed. "This area will be swarming with them soon."

"That is too bad," Zolbar said, getting to his feet. "Well, if there's nothing else, Minister…"

"Could I offer you some advice, Doctor?"

"I consider you a true friend. Of course."

"Whatever you unlock, you will be responsible for. Make sure you can control it."

"Knowledge is dangerous, Minister," Zolbar said cheerily. "But it is always discovered at some point. Either we'll find it… *or they will*."

Subject: Peaglo Gutierro,
Warden of Scoraleza

Comments: Peaglo Gutierrio is the great-
                        grandson of King Watto Gutierro,
                        the last king of Scoraleza.
                        All information regarding
                        Gutierro is more than two
                        years old and unreliable.

                        Coordinates for Gutierro Castle:
                        28.14.33.6N 1772322.5W

Urgent, direct to Admiral Tyson Bannon

                        ~ Signed, Lieutenant Alber Johns,
                                Sky Fleet Communications

                        24th Rotation, The Blooming Season

SEVEN

CAL'S RUBBER SOLES SQUEAKED ON the marble floor as he crossed the Casa Royale's open-air lobby. It had once been the most prestigious hotel in the country, frequented by wealthy tourists and diplomats. Now it was a ghost of its former self. Still the staff carried on with professional, seemingly blissful ignorance of the revolution.

A pretty young woman smiled at him as he leaned against the polished front desk.

"Any messages for me? Room 225."

"Let me see, sir," she said in perfect Basic. She pushed away from the desk and scanned the network of open mailboxes behind her. "I do not see anything, Mister Coleman."

A square-jawed man in a tailored suit appeared from the back office. "I'll take care of it, Sophia. Could you give us a moment?"

The woman looked confused, but she nodded and slipped into the backroom, closing the door.

The manager slid a small scrap of paper across the reflective desk.

```
permission to photograph scoraleza at your
discretion stop conditions on the ground extremely
hazardous stop still waiting on poppin stop
                                       - johns
```

To say Cal had asked for permission to engage Gutierro was a generous interpretation—the name on the front of the notebook taken by the Heilish agent was his only clear lead now, and he'd follow it regardless—but he supposed having clearance from command was better than not having it.

His other concern was Patterson, who should've reported home by now. If the Heilish had moved on the cypher man the same time as they had tried to take him and Antonia, Cal had a sinking feeling they wouldn't see him again.

Damn those bastards on the board… all tucked in their snug beds on Brunswick.

"Any return message, sir?"

I can't think about this now.

"Perhaps later," Cal said. He folded the telegram, slipped it into his jacket and palmed fifty Confederate credits to the manager. "Inform me immediately if there are any further messages."

"Of course, sir."

Cal padded out of the lobby into the sticky night air. He and Antonia had spent the afternoon tearing apart her hotel room.

"The Heilish had to have been watching you close," he'd said when she questioned the search.

"But if they had planted a listening device here, what good is finding it now?"

Of course, listening devices were not the only thing he was searching for. He needed a reason to trust her. Anything would do.

He bounded up the exterior concrete steps to the second floor and stopped outside a door emblazoned with a gold-plated '225'. He knocked sharply and said, "It's me."

The deadbolt clicked and Antonia opened the door wide. She'd changed into a too-thin, too-short, too-intoxicating nightgown, and made sure she stood in the doorway long enough for Cal to notice it fully.

"Anything?" she asked, stepping to the side at last.

Cal moved past her, pulling off his sports jacket before tossing it onto the opulent king-sized bed.

"No word from Patterson yet."

Antonia sat down on the mattress and crossed her smooth bare legs. "I see."

Cal indicated her nightgown. "You've made yourself comfortable."

Antonia eyed him playfully. "It's hot here. But if it's easier for you, I could go back to my hotel…"

He shook his head. The company had arranged a two-bedroom suite for him and Patterson with a shared central washroom, and he'd rather not lose anyone else. "Easier to stay on top of you this way."

"Promises, promises."

Her battered, emerald-green purse lay next to the lamp on the nightstand. Cal strode over to it and plucked out her pistol.

"Looking for something?" she asked, reaching for the weapon. He handed it over. It wouldn't do her much good without the firing pin that was resting in his pocket.

Cal made a show of looking inside the bag. "The lining is ripped."

"Blue-haired bastards," she said. "That bag cost me nearly twenty-five credits."

"I could take a look for you."

"Take a look?"

"Fix it."

She took a moment to process what he was saying before asking, "You sew?"

Cal ignored her incredulity. "Got a needle and thread in my bag," he said. "Won't be a perfect match."

"Things so rarely are." She chuckled. "You are full of surprises, Commander."

"It's a hobby." Cal squatted down and pulled his suitcase from beneath the bed, flipped it open, and gathered what he needed.

Antonia uncrossed her legs and started towards the connected washroom. "It makes sense. You're good with your hands."

"Knock it off," he said, sitting at the room's small writing desk. Antonia had left a half-eaten tray of food there: red bananas, sliced apples, and bacon. The bacon still looked crisp. He picked up a stiff slice and crunched down. "You call this dinner?"

"Try the fruit. It's fantastic here. One of the few things I can stomach," she said. "What did the company have to say about the Heilish?"

"Nothing. I think we threw them for a loop with that one," Cal replied, unspooling a long bit of black thread.

"What about Gutierro?" Antonia called over the sound of running water.

"I've been cleared to *photograph* him and the palace," he said, snipping the thread. "So, we should probably pay him a visit." He finished quickly and checked his work by running his thumb along the inside of the lining near the lip of the bag. "All fixed."

"Already?" Antonia said, bare feet slapping on the tiles as she wandered back into the room.

He held up the bag by its wide strap and she took it, peeked inside. "It looks perfect. You *are* handy." She dropped her gun back into the bag and tucked it under her arm. "Now I'd say it's time you start trusting me."

"Try not to take it personally." He took a bite of a crisp slice of apple. "You're right. This is good."

"I told you," Antonia said, with a satisfied grin. "So, do you think we'll need a ship? I've made some contacts. We can charter something from the harbor."

Cal shook his head. "I'm not risking another trip out of Cyio, not when we know the Heilish could be watching. I've got a better idea."

"That's no good," Cal said, observing the boat rocking against the dock. "I need something that flies."

The girl was young, about ten, with a heart-shaped face and dusky skin. She translated Cal's words for the sweaty merchant, and his second and third chins shook violently as he barked something back in Aruminian and waved his arms wildly.

The girl forced an awkward smile. "Mister Pedrez asks… *why?* We can provide you a very nice seacraft. He insists there are no *laba* this close to shore. He could also provide horses or a motor car for the right price."

Pedrez continued to shout. The girl paused, trying to work out a dignified translation. "He also wishes to reiterate that his requirement of a deposit is non-negotiable."

"Boats and cars and horses will take too long," Cal said. "You've got ships here that can fly. I've seen them."

The girl winced before relaying the message to Mr. Pedrez, who spat into the dirt and stormed away, muttering. The translator made an awkward curtsy and trailed after him.

"You're not going to find a pilot here," Antonia said.

"I don't need a pilot. I need a ship. I flew on frigates for years before entering Special Section."

"Does it look like there are any frigates here? We should have left out of Cyio."

"You mean like Patterson?"

"We don't have any idea what happened to him."

"Uh-huh," Cal said, growing annoyed. The cypher man was the last thing he wanted to think about.

Patterson took his oath just like you did. It's not your fault.

It's part of the game.

A high voice brought him back into the now. "Hey, pretty lady… nice lady."

A boy, thin as a reed, was looking up at Antonia from waist-height. "I hear you looking for a ride." He adjusted the smudged Pantopolis Rounders cap clamped down on his mop of black hair.

"You know where we can find one?" Cal asked.

"Yeah, Mister. Me."

"You're kidding," Antonia said.

"I no kidding, lady. I got the best ship in Lana."

Cal looked him up and down "How old are you?"

"Are you funny, Mister?"

Cal raised his eyebrows and waited.

"I'm seventeen."

"No, you're not," Cal said with a hint of a smile. "What's your name?"

A muscle in the boy's jaw jumped. "Nadir."

"Just Nadir?"

"Nadir Alameidar."

"Can we purchase your ship?" Antonia asked. "Is it for sale?"

"You want to buy it, lady? You can no afford it. How you expect me to live with no ship?"

"Show it to us," Cal said. "Maybe we can work something out."

The boy's eyes narrowed. "I'll show you, Mister. But I'm no selling it." He waved his arm, beckoning them to follow. Seagulls screeched overhead, and a group of bare-chested fishermen unloading their haul of flapping fish paused to watch them. The biggest among them said something in Aruminian and bawdy laughter ensued.

"Something funny?" Cal asked the kid.

"They jealous they no speak Basic," Nadir said. The laughter grew and Nadir added, "They are big *gulas!*"

"You seem popular," Antonia said.

Nadir kept walking ahead of her. "It is not me who is popular, I think. This way, please." He pointed to a ship at the far end of the harbor.

The thirty-foot skiff floated two feet above the water, the sail barely inflated and the waves licking at the hull. It looked as if it had once been a tour boat. The hull had been sloppily painted over, but the ghost of the word *Magnificash!* was still scarcely visible.

Antonia put her hands on her hips. "You want us to ride in that?"

"It's good ship, lady. Best ship in Lana."

"You mentioned that," Cal said. "How high can it get?" The craft was leaking more lift gas than would have been considered normal.

"Real high, Mister. Real high."

"Could we get over the trees?" Antonia asked.

"You very funny, lady. Verrry funny. Go see if anyone else down here speaks Basic and wants to fly you. You go and see. Go and see. I will wait."

Cal stepped close enough to smell the mold on the base of the hull. "Can it get us to Scoraleza?"

The boy looked as if he'd been asked if he could deliver them to hell. "Scoraleza? Why you want to go there? They are crazy people there, Mister. Crazy people."

"Or you can sell it?" Cal said, shrugging.

The boy's eyes flickered as he worked through his options. "How much you have?"

"For the ship?"

"I told you… *I no selling*. You have money?"

Cal nodded.

"How much?"

"I can pay you two thousand Confederate credits now, plus another twenty when we return."

Nadir rocked back on his heels before leaning closer in. "You walking 'round here with two thousand credits?"

"I thought you were afraid of Scoraleza?"

"I can be afraid of more than one thing at once, Mister. But the people here will only rob you."

Cal folded his arms across his chest. "Do we have a deal or not?"

"Kids do not go to Scoraleza. Kids that go to Scoraleza, they no come back."

"Kids? I thought you were seventeen."

Nadir pulled down on the tip of his cap. "Okay, Mister. Okay. You show me money, now."

"Then I guess we just hired a ship," Cal said. "When can we leave?"

Dr. Margo Silverfinch's room at Castle Gutierro was lovely. She doubted there was a room in the palace that wasn't. The royal residence wasn't the sort of place to have a dungeon. Not, when dirty, menacing prisoners could be housed outside.

Unfortunately, outside was somewhere Mag's captors had shown an annoying reluctance to expose her to. Still, they'd gone strangely easy on her. She'd told them nothing, and they had spent almost no time trying to squeeze information out of her.

Whatever the reason for the soft handling, it was certainly a bad omen for Michaels and Nia. Even if they couldn't crack Mag's code, Michaels was a fresh agent and wouldn't last long under intense *questioning*.

Mag had asked specifically if Nia was dead, but Bulkarni only had allowed a cryptic, "I assume so," before presenting her to the duke.

"Careful with the doctor," Bulkarni had told the duke. "She's as slippery as a fish and she's your responsibility while she's here."

The duke had not appeared concerned. Nothing seemed to concern the duke. "Okay, Flat Top. Okay," he had said. "We'll keep her very close for you."

Bulkarni had lifted a warning finger. "Not too close."

The duke rolled his eyes and chuckled. "You are so grumpy, Flat Top."

And so, they had kept Mag locked in tight ever since.

She looked out of her window at the four runs of cart tracks stretching across the barren lawn, and the red mist dissipating above the tropical trees on the far side of the compound.

Taking on this mission without Bannon had been a mistake. For all the headaches he'd caused, life with him had never been as excruciatingly boring as this. He could talk, or punch, or run his way out of seemingly anything.

So why couldn't she?

She had attempted to fashion her sheets into a rope or a weapon, but it had taken too much time and ended up useless. Now her cotton mattress sat bare on its bronze bed frame.

He should be here.

She hated needing him like this.

I told him those formulas were nugging worthless.

There was a sharp knock at the door.

She ignored it. There didn't seem much point in granting permission for her captors to enter. This was a cell, regardless of how pretty it appeared.

The rapping repeated. Faster and with more force.

"Doctor Silverfinch, are you decent? May I enter?" She recognized Vihaan Bulkarni's deep Marabeshi accent.

She had had so many close calls. The cannibals in Wickson. The pirates over Habab. To meet her end at the hands of this pudgy Marabeshi banker… it was humiliating.

She slipped over to the drab mattress and sat down, arms folded as the brass doorknob turned.

It wasn't Bulkarni who entered, but a young Aruminian rebel. He held his rifle close to his sleeveless t-shirt and surveyed the room, before nodding his head. Only then did Bulkarni waddle in, the bells on his short-brimmed *barishe* jingling from side to side. "Did you not hear my knocking, Doctor?"

"I heard it."

"I was concerned you might have been taken ill."

"Touching."

Bulkarni pulled on one of the bells hanging from the corner of his hat. "I… I thought you might be hungry."

I'm starving.

Bulkarni smiled nervously. "Something sweet perhaps? Aruminian chocolate is always something I enjoy when I visit."

That sounds amazing. Chocolate was about the only thing they did well here.

"Okay… yeah, sure."

Bulkarni pinched the two front corners of his *barishe* and pulled it off. He signaled to the corridor. "Bring some of those desserts up," he called. "And something a bit heartier as well." He eased himself onto a red velvet chair alongside the window. "I am sorry that this has happened to you," he said, placing the tinkling hat delicately on his lap.

"We all know what the stakes are."

"Yes… yes indeed." He didn't seem at all the cold man he had been after he picked her up. Something had changed. "I wanted you to know I've petitioned to have you accompany me when I return to Mupai."

Mag forced a smile. "I'd prefer not to move around, if it's all the same to you."

"Fortunately for you, it is not." He eyed her seriously. "No one is coming to help you, Doctor. As a prisoner in Marabesh, you will be a chip that can be bargained with."

Mag let out a hopeless chuckle. "I don't think you know President Tumar as well as you think you do."

"You do not understand us," Bulkarni said. "You'll be kept safe. We're not savages."

Mag smirked. A people that controlled its labor population with drugs would seem to be quite savage.

A guard entered with a small silver tray. "It will be a few more minutes for dinner," he said, placing it on her lap. "But these are very good." He bowed and retreated into the corridor.

Several jagged, charcoal-colored morsels were arranged in a diamond arrangement. Mag popped one of the treats into her mouth and was reaching for a second even as she bit through its thin, sweet shell. "Something has happened," she said, mid-chew. "Why don't you tell me what it is?"

"So eager to talk to me, now?"

Mag gave him what she guessed was a rather grotesque, chocolatey smile. "I'm in a good mood all the sudden."

"I regret that we've met in this way."

"You're not nearly as charming as you think you are," she said. Nia Santos would have certainly agreed with her.

The Marabeshi banker sighed, deeply. "I hope to get to know you better on our journey home."

"It'll take more than candy for that."

He put up his hands defensively. "You misunderstand me, Doctor."

"Do I?"

Bulkarni licked his lips. "Yes. We drew some blood from you when you arrived."

"I remember," she said. The squeamish banker's tan face had turned a bilious shade of yellow as the needle went in. "Why are you looking at me like that? What's wrong?"

"Nothing is wrong per se," he said, shaking his head. *"You're pregnant."*

During the day, they sleep in the trees,
keeping out of the breeze.
But when night falls it's time to run,
a hungry tbizah is no fun.
Cry as you will, they hear no pleas.

~Old Smithon nursery rhyme

EIGHT

THE KID, NADIR, HAD BEEN right. Mostly.

His boat *had* managed to clear the tree line… but not by much.

Antonia rolled her eyes as the branches of a red borcanda tree scratched against the keel. "Keep an eye on him," she warned, before retreating into the skiff's cramped berth.

The boat tacked towards the horizon, the wind moving in swirls across the rocking deck. Nadir abandoned the wheel and knelt next to a knee-high wooden chest. He tugged off his grease-stained Pantopolis Rounders cap and stuffed it inside, before pulling out a pair of flying goggles.

"You're a fan?" Cal asked. The kid looked confused, and Cal pointed to the hat. "Nutball, you like it?"

The kid frowned. "You do not need to pretend to bond with me, Mister. You do not watch nutball, I think."

Cal couldn't stop himself smirking. "Why so sure?"

The lid of the chest creaked close. "This business, Mister. Business. I take you, I bring you back. You pay me. That's it."

"I know all about business," Cal said. "I also know all about the Rounders. I *live* in Pantopolis."

"You do not," Nadir said, settling the goggles over his eyes and returning to the helm. He took hold of the wheel. "Who is their regular catcher?"

"Razzy Wright."

Nadir sneered. "Everyone knows him."

"You asked," Cal said, chuckling. "Six foot two and two hundred pounds. Three ninety-three average and twenty-two knock-arounds last year, making it a hundred and forty-five total for his career. He'd have a lot more if play hadn't been suspended during his second and third seasons."

Nadir released the wheel, and it spun freely, one of the grips striking the back of his hand. *"Ah!"* he said, shaking out his injured knuckles before retaking the wheel. "You know nutball?"

"I don't know why that should be surprising," Cal said. "It's a Smithon game. My house is about two miles from the park."

"Two miles from the park?!"

Cal struggled to hold back his amusement. He'd met Razzy Wright briefly during the player's rookie year, but it seemed better not to mention that particular bit of trivia. "How do you know so much about the game?"

Nadir dropped back to the chest and ripped it open. He held up a stack of thin newspapers tied together with white thread.

"You read the box scores," Cal said.

"It's all there," Nadir said. He pulled out a knob-sized nutball wrapped in horsehide and held it up. "Have you seen Razzy Wright hit a ball like this?"

"A nutball?" Cal nodded. "Yes."

"On the ground?" Nadir asked, pointing downwards. "Not in one of those skyparks?"

"Of course," Cal said. Major teams were only permitted to play on the ground.

"And your nutballs are like this?"

"Let me see," Cal said, holding out his hand. The kid passed over the ball and Cal tossed it up and down. "The exterior's a bit rougher but it weighs essentially the same. Similar material."

Nadir took back the ball and waved it at him. "You've seen Razzy Wright hit one of these six hundred feet?"

"Well, I don't see every game, but it's not out of the question. I've seen him get a hold of a few of them. When he does, they can go a long way."

Nadir seemed different now, like an actual kid. "Amazing."

"You play with other kids?" Cal asked.

Nadir stormed back to the wheel and tossed the ball underhand back into the chest. "Yeah, Mister. All the time. Then we all go out and get ice cream."

And that was that.

Cal eased himself down against the swaying bulkhead and rested his eyes. He'd taught himself to sleep almost anywhere, but he had managed to get little more than a few hours the night before, even after disarming Antonia.

There had to be something to explain away that duress code from Michaels…?

There was a soft bang, and Cal's eyes shot open.

"Mister! My spyglass…" Nadir said. He kicked again at the wooden chest with the toe of a spikeless cleat.

Cal crawled over and flipped open the bronze latch. Inside a refracting telescope sat on the kid's stack of newspaper clippings. He was extending the scope as Antonia's head rose from the open hatch alongside him. The wind whipped her hair in a swirling frenzy.

"What is it? Are we there?"

"Yeah," Cal said, thumbing the wheel of the scope. A distant man-made blob came into focus. "And they've got visitors."

Cal passed her the scope. Hanging above the flat roof of one of the castle's four towers was a fat, windowless airship.

"It looks like a cargo ship," she said, squinting. "Marabeshi."

Cal turned to Nadir. "This is it. Start looking for a place to set us down."

Nadir cranked the boat's elevator winch, and a puff of red mist exhaled from the top of the flapping sail. "There is a lake," the kid said as he cranked. "It will work good for you."

Cal leaned over the narrow gunwale as the pressure from the descent built in his ears. Dense palm trees reflected off a pea-green puddle beneath them.

"How far to the palace, do you think?" Antonia asked.

Cal took back the scope, just managing a final look before they dropped below the tree line. "About three miles."

"So, what exactly is the plan here? We shouldn't risk exposing ourselves before we can get a message back to Pantopolis."

She was right—that would be a problem. So much of their work was about finding snippets of information, snippets that, when combined with other snippets, would come together to form a whole. And locating a Marabeshi cargo ship engaged in secret intercontinental commerce was more than a snippet. It meant the Marabeshi were conducting trade in violation of the Peromay Pact. Whatever they were trading, it wouldn't be good.

They had to get word back to the Confederacy.

"Hold tight," Nadir called out. The sails released a final belch of warm lift gas and Cal gripped the gunwale as the boat plopped down onto the mossy green muck.

The trees were dense around the lake, but a single dirt road had been carved through them. It ran straight towards six rotted pylons of a long-gone dock. Cal guessed it would take him about three hours to reach the castle if he was going to stay covert.

Plenty of time.

"Stay with the kid," he said, looking up from his watch. "I'm going to need… let's say eight hours. If I'm not back by nightfall, head back without me and send in the troops."

Nadir shook his head. "It doesn't have to be pitch black for the tbizah to hunt—"

"You want your money, right kid?"

Nadir's mouth made a thin line. "Okay, Mister… okay. I stay as long as I can. But first sign of boil boys or big cats—"

"Fair enough," Cal said clasping his wide provision-belt around his waist. As he checked to ensure his Enforcer's ammo stocks were full, Antonia bent low to make eye contact with him.

"I don't know how many times we need to go over this," she said, "but you're not going anywhere without me."

A sharp frond scratched Cal's jaw as he pushed through the branches. The wide, rigid leaves were gritty with industrial-smelling pink dust, and somewhere up ahead came the faint sound of sizzling.

pizz…

pizzzz…

pizzpizzpizzzzz

Antonia coughed. Cal raised his hand sharply to silence her. She gave him an apologetic look, which he held for a moment before continuing through the underbrush on the balls of his feet.

The air took on a pink haze that grew thicker with every step. He didn't realize the chasm was there until he almost fell into it. Pulling a wide, stiff leaf out of the way, he found himself no more than two paces from the edge of a huge, elliptical hole in the ground, stretching hundreds of yards across. Black smoke rose from the pit, discoloring the already pink-tinged air. The sizzling came beneath him.

pizzzzzzz…

pizz… pizz… pizzzzz

Cal flapped his hand at Antonia to preventing her from stumbling after him towards the cliff edge, then crouched down silently to survey the scene beneath him.

Wide earthen shelves, lined with four cart tracks, snaked around the cone-shaped excavation in wide rings. Ten feet below him at the top of the pit, a mechanical turbine, coated in a thick layer of pink dust whined loudly, its blades spinning in a blur. A sweat-slick worker hefted a bucket towards it. He hoisted it up to the turbine intake and dumped in the contents.

pizzzzz…

Dropping the empty bucket, he slapped close a metal grate that covered the blades. The tracks—newly laid, by the look of them—disappeared into the dark mine that fell away behind him. He stepped to the edge of the dirt shelf and shouted deeper into the blackness: *"Lastá tanto!"*

Antonia froze as the worker turned back and cocked his head slightly up, but he didn't seem to notice her. The few villagers Cal had seen during the hike had not paid them much notice either. The *gular* now came in a decidedly Aruminian variety.

The worker slid, trance-like, to an accelerator lever almost as tall as he was. He threw the switch and stepped between the tracks as a cart loaded with red rocks hurtled past him, tiny wheels screaming against the rails. The Aruminian *gular* stared blankly as it screeched past him and rumbled out of the pit leaving behind a cloud of red vapor.

Brassite.

Cal took Antonia's arm and pulled her back through the underbrush. "They're mining lift gas," he whispered.

Antonia nodded. "Marabesh doesn't have anything like this."

"No one does."

There were more brassite mines in the Confederacy than anywhere else in the world, accounting for their extensive air fleet, but the stones were typically found only in small, isolated pockets. This was on a whole different scale.

Cal unsnapped the canteen from his belt and took a deep, sloshing sip. "They've got one cargo ship up there. Fully loaded with brassite, it would be enough to keep the Marabeshi fleet afloat for at least a month."

"That means they could have—"

"A lot," Cal said, handing her his canteen. "It means they could have a whole hell of a lot."

Antonia took a sip and handed it back. "We have to get word back to the Confederacy."

"I know." Cal licked his lips. "I want you to get back to the kid. Get word to the company. I'll be fine."

"Cal—"

"You know at least one of us has to make it out of here, right?"

Her eyes narrowed. "Alright… I'll go."

"Send a transport to rendezvous with us back at the pond in forty-eight hours. We'll hole up till then."

Antonia's eyebrows formed into high thin arches.

"Go."

Antonia turned away and Cal said, "Wait."

She looked back in time to catch her weapon's firing pin. Slowly the realization dawned on her. She ripped open her purse and threw the pin inside. "I hope to hell you know what you're doing."

Cal watched her turn back through the underbrush and storm off. He gave her a few moments to get clear and leaned back over the edge of the chasm.

The miner had gone.

All clear.

Cal dropped next to the turbine, and fell into an awkward, painful roll as the next cart roared into view. He stumbled forward and hauled on the heavy switch he'd seen the miner use, pulling it to a more central position. The cart jerked, slowing to a more trolley-like speed. Gripping its gritty edge, he climbed into it, landing on a deep pile of sharp red rocks.

As the cart rose out of the chasm and into the searing hot sunlight, Cal worked his back deeper into the stones. They embedded themselves in the soft folds of the skin beneath his chin whenever the cart lurched forward. Finally, it squealed to a violent stop, sending more rocks rolling across his chest.

Cal unsnapped his holster's retention strap and slipped out his revolver and drew it across his chest.

Blood pounded in his ears.

The cart shook back to life and rattled forward, and overhead the sunlight blotted out as Cal passed beneath the sharp points of a portcullis and into a stone structure.

All he could do was take this one step at a time, and step one had been getting into the castle.

That wasn't so hard…

One time, Mag thought. *It had just been that one time.*

Months earlier, she'd have known what Bulkarni had said was a ruse. A sick mind game cooked up by the Marabeshi. But not now. Right now, it made perfect sense.

Just perfect.

I don't feel any different, she thought, pacing back and forth across the room. But she was a doctor, she knew that at four weeks—*and it could only be four weeks*—it wasn't unusual to notice no change at all.

"Damn it," she muttered to no one.

The good news was that it meant the Marabeshi wouldn't hurt her for at least the next eight months. Scarishnu forbade violence against innocents. Doping them with mind-sapping drugs was fine, but not violence.

There was hope. Hostilities between the Confederacy and Marabesh could cool. There could be a prisoner exchange.

A lot could happen in nine months.

Except they are not going to admit they have you. They are going to lock you up in a comfortable cell for nine months. Then they are going to steal your baby. After it's born, they are going to kill you. They will give it altim and then –

Rap-rap-rap.

The knocks were fast and light and followed by three more in quick succession. The food slot at the base of the door slammed open.

"Mag!"

"Bannon!" She dropped to her knees and looked through the gap, finding his steely eyes staring back.

He pushed his hand through the slot as far as it would go. "You okay?"

"I'm… I'm fine," she said resting her face against his red-tinged fingers. "You found the mines."

"Yeah. Got your note and found Nia Santos too," he said, pulling his hand back.

"My note? What about Michaels?"

"They got to him before I could. He's dead. Nia, too. Someone dosed her water with poison before you stashed her at the church."

"We can talk about it later," Mag said. "Get me out of here."

"The door's wired but I think I can short it out."

"Thank The One," she said, resting her back against the door. "How'd you get in here?"

"I only saw a few guards," he said. "Most everyone working in the castle are *gular*."

"What did you do about Antonia?"

Cal sucked in a breath. "What about her?"

"You haven't decoded the message."

Mag recognized the bitch's sweet voice through the door. "Your instincts were right, Cal," Antonia said. "You shouldn't have trusted me."

URGENT

To: Vihaan Bulkarni

Your request for extradition of Confederate
hostile Dr. Margo Silverfinch is denied.

Eliminate all hostiles and traces of
contact. Bring in Hunt for debriefing.

With Respect

Sulban Kubar, Secretary of Intelligence

NINE

Cal trudged down the glass-lined corridor, acutely aware of the yellow eyes that tracked him from the darkened menagerie beside him. The tbizah expelled plumes of air that misted the panes as it crept close.

"Movenda."

Cal took a hard punch to his good shoulder and wobbled onwards.

Antonia looked back at him, smiling shamelessly. "That means, *move along.*"

"I gathered that," Cal said, straightening his back. She'd managed to gather six armed men as backup by the time he'd made it to Mag's room. They wouldn't be enough to save her.

They reached a fork at the end of the corridor, and as they took a turn, the tbizah sat and twitched its tail, never taking those eyes off them until they'd slid out of sight.

They walked over plush red carpeting and past towering oil paintings. A man with long black hair was a fixture in all the portraits. In one, he rode on horseback, playing some sort of game with long wooden clubs. In another he was seated in a meticulously tended garden with a young woman and four smiling children.

Cal looked down at Mag, who was slumping along beside him. "He doesn't seem so bad."

"He probably wasn't." She sounded helpless. It wasn't like her.

"What's that supposed to mean?"

"You'll see."

He walked on in silence, lost in thought. *One step at a time… one step at a time.*

And the next step was simple.

Kill that treasonous bitch.

Just ahead of him, Antonia pushed open a pair of towering oak doors. "My, Lord Duke," she said as they swung open. "I present Commander Callum Bannon of Sky Fleet's Special Section."

The room beyond the doors was a study, dominated by an over-sized desk and a matching bookcase devoid of books. The Aruminian sitting behind the desk was not the man in the portraits. This man was bald, shirtless, and had skin the color of black oil.

Resting his heavy backside on an oversized bronze globe in the far corner of the ornate room was a man Cal recognized as Vihaan Bulkarni.

"Commander Bannon," said the bald man behind the desk. "It is so good you made it. My friend, Secretary Bulkarni tells me you're a special catch." He stood and slipped around the desk. He was thickly muscled, almost as thickly as the guard now holding Cal in place.

"Don't you have any portraits of your own?" Cal asked, forcing a smile.

The duke looked confused for a moment before grinning brightly. "Yes… my predecessor did rather enjoy having his likeness captured. Yanko thinks I should take them down, don't you, Yanko?" The man holding Cal grunted a response and the duke waved a dismissive hand. "Yes, yes. I've forgotten. Yanko doesn't speak much Basic."

Yanko grunted again.

"Did the pet outside belong to him too?" Cal said.

"Oh, her…" The duke laughed. "At least I think it's a she. Yes, she belonged to my predecessor also. He was quite… *eccentric.*"

"His wife was *electric*," one of the grunts said behind Cal. "Quite the squealer."

"Please, Batche," the duke said, playfully, his perfect smile widening. "None of that talk. My kids run around in here. But I have been remiss," he went on, turning his attention back to Cal. "My name is Mobatam. You have heard of me?"

Cal frowned. "Afraid not."

"There's no sense talking to either of them," Antonia said. "Bannon is just as resistant to *altim* as Doctor Silverfinch."

Mobatam leaned in close. He smelled like Cal's father, all sweat and cigars. "We'll see." His arm flashed out, striking Cal's injured shoulder.

All the air shot out of Cal's lungs, and Yanko dropped him to the polished stone floor, where he knelt, taking ragged, gagging breaths.

"Pick him up," Mobatam said. The brute gripped Cal's upper arms and yanked him back to his feet.

Mobatam came forward again, hanging over him like a buzzard. "Still hurts, I guess?"

Cal could only manage a few desperate gasps of air in response.

"I mean it," Antonia said, folding her arms. "You won't have any way of verifying any information you get from him. Besides, he doesn't know anything about the other factions, and next to nothing about the provisional government. Kill both of them. *Now*."

"You kill us…" Cal said, regaining his breath. "There'll be… there'll be… no one to protect you from the Marabeshi."

"Is that true?" Mobatam asked, looking to Bulkarni. "Are my Marabeshi friends planning on betraying me?"

Bulkarni looked annoyed. "Of course not," he said, placing his hands in the pockets of his khaki pants.

"Think about it," Cal said. "You're supplying Marabesh with lift gas in exchange for *altim* so you can… what? Turn everyone in Aruminia into mindless sheep? Make your revolution go a little easier?" Cal studied Mobatam's face, saw his guess was on the money. "And what happens when Marabesh has all the gas it needs? They'll cut off the *altim* supply and your people will tear themselves apart."

Mobatam nodded. "I appreciate your concern. But rest assured we have enough of that sweet dust on hand to unify the resistance. Once that's been accomplished, we can release some of our more *uncommitted* people."

Mag scowled. Despite bound hands, she tugged at the octagonal charm dangling from her bracelet. "The Confederacy will not stand for an out-of-control dictator as their neighbor," she said. "They will *kill you.*"

"Who says I'm out of control?" Mobatam asked. "Mister Bulkarni, am I out of control?"

"No. Of course not."

Mobatam retreated to his seat. "You see? All I have are friends. Friends everywhere." He dropped into the chair and put his feet up on the desk. "Now what to do with you? My Marabeshi friend here wants to take the good doctor home with him. But what about…?"

"There's been a change of plans," Bulkarni said stiffly. "Eliminate them both."

"You're making a mistake," Cal said.

"Oh, I don't think so, Commander." Mobatam took a moment to consider Mag. "Because you see, even after I kill you and your little sweetheart here, your country will do what it always does."

"And what's that?"

"Try to play nice, try to *make a deal!* Corporatists love a good deal." Mobatam craned his neck to see over Cal's shoulder. The oniony stench from Yanko's breathing intensified. "Make it quick for them."

Yanko grunted.

"What, not going to let your pet bitch do it?" Cal said, pulling himself up straight.

Mobatam leaned back in his chair, flicked his gaze at Antonia. "You know something, I think I like that idea. What say you, Commander Hunt? A little reward for tolerating him the last few days?"

Antonia thought for a moment and nodded. "Very well."

Nadir pulled on the slick hempen rope and dragged the cage up onto the deck. Behind him, the maroon-speckled *karanjeugos* he'd already collected were clicking and snapping at each other in search of freedom. He opened the wire door and dumped in the fresh basket of twenty crustaceans on top of his earlier catches.

The secret to getting the big payouts with *karanjeugos* was patience. The commercial fisherman from Cyio collected more, but most of those were sad, tiny things. Picking through and tossing back the scrubs was the key.

Nadir lowered himself over the side to his tiny raft. He estimated he could collect another fifteen or so *karanjeugos* before his keeper cage was filled.

What would he do then?

He had two thousand credits and even without it, the money from his haul would be enough to feed him for months. But one thing he knew for sure: the man from the Confederacy was not a member of the World Press. Nadir had seen Smithon journalists before. And scientists. And humanitarians. This man was none of those things.

He decided that at the first subtle sign of dusk, he would be gone. Twenty thousand credits wouldn't do him much good if he was dead.

He picked up his rafting stick, stabbed it into the water, and pushed his way closer to the shore.

The insects grew louder towards land. It was mating season, and the steady hum grew impossibly deafening… but there was also a metallic smell filling his nostrils.

Not insects…

Black exhaust billowed above the underbrush and Nadir's arms burned as he propelled the raft towards the shoreline. He leapt off the raft, landing in swampish, green muck just as a flatbed truck rolled onto the beach.

Nadir barely reached the cover of a tree before two armed men jumped off the back and two more exited the cab. One of them was the biggest man Nadir had ever seen.

"There's a raft there," the big man said in Nadir's native language, spitting out each word with angry precision. "The boy must have heard us and jumped. Fan out. Find him."

Nadir squeezed himself against the tree's rough bark. His fingers grew numb, locked around the shaft of his rafting stick.

The crunching of the underbrush grew louder, until it was almost on top of him.

Nadir spun, bringing the stick around in a sweeping motion. It connected with the glistening, sun-burned midsection of one of the hunters, who instantly doubled over. Nadir brought the stick down again hard on the man's unprotected neck.

"He's over there!"

Nadir scooped up the fallen man's rifle and rushed through the trees, branches clawing at his face and arms.

Footfalls raced up behind him, and thick fingers grabbed his shoulder. The big man threw him like a sack of straw, through sharp, scratching tree limbs. Nadir slammed into a tree trunk's jagged bark.

He tried to lift his weapon, but the beast slapped it away, sending it flying into the undergrowth.

"You are a lively brat," the giant said, lifting Nadir up and pressing a forearm into his neck, pinning him to the tree.

"I can no… breathe."

The big man smiled. "Will you be a good little boy?"

Nadir didn't think long before nodding, his chin barely dipping into the man's sticky forearm.

"Good," his captor said, and flipped him over his shoulder. Nadir's nose pressed against the matted hair on the man's back, and he could taste the salty sweat running down the shifting shoulder blades.

"That punk knocked Manuel cold," came another voice.

The giant slung Nadir down on the flatbed of the truck, so hard that he bit his tongue as his head bounced against the tailgate.

"Stow the raft and check his boat," the monster ordered, before lowering his lips to Nadir's ear. "Is that true, little man?" he whispered, his breath stinking of fish and dust. "Did you put Manuel down?"

Nadir sucked the blood off his tongue.

"We have need of young men like you. Scrappy types who need discipline."

The other man appeared, cackling. "It's the mines for you, bucko."

Nadir kicked out and slid up the flatbed. "No…"

The big man locked one hand around each of Nadir's ankles and yanked him back into place. The truck clanged as one of the others jumped into the bed and dug his palms into Nadir's shoulders. "Keep a firm grip," the giant said, releasing the boy's kicking foot. "He's feisty." He straddled Nadir across the stomach and reached into his pocket. "You'll like working with us." He pinched Nadir's cheeks and forced his mouth open. "Hold still now."

Nadir thrashed as the man sprinkled yellow powder into his mouth. He sneezed and kicked out again, but it was no use.

The man laughed and climbed to his feet. "That's it. You'll understand soon. *You'll understand everything.*"

"Hey," a distant voice called. "That kid's got some of the biggest *karanjeugos* you ever seen."

Nadir turned his head towards the sound. Someone was holding him down. He'd been struggling. Fighting.

Why was he fighting?

The colors in the reddening sky above him seemed to explode with an exhilarating vibrancy. Everything was… perfect.

A bewitching playfulness came into the giant's eyes. "There. You see?"

"You slept with her, didn't you?" Mag said, looking straight ahead at the hairy backs of the two guards escorting them. "I mean, again."

"What?" Cal said. "No!" *You can't be serious.*

She shook her head. "You are unbelievable."

I'm unbelievable? "You know, we do have some other problems going on right now."

Antonia's cackles echoed off the stone walls. "You two are so cute."

Cal lowered his voice to a whisper. "I came here to save you."

Mag's head bobbed like a fishing lure. "And that's going great. Just great." Her eyes trailed down to the bindings wrapped around Cal's wrists and then rose to meet his gaze. The message in them was clear.

Are you close to getting free?

Cal shook his head. The cords had loosened, but not by much. He'd got out of similar knots before—*with more time*—but at this point, he'd only been able to get his hands a few inches apart.

Enough to get them around a neck.

"You shouldn't have come here," Mag said.

Antonia laughed again. "He would never leave *you*," she said. "You're his little nug-a-nug partner."

Keep laughing, bitch. "I would have done the same for you."

Antonia came to a sudden stop, causing the escort party to stumble to a staggering halt. "Oh, I don't think so. You'd have never brought that kid along—risked his life—to save anyone but *her*."

"What kid?" Mag asked.

Nadir was smart, Cal thought. He wouldn't have risked going far from his boat. No, they didn't have him, or he'd be here too.

The two guards ahead of them split ranks in unison, and Antonia stepped between them, so she was facing the two prisoners. She looked down at Mag, whose thumb was toying with her charm, and her eyes widened in realization.

"You haven't slept with him, have you?" She looked at Cal with mock astonishment. "But Cal… you sleep with *everybody*."

"It would seem so," Mag said.

"You are an odd pair." Antonia took a moment to consider them before her eyes softened. "Okay, Cal… when we get where we're going, I'll do you first."

We'll see.

"What I heard about you was true." Antonia chuckled softly. *"You really had no plan at all once you got in here."*

"Why did you do it?" Cal asked as they moved off again. "Betray your country?"

"It was nothing personal."

"Why then?"

She thought for a moment. "Sometimes you're just *stuck*. I won't be stuck again."

They walked on, deeper into the palace. Soon machinery noise came pounding off the walls, growing to a roar when they reached their destination: the same shipping bay through which Cal had entered the palace.

"Through here," Antonia said to her escorts. "I'm less than excited about the prospect of dragging this on any further."

At the center of the hot, stinking bay a vertical conveyor belt traded full and empty carts up and down a grinding shaft.

"Step over here, Cal," Antonia shouted over the mashing machinery. She waved with her gun hand at the conveyor sending empty, gritty buckets back down the chute. "Make it easy for me, I'll make it easy for you."

Cal stepped up to her, his back to the roaring gears. "Can we go together? Mag and I?"

"You want me to shoot you both at the same time?"

Not exactly. "You've got two hands, right?"

Antonia gave a hint of a smile. "You're so much more romantic than you used to be." She turned to the guards, who were lurking at the chamber's entrance. "Send her over here too."

Mag shuffled forward, head down.

"And could you give us a moment alone?" he said. "Please."

Antonia's mouth twisted. "You're pushing it, Cal."

Come on. You've won and you know it.

Antonia shrugged then nodded. "You've got thirty seconds," she said, and wandered back to her retinue.

Mag whispered, "I... I have to tell you something."

"This is really not a good time."

Mag coughed out a laugh. "When would be a good time?"

Cal smiled. "Later."

Tilting his wrist, he twisted the bezel of his watch.

A rhythmic beeping started somewhere over Mag's shoulder, growing rapidly in tempo. She turned in time to see Antonia's eyes glancing around wildly, before landing on the purse resting on her hip.

The beeping became a long, drawn-out buzz, and Mag dropped to her knees, only able to cover one ear with her fastened hands.

Antonia's mouth opened in shocked understanding before her midsection popped in an explosion of blood and bone.

Cal plowed through the hot pink mist to the blast point.

Two of the men were dead. The others were screaming. Cal scooped up the nearest weapon with his still-bound hands: a short-barreled pistol. He fired three times, killing the screamers before turning his aim on what was left of Antonia. Her mouth was moving but there was no sound.

"No plan, huh?" He shot her in the head.

Frisking a dead guard, Mag produced a flat knife from his pocket and set to work on Cal's bindings. "How'd you get a bomb in her bag?"

"New hobby. I stitched her up." Cal's wrists came free, and he slipped the pistol into his empty holster before taking the knife and sawing at Mag's restraints.

"Okay," she said, as the cords fell away. She picked up a pistol before pushing a sweaty lock of hair behind her ear. "Now let's get out of here."

TEN

VIHAAN BULKARNI HAD RELUCTANTLY ACCEPTED Mobatam's invitation to dine in the east tower. He loathed the man but supplies on the transport barge would be limited and he planned to leave with the corporatist defector as soon as the ship was loaded. He guessed the food in the castle would probably be better than on the transport.

Probably.

Dinner at Castle Guttiero had proven to be something of a mixed bag after the change in management. The rebel leader sat back with his dirty boots up on the massive dining table he'd inherited and took a sloshing sip of black beer from a dented crystal mug.

Bulkarni looked up at the portrait, framed in gold, hanging behind Mobatam. In the painting, the palace's former owner was smiling ear to ear and holding up the bloody carcass of one of his country's terrifying cats by the scruff of its neck.

"You look sad, my friend," Mobatam said, taking another long swig.

Bulkarni's back stiffened.

Mobatam regarded him with faint amusement, tugging on an elongated, drooping earlobe. "Is it because the woman was with child?"

"I appreciate your concern for my spiritual wellbeing," he said, using his most even tone. "… but it is not necessary." Bulkarni saw little point in debating the teachings of Scarishnu with a hoodlum whose nickname—*Furlúco*—very roughly translated to '*he who boils*'.

It had been a shame Gutierro had been so timid when Bulkarni had approached him with a similar partnership proposal. It was a decision Gutierro no doubt had come to regret when he'd learned how Mobatam had earned his unofficial moniker.

"We'll be served soon." Mobatam wiped beer from the corner of his mouth with the back of his hand. "I'd ask you to remove that *thing* from your head before dinner."

Bulkarni's eyes narrowed. He took the opposite corners of his *barishe* between fingers and thumbs and lifted it from his head, placing it delicately on the table.

"Why do you wear such a thing?" Mobatam asked. "Looks terribly *inconvenient*."

"My father wore one. His father wore one. My son wears one. I wear one."

Mobatam pursed his lips. "Funny."

"What is *funny?*"

"Your sense of *honor*. Your little game of—what do the corporatists call it?—'*Pug-a-Lug*' with that whore from Lana has caused so much trouble for our very profitable arrangement. I thought you were a family man, Mister Secretary."

"Nug-a-Nug," Bulkarni corrected him bitterly. "And I'd ask we not discuss my family."

Mobatam smiled, revealing bleached, crooked teeth. "That is too bad. My son is of age. I had hoped you might have interest in a union."

I'd die first. "I do not believe that would be *appropriate*."

Mobatam regarded him coldly for a long moment. "You know something? I am beginning to agree with you."

The doors behind Bulkarni clicked open, letting in a cool gust of air.

"Good evening, father," said the eldest of Mobatam's brood as he made his way towards the head of the table. He made a quick, deep bow to Bulkarni before sitting.

Mobatam's middle child was next, bounding into the room and taking the ornate chair next to his brother. "What's for dinner?"

Last in was the rebel's matronly wife, dragging along the youngest boy. "It is good to see you again, Mister Secretary," she said, attempting a curtsy as her toddler worked to wiggle free of her grasp. "It is always good," she yanked the child, hard, back into place, "to have you at dinner."

"What is for dinner?" the middle boy repeated.

"You'll eat what's served," his mother said, pulling out her chair.

"Okay… but *what will be served?*"

Bulkarni had wondered that himself. The new 'duke' had lived the life of a bandit. There was almost nothing he didn't find exquisite.

Mobatam leaned over the table and gripped the middle boy's shoulder. "Baby *laba.*"

Bulkarni's heart sank. In silent agreement, the boy stuck out his tongue and mimed retching.

Four *gular* filed into the dining room and placed gold-rimmed plates in front of each of them. Bulkarni frowned at the shiny, slithering squid on its bed of crushed ice. "Looks *delicious*," he said, as a tentacle slapped at the accompanying cup of oily dipping sauce.

Mobatam's wife gave a knowing smile. "It took me some time to get used to as well."

"Yes," Bulkarni said. The wet lips of the creature made a grotesque kissing sound. "In Marabesh, we prefer our dishes a bit less lively."

"Lots of protein," Mobatam said, squeezing his youngest son's left bicep. "Make you strong. Expensive, too."

"The exorbitant price does little to make it more digestible," Bulkarni said. "I'm afraid I won't be—"

The doors banged open. "Mobatam! The corporatists are loose!"

"How?" Bulkarni swung around. "All you had to do—"

"Some kind of detonator, we think. Planted on the woman."

Mobatam stomped to the door, pulling Bulkarni to his feet as he passed him. "Keep two men with my family. Lock down the castle."

Cal and Mag rode up to the west tower's top level in a single, loaded bucket. It was a tight fit, but Cal wasn't going to risk separating from her again.

At the top of the chute, the bucket tipped forward, dumping them onto a coarse mound of red rocks. They tumbled end over end, Mag landing on top of him with her full weight and driving hard stones into his back.

He scrambled to his feet as the cart they'd rode on clanked over the top of the conveyor belt and back down the shaft. They needed to move fast. It wasn't going to take long for Mobatam to figure out they were free.

Let's hope they guess I'm heading for the front gate.

He stalked out of the chamber and into another room filled with the screech of rotating metal wheels and the thump of pulleys and gears. He stopped dead, suddenly enough that Mag walked into the back of him.

Someone was coming.

He shoved Mag back through the open doorway and slapped a hand over her mouth.

Moments later, a bearlike laborer with arms thicker than docking cables walked head down past the opening, pushing an empty wheelbarrow.

Cal waited for the sound of a scraping shovel and brassite banging against the metal wheelbarrow before scurrying out of the chamber and along the corridor. At the end of the hall, he found a corkscrewing industrial ramp that curled its way upward to the roof of the tower.

"Where are we going?" Mag whispered, following him up the red-stained ramp.

"We're gonna fly out of here."

Outside, the transport ship hovered above the tower's stark white, rubber roof. The ship was held in place by four taut mooring lines, clamped to the roof with hooks the size of anvils.

Cal pulled Mag behind a control board studded with flashing blue and red lights. His eyes traced the muddy red trail up the transport's lowered gangway. The edge bounced gently against the roof as the transport bobbed in the hot breeze.

Mobatam didn't have much in the way of airships, and certainly nothing designed for combat. If he and Mag could get the transport in the air it would be all over: they'd fly it straight up and out of firing range.

"One man on the deck," Mag whispered.

Cal nodded and wiped beads of sweat from his forehead with his wrist. Sure enough, he spotted the top of a *barishe* moving past the pilothouse window. "There'll only be the one of them," he said. "These things have minimal crews. More room for cargo."

"Maybe," she said doubtfully.

"Do you think you can disengage the mooring clamps?"

Mag looked over the control panel. "I should be able to, but I'll have to do them one at a time. And our friend on deck is going to notice."

"I'll take care of him. Start working on it. I'll be right back."

Mag pulled herself up to the controls and began flicking switches. "Hurry."

Of course he was going to hurry. "It's no problem."

Keeping low, Cal sprinted across the blistering roof and gripped the warm yellow ladder running up the hull of the swaying ship.

"*Quema bae votché.*"

Shit.

Cal turned.

The Aruminian man behind him was not *gular*. Not a guard either. He was unarmed save for the industrial winch he was holding. He lifted it over his head, letting the tool's razor-sharp hooks rattle. "*Quema bae votché.*" he said, sweat running down the tip of his sunburnt nose.

Cal held up his hands as the man's eyes dropped to his holster and went manic.

"Hold on a sec."

The Aruminian took a sweeping swing with his winch. Cal ducked and spun. He flashed a foot at the man's groin, connecting instead with a thick chunk of thigh.

The man howled and released another wild, rattling swing. Cal slipped to the side and connected with a cracking strike to his jaw. The winch sprung back striking the man above the nose. He fell backward and his head smacked hard against the roof.

Cal settled a hand on the butt of his pistol, ready to draw if the man moved again.

He didn't.

Back to the next step: get the hell out of here.

Cal started up the ladder again making it to the third rung. The sharp squeak of wheels cut across the wind. He looked over his shoulder to the source. It was the bearman from downstairs. He let his wheelbarrow tip forward, sending its load of dusty red rocks clattering across the roof.

Cal hooked his elbow under a rung, working to pull his pistol free.

The beast stormed forward. *"Vatche mal!"* He wrapped hands the size of oven mitts around Cal's upper thigh and tore him free of the ladder.

Cal fell back to the rooftop, tumbling to break the impact. Even so, he was stunned for precious seconds.

Rolling away, Cal pulled his pistol free, but his huge attacker closed the distance in seconds. A hammerlike foot hit Cal's wrist, sending the weapon spinning away in the sticky wind.

"Puergo!" the man shouted. *"Vatche mal, Puergo."* He entered a fighting stance and stepped back, allowing Cal to haul himself up.

Cal stood slowly. This one wasn't going to be so easy.

A shout came from the ship's deck. As his opponent half-turned towards the sound, Cal threw a punch, putting his full weight behind the blow. But for a big man, the brute was fast. He twisted away, letting Cal's swing whistle past him. The return shot smashed the air out of Cal's lungs. The back of his head hit the surface of the roof, and light popped behind his eyes.

Definitely not going to be easy.

As massive hands yanked him back to his feet, he was dimly aware of the docking strap to his left snapping free.

"Masá ta malya!"

Cal buried his teeth deep into the man's upper arm.

"BAAA!" The thug howled and threw Cal into the shadows beneath the ship. Across the rooftop, a second mooring line

snapped free and blue flames erupted from the ship's undercarriage thrusters.

Cal threw himself clear of the blisteringly hot shade as the third line tore free. With only one line remaining, the ship spun and twisted upwards, the three unhooked straps swinging in wide arcs.

That's not good.

The behemoth threw his body at Cal, driving both of them into the smoke forming beneath the spinning ship.

Mag leapt and caught the ladder's lowest rung moments before it would have risen out of reach. There had been no time to disengage the last strap. The idiot pilot had panicked and engaged the maneuvering thrusters.

Mag pulled herself onto the spinning deck and noted he hadn't calmed down much. He was at the bow, leaning far off the edge, firing wild shots at the roof and shouting into his radio.

Mag pulled her pistol and fired a shot clean through the back of the man's neck. His *barishe* slipped off his head and he tumbled over the bow after it.

Colors blurred. The world was spinning in sickening waves.

No problem, she thought, *Right.*

Mag gripped the doorframe of the pilothouse and pulled herself inside. She took hold of the lazily spinning wheel. Outside, the scream of the final line struggling to hold onto the hull was deafening now.

She reversed thrust and steadied the ship and the spinning lines outside settled along with her stomach. Still the wind was getting under the sail. One strap wasn't enough to hold the ship, but it was enough to tear it apart.

Mag darted from the pilothouse to the source of the screeching line. It was pulling hard against the ship's steel plating.

That line's going to tear us apart.

She leaned out and took careful aim before firing at the groaning strap.

Miss.

The ringing in her ears was unbearable.

She took aim again.

Cal's left eye had swelled shut, and his left arm was near useless. Knocked to the ground again, he dragged himself across the roof, as the whirring straps settled against the screaming transport's hull. He faintly heard the sound of gunshots.

This was it.

The behemoth's long shadow trailed after him. *"Le Voe te Magar."*

Cal turned onto his back and wiped the blood from his mouth. "Nug you."

The distant groaning stopped, and the airship cocked hard to port. The blur of a strap sliced across the roof. Cal sat back, catching the behemoth's eyes. They flashed a moment before his torso slid away from the lower half of his body, landing next to his feet with a sickening splat.

The ship's keel smashed into the roof and Cal rolled as a heavy hook sunk into the rubber roofing on his left.

Well, that wasn't so bad.

Cal hoisted himself up, staggering dazily ahead towards the open roof hatch, before his feet rolled over the spilled brassite and out from under him. He landed on top of the rough stones.

"Bannon are you okay?" Mag called as she came down the ladder. "I think we're going to have a problem flying her now."

She was right. The transport's central mast was still intact, but the sail had been torn. A ship that big wouldn't stay in the air for more than a few minutes, even unloaded. It might have been able to trip over the side of the roof but nothing more.

Cal swiped a pile of the gritty stones away.

Damn it.

How in the hell was he going to—lying cocked onto one of its flat edges was one of the strangest stones Cal had ever seen. He pinched the brassite nugget between his fingers. It looked like an oversized eight-sided die. One side wasn't quite perfect but could be filed down. It's match for Mag's charm was uncanny.

Mag pulled him to a wobbling stand as he stuffed the stone into his pocket.

"It's… it's okay," he stammered. "Next step… a distraction…"

"What were the other steps?"

"Don't worry about…"

Shit.

A small airship barely above the tree line, was charting a course toward the castle through the reddening sky.

Mobatam had picked up a dozen more men on his way through the castle to the mining tower. Still more men had secured the castle's entrances and exits, but they'd quickly learned the corporatist wasn't headed for the front door.

As the rebel leader strode through the building, a voice crackled over the hand radio hanging from his belt: it was Richio, his head of security.

"Furlúco! There is smoke on the roof."

Mobatam raised the radio to his mouth and barked, "We're already on our way. Make sure no one makes it out of the tower." He released the transmit button and glared at Bulkarni. The clumsy fool had been huffing and puffing to keep up with them. At least he'd been quiet since losing contact with his frantic pilot.

The radio blasted again. *"Should I send more men to the mining tower?"* Turning the corner into a new passageway, Mobatam was about to answer when he became aware of two things: an imposing stench of ammonia, and that his boots were crunching over broken glass.

He stopped dead as his brain caught up with his senses.

They were in Guttiero's menagerie corridor.

At the end of the hall, the white *tbizah* sat on her haunches beneath a towering portrait. The cat licked a paw and rubbed it against a matted ear.

Mobatam gripped Bulkarni's arm and pulled him close. "Do not move," he whispered. "It cannot see in the—"

"*Mobatam?*" The radio buzzed again. "*Mobatam… do you copy?*"

The cat barreled down on them.

"Shoot it!" Mobatam yelled, knocking back into Bulkarni. "Shoot it!"

Flashing shots rang through the hall, but Mobatam wasn't waiting around to see if they hit. He was an instant behind Bulkarni, who had already bolted to the nearest room, stumbling in behind the Marabeshi banker and slamming the door behind him.

They were in the study.

Gunfire echoed off the walls outside as Mobatam vaulted his desk, shoved it on its side and heaved it towards the door. Bulkarni barely got out of the way before the heavy furniture thumped into place.

The banker tore his ridiculous headwear from the floor and clamped it back on, fear etched into his features. "They let the cat out of the—"

"No shit, Flat Top."

ELEVEN

NADIR WATCHED THE ORANGE CLOUDS move across the blood-red sky.

No… the clouds are not moving. They are dancing. Beautiful, dancing marshmallows.

Everything was beautiful.

He turned his head, resting his cheek against the warm wooden deck boards. Even his captor's boots were beautiful. The mud caked around their soles oozed like thick, melting fudge.

He looked up at the sky again. Twinkling stars were beginning to peek out. "How long until we're there?"

"A few more minutes," said the gentle giant behind the helm. "I need to find a place to set down our new fishing ship. If these *karanjeugos* are as good as they look, we may have no need for you in the mines. You have a special talent."

Nadir couldn't remember what he'd been fighting about in the first place. He didn't need freedom. He had been free, but he had no place free to go. He had nothing.

"Would you like to present your bounty to the duke?" the giant asked. "There may be a reward for these."

"Really?"

The hulking man nodded. "It's possible."

"More of the…" Nadir couldn't think of the word. *"Magic dust?"*

"Oh, that wouldn't be much of a reward," the man said, turning the gas release valve. "Scoraleza is an all you can eat buffet as far as that goes. But there may be a place in the culinary barracks for you. Soft mattresses… pretty women. They all have thick, juicy hips there. You'll like it."

"Girls?"

"Pretty ones."

There had been girls in Lana, but they never seemed to have much interest in Nadir. Why would they? Feeding himself was challenging enough. What could he offer them?

"Hold onto something," the man said, cranking the winch. "I'm landing."

The wind whistled as the boat touched down on the water. Cool, crystalline water spray splashed over the side, across Nadir's face. He lifted himself up. "Amazing."

The palace near the shimmering cove they'd landed in had the look of an elaborate musical instrument. All shiny spinning gears and pistons. Its towers seemed to stretch into the reddening heavens, but no, that was impossible. Nadir was already in heaven.

"What is your name?" he whispered.

"Tobar," the big man said. He turned the wheel and angled the craft to the dock at the edge of the lagoon. He indicated the wire cage of feisty crustaceans. "Are you as practiced in preparing these as you are at catching them?"

Not at all, Nadir thought. "Yes."

Tobar smiled his golden smile. "Really?"

Nadir looked down at his feet. "I've never had one."

Tobar rested his backside on the lip of the rocking boat. "Well now, see, that's not right. That's not a thing I… can let…" His words tailed off.

"What is it?"

Tobar pointed at the top of the tower. Nadir hadn't noticed the smoke curling above it—how could he have missed that?—or the cargo ship that was moving away from it. It was the same ship he had seen before he'd landed. A lifetime ago.

The sputtering airship drifted towards the ground, spiraling like water flowing down a drain. It hit a canopy of branches and flames erupted across its bow.

"Don't move from this spot," Tobar said, kicking his leg over the side of the boat.

"Can I come with you?"

"Stay here. I'll return in a moment."

Why would he go anywhere? This was where the magic was.

Nadir watched the smoke billowing from the trees and listened to the shouts of men in the distance. He wasn't sure how long he'd been watching when Tobar, covered in soot and ash, lifted himself back over the gunwale.

"What happened?"

"Your friends are loose."

"Friends?"

"Yes. I need you to…" Blood sprayed across the deck as something dark and red emerged from the front of Tobar's neck.

A flat knife.

Tobar clawed at the protruding blade as a red-headed woman climbed aboard alongside him.

"He's here," she said to someone behind her.

The knife disappeared and Tobar dropped to his knees.

Nadir scrambled and slipped backwards across the deck, huddled himself against the bulkhead. At first, he didn't recognize the man who'd killed Tobar: his face was a bruised and swollen mess. Then he spoke.

"You alright, kid?" he asked in Basic.

"What have you done?"

"I don't speak Aruminian, kid," the man said, climbing over the side and into the boat.

"You killed him," Nadir said, slowly sounding out the words in the man's language.

The woman kneeled beside him, and holding the lids open, peered into each of his eyes. "He's been drugged."

Nadir pushed her away and grabbed the side of the boat, ready to vault over and into the water, but the crook of an arm slid around his neck, pulling him back.

"Sorry, kid," the man said.

Nadir focused again on the Basic words he needed, translating them in his mind. The man would understand. Nadir would make him understand… but the world was going cloudy around him. "I want… *I want to stay.*"

"I know, kid. I know."

Zichor lowered his spyglass and ran a hand through his long greasy hair. He turned to his leader. "They're well out of range, *Furlúco.*"

What the hell is he talking about? Bulkarni thought. The skiff wasn't that far away. He could still see a blurry figure standing at the wheel. "How can they be out of range? We control thirty miles in every direction."

"That's true," Mobatam said. "*We do.* But soon it will be dark and the tbizah will be up. It'll be impossible to mobilize a strike from the ground."

So, we go get them when they land, you ape. "They'll be headed back to Cyio to charter a frigate. We'll pick them up there."

"Cyio de Reyes is controlled by the Traditionalists, Mister Secretary."

"But we can't let them get away!" Bulkarni shouted. "Our entire operation will be over!"

Mobatam smirked. Zichor moved behind Bulkarni and pinned his arms behind his back.

"What the hell are you doing?!"

Mobatam frowned. "I'm afraid, Mister Secretary… our operation *is* over."

Bulkarni thrashed against Zichor's grip. "It's over when I say it is! Do you have any idea what you're doing?"

"I am aware, Mister Secretary," Mobatam said, his eyes crinkling as he smiled. "It seems you are under the misplaced assumption that you are in charge. But this is my castle. This is my country. Mine."

"You ungrateful…"

Mobatam barked with laughter. Bulkarni's mind raced, trying to organize his thoughts. "Keep laughing if you want," he said. "Do you think we're going to let you get away with this?"

Mobatam composed himself then lifted off Bulkarni's *barishe* and placed it on his own glistening, bald head.

Bulkarni took a breath. "Whatever you're thinking of doing…"

"Oh, relax," Mobatam said, waving a hand. "Most of what they say about me is just for show, Mister Secretary." He looked to Zichor and held up his hands defensively. "I cook a *few* people and suddenly I'm almost expected to do it."

Bulkarni's knees wobbled beneath him.

"It's honestly more for appearances than anything else," Mobatam said. "Anyway, you're too valuable a commodity to kill."

"My people will not waste time trying to trade with you after this. Not even for me."

Mobatam nodded. "Oh yes, I know they won't. I would assume it is very likely they'll be steering well clear of my lovely country for some time. But the corporatists… *I think they might like to talk to you.*"

Cal was crouched low in the ship's tight berth, hands on his knees. Mag was in front of him, legs folded underneath her as she placed a flask of water to the boy's lips. Cal could smell the salt and seaweed on the back of her smooth neck.

Nadir's eyes fluttered open, and almost immediately he began thrashing wildly against the thick cords holding him in place.

"No sense struggling, kid," Cal said. "I'm good with knots."

Mag leaned forward to examine Nadir, but he twisted away. "Who are you?" he spat.

"My name is Margo Silverfinch. I'm a doctor."

"A doctor?" Nadir said, trading wild looks between them. "What happened to the other lady?"

Mag looked back to Cal, unsure what to say. He forced a smile and said, "She had to blow off some steam."

Mag rolled her blue eyes back towards her patient.

"I… I need *more*," Nadir said, writhing against his bonds. "Send me back!"

"I have some here." Cal fished a small case out of his pocket and held it over Mag's shoulder. He had found a small supply of the powder on the man who had taken the kid's ship.

Mag frowned. "Bannon…"

He held out the case. "Give it to him."

She sighed and took it. Opened the lid. "There isn't much here."

Nadir's squirming slowed, his eyelids batting fast as humming-bird wings. "How much? How much is it?"

Cal rested his forearms on his knees. "It'll be enough to hold you over. I still owe you your payout, kid."

"I no care about that anymore, Mister. Take me back."

"Back to the mines?"

"They not sending me there!"

Cal put his hands up. "Okay… okay, kid. Calm down."

Nadir's body shook, as if he was freezing. "I calm. I calm." He eyed the case hungrily. "Give it to me."

Mag shook her head. She licked the tip of her pinky and dabbed it into the powder. Then she held the dust under the kid's nostril, allowing him to snort it off her finger.

Euphoria washed over him, and he rested his head back on his sweat-stained pillow.

"Do you remember my name?" Mag asked.

"Doctor Margo Silverfinch," he said sleepily.

"That's right. I'm your doctor."

"Yes… you are my doctor."

Cal gripped his partner's shoulder and squeezed. "Can you handle this? Someone's got to steer this thing."

Mag nodded. "I'll be up in a minute."

He turned and popped the hatch. Moonlight puddled at the base of the short ladder, and he hoisted himself up into the warm air.

Taking the shifting wheel, he was pleased to find the light gusts had not pushed them too far off course. He nudged the helm slightly to starboard, towards the constellation of Cyocles fighting Yorono… *and home.*

Cal had always thought the pattern of stars depicting the two warriors looked more like two beetles wrestling, but it was an easy one for him to recognize. Cyocles and Yorono had been one of the first constellations his father had taught him.

That seemed like so long ago now. He felt so *tired.*

Mag had been right. It was time to stop.

He reached into his pocket and felt for the oddly shaped stone, rubbing a thumb along its rigid edges. Would she know what it meant?

She should.

She seemed to know everything.

Mag emerged from below deck. The wind whipped the pink dust off her clothes in a haze.

"How is he?" Cal said.

"Sleeping. Very relaxed now." She lowered the hinged hatch. "You need me to take the wheel?"

"I can do it," Cal said with a smile. "I took a few punches. Doesn't make me completely helpless, you know."

"I know… I know you're not." she said, biting her lip. "Looks like we're going to make it home *again.*"

"Never a doubt," Cal said cheerfully.

"Thanks… thanks for coming after me." Her voice cracked. Cal could see how scared she'd been, how much this had shaken her, but he knew better than to mention it.

"I'd have shown up faster if you had let me know you were going on assignment. No message. Nothing."

"It's Special Section, remember? Besides, you were busy with your friend. *The singer.*"

"Come on, Mag."

"Don't do that. You don't get to pretend you didn't know that would bother me."

"I… I know."

She looked up at him and touched his face. "You look like hell, Bannon."

He smiled, relieved she'd broken the tension. Things would be different this time. "Just need a drink and some sleep."

"That would be nice." She looked back to the hatch. "What are you going to do with our patient?"

"Pay him what I owe and bring him home to get vaccinated."

"Bring him back with us to the Confederation?"

"At least temporarily."

She coughed out a short laugh of disbelief. "Do you go anywhere without bringing someone back?"

"It's my fault he's here. It was the price of getting you out."

"I know… I just don't want you in trouble because of me."

"Trouble with you I think I can handle."

She wrapped her arms around him, and Cal rested his chin in her hair. "I thought we were dead," she said. "That Hunt had us. She fooled everyone."

"She fooled a few," he said. "But you're the only one I trust."

"Cal," she said into his chest, "I'm leaving the service. My contract's up. I'm going back to private practice."

"Good."

"Good?" she squeaked in surprise, pulling away from him.

"Yeah, But we can't—"

"I'm pregnant."

"You're…"

"Pregnant."

"You're… you're sure?"

She pursed her lips. "One hundred percent? No. But pretty sure."

"That's no answer!" he snapped, his imagination driving him to fury. "It wasn't one of those maniacs?" She shook her head. "So how? *Who?*"

"You don't know him," she said, before raising a hand to correct herself. "Well, you don't know him well."

"Who the hell is it?"

"Simon Handley."

"Simon Handley? *Simon Handley from accounting?*"

"He's not from *accounting*," she said, raising her voice. "He works for the CFO."

The deck shifted beneath Cal's feet and the ship pulled sharp to the left. Mag sprang forward and took the wheel. Cal could only stand. A vein was throbbing hard in his knotted forehead and his tongue had grown numb.

"He… I mean… are you happy about this?"

"Yeah… I think I am."

"That's… that's good," he said quietly. He felt the stone in his pocket and shivered against the cold, tropical wind.

Surveillance Report

Eyes Only: Admiral Tyson Bannon

Coordinates: 31.46.03.5N35.13.01E

Subject: Unidentified Heilish construction

Location: Disputed territory. Sea zone claimed by Sanland and Heiland, at near the center of what the Sanlish call Lucy's Bay, and what the Heilish refer to as *Pare Eine*.

Physical Description: A windowless, metallic sphere. Means of propulsion unclear. There is no tower connecting it to the surface.

Awaiting further instructions.

~ Lieutenant Martan Tims

Communications, CAS Cyocles

TWELVE

PATTERSON'S CELLMATE WAS ALIVE BUT not. The journalist was staring at the wall again, unblinking.

Once, Patterson had asked him what he was looking at. The man had claimed he wasn't looking at anything. That was when he'd still been talking.

The reporter had been quite chatty when he first arrived. He'd introduced himself as Parker and told Patterson he was an independent journalist from Salzburg. After a week, the reporter was still speaking with a strange confidence, though his words were often jumbled and incoherent.

After two weeks at Yalespitz, Parker still spoke, but only when spoken to.

That had been months ago.

Now Parker said nothing. He did nothing. He slept as quietly as a dead man. The only sounds he made were while crunching on his evening meal of crackers or relieving himself at the steel toilet built into their cell wall.

Patterson found he didn't miss talking to the man, which struck him as odd. He'd never been so alone, but there was nothing to be gained from talking to a dead man. Even one that slept and ate.

Instead, Patterson filled his waking hours with aerobics, strength training, and meditation. He'd never meditated before and had never been an athlete, but it seemed the right thing to do. It was the only thing to do. His former noodlelike arms now rippled with muscle. He was not vain. It was a statement of fact.

"

He understood everything now. The answer to every puzzle was right there in his mind.

He knew now that he could escape. There were so many opportunities, everywhere, all around him, all the time. He estimated an eighty-three percent chance of escape on his first attempt. And yet, it seemed wrong to try.

He would miss his appointment with Dr. Zolbar.

The cell door opened and two familiar *wehrcomache* entered: Han and Kal. Han was stocky, balding, and stank of a revolting blend of Heilish whiskey. "It's time, Patterson," he said, looking down at his feet. Neither of the two *wehrcomache* would make eye contact with him.

Patterson could have taken the rifle from Han then. He would eliminate the still armed Kal first. He estimated there was then a ninety-two percent chance Han would beg for his life rather than risk running. Patterson would learn a lot more at that point. The extra knowledge would give him a thirty-five percent chance of being back in Pantopolis with Beth and Paul in under a week.

But again, if he did that, he'd miss his appointment. Patterson couldn't do that. It would be like cutting off the oxygen he needed to breathe.

He finished a final set of sit-ups, got to his feet, and extended his wrists. Kal shackled him silently and the guards led him into the corridor, away from his undead cellmate and the buzzing fluorescent lights of his cell.

The illumination outside was dimmer and softer. There were no windows.

So many corners to hide in.

They passed the docking bay. The overhead doors of the hangar were shut as usual, but the high-altitude air chilled Patterson's skin.

There was a seventy-five percent chance he was on a cloud-reacher in either Scranzland, Dranbad, or Kurat.

Yet, the most logical location for a covert facility on a populated habitat would be near the roaring wind turbines at its center, and Patterson had been unable to hear any such sound.

He knocked on the doctor's door and pushed down on the stiff, brass latch with his bound hands.

The door groaned open. From behind his desk, Dr. Zolbar peeked up at him over his reading optics. "Ah, Lieutenant. Good." He extinguished his cigarette into a crystal ashtray and beckoned Patterson inside. "Please, sit. How long has it been since our last session?"

Patterson lowered himself into one of two vacant leather chairs. Behind him, the door latch clicked into place again. "Two days, two hours, eight minutes."

Dr. Zolbar flipped through several pages of his legal pad. "Yes, Lieutenant," he said, scratching a note with his pen. "That would seem to be about correct. You are progressing quite well. How do you feel?"

Patterson understood everything, yet this question. It was nonsensical. "How do I…? I don't…"

"You look quite fit, Lieutenant."

"Yes. Quite fit."

"I'd estimate you could lift me with a single arm."

"Yes. I could."

Dr Zolbar's pen scritched faster. "It is good you are doing so well. Would you like to play a game with me?"

"That would depend."

"On what?"

"A great many things, Doctor."

Dr. Zolbar smiled and opened the top drawer of his deck. He produced a standard sixty-card deck and slid a thumbnail across the seal. "We will play *parsnipper*. Are you familiar with the game?"

"No, Doctor."

"I will teach you." Dr. Zolbar dealt out ten cards each, face down. "First, we must select a card from our hand to discard. These will be our respective trump suits. If we select the same trump suit, we will discard our hands and draw fresh cards from the deck and then proceed to Round Two. There will be three rounds total."

Patterson slid his cards across the tablet towards him. Curling up the edges, he peered underneath.

Hearts: 9
Swords: 4
Shields: 2, 4, 7, A
Leaves: 3, 4, 6, 9

He had not been dealt any Bells.

"The goal of the game will be to take tricks," Dr. Zolbar said as he rearranged the cards in his hand. "After we've selected our trump suits, the lead player will select a card to play. The responding player must play a card of the same suit or his trump suit, if possible. If not, he may play any card. The highest value card wins the trick and control. Capturing a player's numbered card, two through nine, is worth a single point. Holy cards are worth two points, and the ace is worth three."

"A simple game," Patterson said. "I understand."

"You sound quite confident." Dr. Zolbar laid his pen on a fresh pad and slid it over to Patterson with a bony finger. "Would you care to keep score?"

"Of course, Doctor." Patterson took the pad, then drew the Two of Shields facedown from his hand.

"Good. We will reveal trump cards simultaneously." They flipped their cards. Dr. Zolbar revealed the Five of Leaves. "I will lead play," he said. "As you see, my trump suit is Leaves. Yours is Shields."

He won the first two tricks, capturing Patterson's Nine of Hearts and Four of Swords.

"Going first allows you to set the tempo," Patterson said.

"Life is so rarely fair." Dr. Zolbar revealed his Five of Hearts and Patterson captured it with his Six of Leaves.

The game became much clearer as the tricks progressed.

"Are you not keeping score?" Dr. Zolbar indicated the untouched yellow legal pad.

"I *am* keeping score."

At the end of the round, Patterson was ahead five points to four. The doctor dealt another ten cards to each of them, and after the second round, Patterson's lead had grown, thirteen points to eight.

"You are taking to the game quite well," Dr. Zolbar said, as he dealt out the remaining twenty cards.

Patterson examined his hand. "It is easy," he said. "You have not been shuffling."

Dr. Zolbar leaned forward and rested his elbows on the desk. "Do you know my cards?"

"Yes," Patterson said evenly. "You have the Four, Eight and Father of Hearts, the Eight and Nine of Swords, the Mother and Father of Shields, the Two of Leaves, and the Four and Six of Bells. I suspect you will select the Four of Hearts as your trump card."

Dr. Zolbar chuckled and clapped his hands together. "It seems you're too good for me, Lieutenant. Have you always been such a natural card player?"

"No, I haven't."

"Well, no matter. You are very gifted, Lieutenant. Truly."

What have you done to me?

Dr. Zolbar pulled his bag of candy from the top drawer of his desk. "Something sweet, Lieutenant?"

Patterson extended his bound hands and Dr. Zolbar dropped a sky-blue ball into his palm. He popped it into his mouth. It tasted like powdery nothing. He swallowed the flavorless ball, only half chewed.

Dr. Zolbar selected a matching candy. "How have your dreams been? Any more nightmares about this white room?"

White room? "I'm afraid I cannot… cannot recall…"

Dr. Zolbar slurped at his sweet and put up a hand. "My mistake," he said, licking his lips. "I must have confused you with another patient."

"Yes. I was confused."

Dr. Zolbar offered him the bag of treats. "Please. Have another."

Patterson picked out a hot pink candy.

"Tell me, Lieutenant, what can you tell me about Sky Fleet's tactical plans in the event of a joint Heilish and Marabeshi assault on Prakesha?"

"I've not been privy to any of those types of advanced plans or discussions."

Dr. Zolbar smiled, his teeth and tongue stained a faint blue. "Yes, Lieutenant. But speculate. Tell me what you think."

Patterson's mind unspooled the query in an instant. "Prakesha is likely a redline for direct Confederate military involvement. Prakesha borders Sanland. The Confederation will not risk losing Sanland."

"Very good. Those would be my thoughts as well. And what do you think the odds of success are, regarding such a hypothetical incursion into Prakesha?"

"Against a joint attack by Marabeshi and Heilish forces, the odds are Prakesha would fall quickly. There is a sixty-eight percent chance it would surrender in under seventy-two hours."

"Ahh…" Dr. Zolbar picked up his pad again and scribbled a note. "I see."

"However, it is unlikely such an alliance would be successful in the long run."

Dr. Zolbar cocked his head. "And why is that?"

"Because both nations are led by men who believe they are The One. Men like that have many enemies and few friends. Least of all each other."

Dr. Zolbar stopped writing and leaned back in his chair. "Interesting." He pulled a medicine bottle from inside his red coat and unscrewed the cap. He placed it on the desk. Patterson picked it up and tipped out two red-and-blue colored capsules.

"Do you require any water?"

"No, Doctor," Patterson said, taking the pills and swallowing them.

"It has been a pleasure working with you," Dr. Zolbar said with a smile. "You remember that I promised to check in on your family?"

"Beth."

"Yes. Elizabeth Patterson and your son…" Dr. Zolbar took a frayed purple folder from the desk beside him and flipped through the pages. "Paul. Yes, that's right. Paul. I swear, I just lose my mind sometimes."

"Beth and Paul are…"

"Dead, I'm afraid," Dr. Zolbar said baldly. "Your sweet wife poisoned the boy and then jumped from Brunswick into the

Pantopolis Sound. There wasn't much left, but I do have the coroner's report here."

Dead.

Dr. Zolbar held out the folder across the desk. Patterson swatted it, sending the paper fluttering like oversized confetti.

"I must say you seem quite agitated by this news, Lieutenant."

"I'm going to kill you. You're lying."

Dr. Zolbar's eyebrows arched upward. "I do not lie."

That was true.

"You do not lie," Patterson said. Of course, he did not lie. He was Patterson's doctor. He was here to help.

Dr. Zolbar cocked his head. "You are not going to kill me?"

"Of course not, Doctor."

"Good." Dr. Zolbar smiled and took stock of his office. "Do not worry about the mess, Lieutenant. You may see yourself back to your accommodations." He returned his attention to his pad and began scribbling notes.

Patterson left the office, blood pumping in his ears. Han and Kal were waiting for him in the hall.

"That was fast today," Kal said.

How could Beth do this? It can't be true. I need to get out of here. But the doctor does not lie.

Kal led him past the docking bay. The bay doors were open. A luxury yacht hovered above the black deck plates twenty yards out past the hatch, held in place by four thick mooring lines.

No one was on deck.

No one was in the docking bay at all.

It was wide open.

Patterson walked on, making calculations in his head.

Kal opened the cell door, and Parker turned away from the wall, considering the group with hollow eyes.

There was a ninety-one percent probability that he could escape if he left right now. The odds would drop by twenty-eight percent if he attempted to bring the reporter with him.

There would be no time to interrogate Han.

Patterson spun, ripped the rifle from the stocky *wehrcomache* and shot Kal an eighth of an inch above his left eye. In a seamless motion, he rammed the rifle into Han's stomach then shot him in the back of the head.

Parker looked briefly at Kal's lifeless body before turning back to the wall. Patterson grabbed his arm. "We must go."

Saying nothing, Parker allowed himself to be pulled out of the cell. He slumped behind Patterson, back to the docking area.

The bay was still empty. The yacht's gangway was down. Patterson would—

"Halad!"

Stop.

Patterson's body went stiff, and his thoughts snapped away.

"Wich lunhen."

Turn around.

Dr. Zolbar stood behind him, next to a much taller man with a neatly trimmed black-and-blue beard that ended in a sharp point below his chin. Patterson had never seen him in the flesh before but recognized him instantly.

Chancellor Ayon.

"You see, My Guide?" Dr. Zolbar said in Heilish.

The chancellor looked each prisoner over. His eyes held for a moment on Patterson's weapon before drifting away. "What tricks can they do?"

"Almost anything we can think of, My Guide. Mister Parker, stand on one foot."

Parker did so.

"Hop up and down."

Parker began hopping continuously.

"When treated," Dr. Zolbar explained, "they will do whatever is asked, My Guide."

Chancellor Ayon made a wide circle around the pair of them. "Can they speak?"

"Lieutenant Patterson can. As I've mentioned, My Guide, the results of my treatments are limited without prior exposure to the Confederacy's *altim* inhibitor."

"We have use for only that one, then," Ayon said, indicating Patterson.

"Of course, My Guide," Dr. Zolbar said, understanding. "Mister Patterson, kill Mister Parker."

Patterson shot the hopping reporter, sending him spinning away.

The chancellor smirked. "I hadn't meant right this moment, Doctor."

"Apologies, My Guide." Dr. Zolbar waved a finger at Patterson. "That's very good, Lieutenant. Now put the gun on the ground."

Patterson bent forward at the waist and laid down the weapon.

"Promising, Doctor." Chancellor Ayon beckoned someone forward from the edge of the hangar.

A wisp of a woman slipped past Patterson. Her high messy blue bun bobbed as she made small leaps between pools of blood. "Really, Doctor Zolbar. You must learn to control yourself."

"Mistress Gubinette," Zolbar said. "It is good to see you as always. I hope your family is well."

"I do not see what is to be gained by these ridiculous demonstrations."

"Apologies, Mistress," Dr. Zolbar put up his hands and shook his head. "Honestly, it was just a bit of fun."

Chancellor Ayon gurgled a closed-mouthed chuckle.

Gubinette licked her lips. "Of course, Doctor," she said acidly. "May I?"

Dr. Zolbar gave a half-bow "Of course, Mistress. Please."

Mistress Gubinette looked down at a thick, heavy binder she carried in both hands. "Lieutenant Patterson—"

"You can step closer," Dr. Zolbar said. "He will not bite."

"He can hear me from here. Please, Doctor."

"Apologies."

"Lieutenant Patterson, do you speak Heilish fluently?"

"Yes."

"How have you come to have this knowledge?"

"I do not know," Patterson said. "I hear the words. I understand."

Gubinette scribbled a note. "Would you say your capacity for mathematical computation has increased in the last few months?"

"Yes. I would say that, if asked."

The chancellor grunted. "He still has free will."

"Some, My Guide," Dr. Zolbar said. "But the mistress has not been properly bonded with him. He has been conditioned to obey me."

Gubinette frowned and returned to her list of questions. "How do you feel, Lieutenant?"

I feel nothing.

I want Beth back.

I want her back so I can kill her.

I want Paul back.

I want to snap all your necks and stuff you with candy.

I want to kill Cal Bannon. I'm sure he's the reason I'm in this hell.

"I feel fine, Mistress."

"You can show me how this bonding is done?" Ayon asked.

"Of course," Dr. Zolbar said. "There is no perfect connection, and a great one takes some time, My Guide. But I can demonstrate for you the pairing I have with Lieutenant Patterson is rather strong."

"Proceed."

"Lieutenant," Dr. Zolbar said. "Who speaks the truth?"

"You do."

"That's right. I speak the truth. And do you approve of your new condition?"

"I approve of it."

"You want to share your new knowledge with all of your countrymen in the Confederacy?"

"Yes. I want to share it with my countrymen in the Confederacy."

"Very good, Lieutenant," Dr. Zolbar said. "Now you will forget the entirety of the last few minutes. You have not attempted to escape. You returned to your room after our appointment and found Mister Parker gone."

And so it was.

PART TWO

... must come down

CONFEDERATE MEDIA ARCHIVE

SUBJECT: MARABESHI SURRENDER, GULAR WAR

DATE STAMP: FIFTH ROTATION, THE DRY SEASON, 1475 OS

"The war with Marabesh is over.

"In the early hours of this morning, Heilish ground forces seized control of Pindon, Mupai's aerial defense base. The facility, largely staffed by gulars, provided little resistance against the heavily armed *wehrcomache* soldiers.

"With Marabeshi air support grounded, a joint task force of twenty airships, led by the Confederation flagship *Bicentennial*, executed what Sky Fleet officials are calling Operation Wet-Drop. The flotilla dropped a payload of vaporized altim inhibitor across the capital city, shattering the chains of induced mind control and sending the liberated gular population into a frenzy.

"Soon after, Marabeshi President Yunai Tumar signed over authority to now acting President Suhain Pinto, who immediately surrendered to the commander of the *Bicentennial*.

"And so the conflict that began more than a decade ago with Marabesh's invasion of Prakesha has finally ended. And while estimates suggest more than thirty million lives have been lost, it is certain that the true cost of this war will not be reckoned for many years to come.

"Reporting live from the cloud-reacher Tarastan in Mupai, this is Ryan Rique of the Pantopolis Radio Network.

THIRTEEN

Jon Merry found Lagard to be a beautiful place.

Back home, the Confederacy's more affluent population opted for the limitless energy offered by the cloud-reachers. That was not so here. In the low-lying towns of Sanland, the homes and shops were still built with wood and heated with coal-fired stoves. Most of the buildings were nearly a hundred years old, each wonderfully distinctive and full of character with angular clay roofs and weather-beaten siding.

Jon had grown up on the ground, but even the farms outside Pinburgh had been updated into standardized, soulless creations over the last several years. That was why he had attended the academy: to travel and see places like these.

It helped that he turned 18 at nearly the exact moment the Gular War ended. It was a blessing that years of conflict were over, that he could join Sky Fleet and be reasonably safe. At least that's what everyone kept telling him.

Everyone but the commodore.

We're always at war, Skyman, the old man had said. *This is where the real wars are won. In the shadows.*

It had been nearly two months since Jon had applied for Special Section, and now those words seemed like hyperbole. Still, the commodore's assignments were more exciting than sitting around, playing cards in Marabesh.

He couldn't risk nugging this up.

Behind him, the captain's radio crackled, and Jon tore himself from the window overlooking the dusty, cobbled streets.

"Receiving," Captain Alameidar said. "Go ahead."

"*The tbizah is in the tree*," an unfamiliar voice responded. Jon had never heard the expression before, but he was learning quickly that the crew of the *Bicentennial* had a language all their own.

"Understood." Alameidar released the radio's transmit button and shot Jon a look. "Ready, Skyman?"

"Yes, sir," Jon said. He still hadn't quite wrapped his head around the discovery that Captain Alameidar was involved with Special Section. Alameidar was not just any captain. He was *the* captain. The commander of the Confederate flagship, one of four remaining Typhon-Class cruisers and the most renowned vessel in the fleet since the *Corralgazer* had been lost.

He'd also been surprised how young the captain was. Out of uniform, in his navy tweed jacket and slim tie, he looked more a man-about-town than a renowned officer. As if his entire life had been played with house money.

The captain led Jon down the creaking stairs of the safehouse and opened the door to the street. "Be careful, Mister Merry."

"Yes, Captain."

"You have your radio?"

It was strapped around his calf beneath his trousers. The commodore had warned him not to use it, except in the case of an eminent threat to his life.

"Yes, Captain," he said.

Alameidar rubbed his neatly trimmed black beard. "Very well. Target is in the pub across the street. Worn gray suit with matching fedora."

"Understood, sir."

"Do not make direct contact. See where he goes, and no matter what, you report back in two hours."

Jon noted the time on his aviator wristwatch. "Yes, sir." He scooted around the captain and out onto the lamp-lit street.

He had watched the pub from his perch near the window for an hour. Five people had gone in and three had come out. None had been wearing a gray suit, so the target had to have entered via the back door, or from one of the apartments above the establishment.

The pub door groaned on old hinges as Jon entered, but none of the four men scattered throughout the pub looked up, including the target. Jon spotted him straight away, even with the man's fedora placed on the bar and his tattered gray overcoat slung over the stool to his left.

Jon weighed taking the free stool on his right, but the commodore would have called that move too bold. And Jon needed to keep the old man happy. Instead, he took a seat at a round wooden table near the center of the taproom. It was best not to hide himself in one of the corner booths. Spies check the corners.

A stocky, bald man was tending the bar, the sleeves of his denim shirt rolled up to the base of his elbows. He leaned across the sticky wooden surface and called out, "What you havin', lad? Beer or whiskey?"

"Beer," Jon said, allowing himself another smooth look at Fedora Man. The target was seemingly immersed in a crinkled newspaper and took a sip from his glass without looking up.

The bartender pulled down on a tap and filled two glasses with frothy beer. He clumped around the bar and plopped down in the empty seat across from Jon, clunking the drinks down on the table.

"Here ye are, lad." His warm, red face split in a wide grin. "How are ye?"

Jon realized he'd sat back a little, startled by the man's sudden proximity. He focused on keeping his voice casual. "I'm doing well, sir. And you?"

"I'm good, lad. Very good," the bartender said, chuckling. "I hope I didna scare ye. Was not my intent." He slid the pint across the table's rough, stained surface and chuckled to himself. "Most folks round here are regulars, is all. When someone new comes in, I make a point to join 'em in a drink. Free of charge. I'm not intrudin', am I?"

Jon looked around the pub. "You've bought a drink for everyone in here?"

The bartender looked over his shoulder. "Have I, lads?" he asked.

A smattering of 'Ayes' sounded around the establishment, with a singular, notable exception.

"Podlick's the name," the barman said. "And what would be yer holy name, my boy?"

"Sam," Jon said. "Sam Masterson. I appreciate the hospitality." He raised his glass. "Thank you."

"It's a pleasure, lad. Truly a pleasure."

Podlick grunted as he leaned forward and the two touched glasses. Up close, Jon noticed a blackish-blue shadow behind the man's ears. He swished the warm, bitter beer in his mouth.

Podlick licked his lips. "Yer accent… yer from the Confederacy."

"Very perceptive," Jon said. "You have met many Confederates?"

"Aye I have, lad, I have. But none with quite yer pronunciation."

"With all the travel I've been doing, it seems I've picked up a few confusing inflections."

"Aye." Podlick pointed a thumb at his chest. "Yer like the ole *Saint* Podlick, ye are. Stay here long enough and yer'll be one of us."

Except Podlick isn't your name, Jon thought. The barman was Heilish and trying very hard not to look it. Few of his countrymen would show their face—or hair—in Sanland. Though the commodore was said to have quite a few in his back pocket.

Jon smiled and said, "A charming thought."

Over Podlick's shoulder, the target counted out a few Sanlish credits and placed them on the bar.

"What brings ye into our cozy lil' town, lad?" Podlick's accent was good, Jon had to give him that. Near perfect.

"A Mister Travers up the road," Jon said. "Are you familiar with him?"

"Aye, I am, I am. How ye know Lenny?"

Keep to the script.

"He served with my father in a joint unit during the war. There were some things left to him in my father's will. I've been transporting them."

"My condolences on yer loss. My condolences." They touched glasses again. "And cheers to 'em both, lad. All those men from the war are heroes."

The target shook his way into his coat and put on his hat.

Jon chugged down the final quarter of his beer and stifled a belch. "I must thank you again. It's rather good." The target stepped outside, the door easing shut after him. "But I should be heading off. Mister Travers was kind enough to allow me to stay but warned me to be back before the calendar turned. Thank you again for the drink."

Podlick squeaked backward in his chair. "Leaving so soon? Why, yer just sat down. Is it na rude to accept my gift and na' stay for a second?"

Jon stood and made for the exit. "Perhaps."

"I'm sure ye—"

But Jon was already out in the street, the door banging shut behind him. He looked in both directions, and spotted Fedora Man three streetlamps away to the left.

Jon leaned against a cool, damp lamppost and waited for the target's footfalls to fade. When they did, he slipped into the shadows and closed the distance between them to two blocks.

Fedora Man trudged up a flight of concrete steps and entered a darkened, twin home. Jon gave him a moment, then skipped up the short stoop and read the address plate: 14 Lagard Place.

The door had a large glass pane, and through it Jon could see a dim light bleeding into a dark foyer.

He hopped down to the sidewalk and made his way into an alley between the buildings. He sat on the weedy grass under the glowing light from the window above and checked his watch. It was another hour and a half until the cutoff, and it would be a brisk ten-minute walk back to the safehouse.

Would the commodore have devised a game of this sort just to test his patience?

Yes, he absolutely would.

During their brief time together, the commodore had done little more than assess Jon's ability to follow his exact instructions. Jon had hoped this time was different. That he had proven himself enough to be trusted with a mission that was actually important.

He'd been waiting in the alley for thirty minutes before he heard footsteps clapping on the sidewalk. A man strolled past the alley and Jon took mental note of his appearance: male, 6 foot to 6 foot 3, 160 to 180 pounds, likely between 35 and 50 years old.

The footfalls slowed at 14 Lagard Place and keys jangled before the door opened. Moments later, Jon detected mumbled voices above him. There was little he could do to hear exactly what was being said, unless he found a way inside. And he wasn't going to fall for that.

Do not get caught. You get caught—you're gone.

Yes, this was a tease to pull him out of hiding. Jon settled his back against the brick foundation and checked his watch again. The second hand slid around the dial seemingly in slow motion. Still another hour to go.

Above him, the light in the window went out. Footsteps clomped up the stairs.

He would give himself an extra ten minutes to get back regardless of any additional surprises he was thrown.

"Aaaaaaaaaaaaahh!"

The scream was high, sharp and shrill. More footsteps slapped against the sidewalk, and a young girl scrambled past the alley in a blur.

Thin, 40 to 50 pounds, between 8 and 10 years old.

She screamed louder.

It's a game.

A man in a newsie cap ran silently past. 5 foot 5 to 5 foot 8, 200 to 220 pounds, 30 to 50 years old.

Trash cans banged together, the sound of someone being slapped.

It's a game.

Jon slunk towards the road, hugging the rough wall. He peered around the corner in time to see a glass bottle roll from an alley a little further up the road. It cycled off the curb and shattered.

The commodore doesn't use kids.

Hell…

Jon retreated into the alley and pulled out his radio. "This is Nixon," he whispered.

The radio blared, *"Receiving you, Nixon. Go ahead."*

"Look, I know this is a test, but there's a girl out here being assaulted. Request permission to terminate the exercise."

"What girl?"

The slapping became rhythmic, flesh impacting on flesh.

"Exactly—what girl?" Jon spat. "She's outside the mission parameters. Request permission to *do something.*"

"Hold a minute. We're going to bring the commodore on."

Another slap. Jon flinched, squeezed the transmit button. "Any time…"

"We're working on it. Standby."

"The girl!"

"We're evaluating the situation."

Damn it.

Jon dropped the radio, sprinted onto the sidewalk and to the alley.

Podlick sat on a trash can, his newsie cap in his lap. A small woman—no bigger than a girl—was leaning up against another corrugated metal can, with her skirt was pulled up past her knees. She was slapping her reddening thigh, over and over.

"Sorry, Lieutenant," she said, the ghost of a smile on her lips.

"Was my accent, alright?" Podlick asked, all trace of his Sanlish tones gone, replaced with clipped Heilish pronunciation.

"It was fine." Jon tapped on the space above his ear. "But I'd use a sharper razor next time."

Podlick rubbed his scalp and smiled knowingly.

"Alright, that's enough, Skyman." the commodore's voice called behind him. "That'll be all for you as well, *Saint Podlick.*"

Podlick helped the petite woman to her feet and sidled around Jon, back into the street. "Sorry, Lieutenant," he muttered as he passed.

"I knew it was a test," Jon said.

The commodore shook his head. "Except you didn't."

Damn this blowhard. "So, I failed?"

Commodore Bannon nodded and unfastened the horn button of his sports jacket. "I'm afraid you did."

"I'm sorry, sir…"

"So am I. You'd performed well to this point. Believe me when I say, I'm disappointed it's over."

"Over?" Jon said. "You mean, that's it?"

The commodore nodded solemnly. "That's it."

"But sir… I only get one chance?"

"One chance is all any of us ever get, Lieutenant."

"What happens now?"

"Your previous assignment was at Porakpur. I assume you'll be sent back there."

Jon's mouth hung open. Porakpur was even more boring than home. "You're sending me back to Marabesh?"

"I think the point is, I'm not sending you anywhere, Skyman."

Captain Alameidar approached behind the commodore, wearing a somber expression.

"You'll accompany us back to Pantopolis for debriefing," Bannon said. "From there you'll be reassigned. Seeing as your previous position in Porakpur has likely not been filled, I'd assume that's the most logical assignment for you."

"Sir…"

Bannon scratched the thinning salt-and-pepper hair at his temple. "I'm not going to debate you. You had your shot. It's over. If you wish to file a complaint or appeal, Captain Alameidar here will provide you with the appropriate paperwork and will file it for you." He turned to the captain. "You can handle that, Captain?"

"Of course, Commodore," Alameidar said, his face sour.

"Good, then you're both dismissed." The commodore spun on his heels and vanished into the night.

The life drained out of Jon, and he sat down amongst the scattered bottles and cardboard, hands on his knees.

"It was a difficult test," Alameidar said. "Not many would have passed it."

Jon gritted his teeth. "I don't believe it was a *fair* test, sir."

"On that we can agree, Skyman."

"I knew it was a trick, and I fell for it."

"In Special Section, not everything is what it seems."

ATTENTION: SKY FLEET BOARD; EXECUTIVE TEAM

Subject: Commodore Callum Bannon

Since Commodore Bannon was given command of recruitment and training of Sky Fleet's Special Section, several members of the board and our executive team have expressed publicly and privately their desire to have this appointment re-evaluated. These concerns are due in large part to a lack of output.

The purpose of this memorandum is to affirm my support for Commodore Bannon and express my confidence in him as both an instructor and intelligence officer.

Though the nature of many of the commodore's accomplishments while an active operative remain both secret and confidential, I will allow simply that he performed with both bravery and distinction during his time on active duty.

However, his contributions as an academy instructor may have been even more impactful. I point out that many of his students have gone on to achieve great success throughout Sky Fleet, including Captain Mario Tether, Captain Rogers Hornby, and Captain Nadir Alameidar.

The need for intelligence gathering never ends even in peace time but given the lack of active threats at the present time, I advise we give the commodore the freedom needed to accomplish his task.

~ Admiral Robert Bishop

FOURTEEN

"COMMODORE, WAIT UP." NADIR JOGGED along the sidewalk to catch up with Cal's brisk pace.

"Not bad performances tonight," Cal said.

Nadir took a breath. "Yes, sir. *From everyone.*"

Cal smirked and continued towards his black sedan. "It doesn't sound like you ran up to talk about the Rounders' relief pitching."

"No, sir. The test—"

"Let me guess. It wasn't fair."

"We both know it wasn't fair, Mister Cal." Nadir leapt between him and the driver's door. "Lieutenant Merry scored higher on the P, B, and Rs than any recruit we've had since you've taken over."

Cal frowned. Several of Nadir's crew who had been part of the exercise were still milling about, trying very hard to look as though they were not listening. "That's more of a reflection on the level of the recruits we've had."

"Standards since you have taken over the program have become—"

"You have an issue with high standards, Captain?"

"When they are this restrictive, sir, I might. What is the point of the P, B, and Rs if—"

"The written test helps us identify potential. That's it." Cal reached around Nadir and gripped the door handle of the sedan. "Now, how soon can the *Bicentennial* be ready to depart?"

Nadir frowned and sidestepped out of his way. "Give me at least two days, Mister Cal. Half the crew is on leave. I was not expecting to ship out so soon."

"Try to have everybody back on board by noon tomorrow," Cal said, opening the door.

"Mister Cal, maybe *you* should go—"

"I don't need shore leave."

"Sir, I think I'm going to have to disagr—"

"Just have the ship ready," Cal said as he settled behind the wheel and pulled the door closed.

He waited for Nadir to take a step back before starting the car and hitting the accelerator. Captain or not, he didn't understand: the next war was going to be even worse than the last one, and Cal couldn't use men he didn't trust.

A few miles down the road, the flickering streetlamps running alongside the cobblestone road gave way to darkened farms and fields. Vienamy's domed habitat peeked over the horizon and as the shape of the cloud-reacher grew, even the farms dwindled away. No one wanted to live in the shadow of such a monstrous city.

When at last Cal reached the base of the tower, he steered towards the parking area and pulled up alongside the valet booth. He stepped out of the sedan, the ground crunching under his feet. The dry dirt hadn't felt rain in more than ten years.

The shack's rickety window slid open, and a scrawny young man leaned out. "Evening, sir. Welcome to Vienamy. Do ya have yer ticket?"

Cal held up his laminated identification card. Puzzled, the valet angled his head to see it, before leaning further out to get a better look. He squinted and took the card, holding it up to the spotlights on the roof. "This ain't a ticket."

"It's a military clearance card," said a woman's voice behind him. As she stood up, the legs of her metal folding chair scraped against the shack's floorboards. Cal assumed she was the supervisor here: she was at least twenty years the valet's senior, with cheeks like raisins.

She took the card and gave the young man a reassuring pat on the back. "I'll take care of this one. Go and park his rental, Louie."

The young man nodded and slipped out the booth's side door.

"Sorry about that, Commodore," the woman said, handing him back his card. "His shift just started. You're out of uniform and we don't get many military ships here anymore. Certainly not anything like the *Bicentennial*." She yanked up on a lever by her knees and the doors built into the cloud-reacher's tower rattled open, spilling out a buzzing, artificial light.

"Of course. Just so you know, there'll be a few more behind me." Cal took back his card and gave her a curt nod. "Evening."

The lift was large enough to carry as many as fifty passengers and was exclusively used to take riders between the deck and the car depot. The small horde of tourists from the passenger liner that made the run between Vienamy and Seven Pools every two weeks used it, but the residents rarely did.

Cal rode the lift up, and his shoulder ached slightly at the increased altitude. The low hum of grinding gears and wind turbines became overpowered by a gathering musical clamor.

da... na... do... dee... do... dee

He tapped his foot as the earworm took root in his brain.

What was *that?*

The doors racked open, and Cal found himself at the back of a shifting mass of bodies. Several onlookers gave him a brief, annoyed look before returning their attention to a band playing on a wooden stage.

Four players thrummed miniature guitars under the glare of the stars shining against Vienamy's dome. The rhythm shifted the weight of the crowd, pulling them left to right and back again.

de... na... na... na... na... naaaaaaaaaaaa... na.

The crowd whooped and cheered.

Cal recognized the tune now: *The Stranger Named St. Podlick.*

How could he have forgotten that one? That song had been everywhere once. Mag had loved it, humming it to herself whenever she'd thought she was alone.

The melody continued in his head as he made his way through the dissipating throng. He thought about how Mag had playfully shaken her hips to the music while on board the *Equinox*, listening to it on a tombstone-shaped radio the night before he'd broken into Busain's vault.

Their last real mission together.

Cal followed a dozen or so of the spectators to the trolley stop, where a blue-and-yellow tram was gliding toward the intersection below a sparking wire.

Since the cloud-reacher dome technology had been perfected almost no one lived inside reachers anymore. Buildings as high as seven stories had been built directly onto the structures. Despite the tenements and towers, Cal could see the top of the *Bicentennial's* elevated central mast as soon as the trolley made its first turn.

The industrial battleship took up nearly half the right side of the harbor and hulked oppressively over the wooden pleasure crafts and transport ships floating outside the dome.

Arriving at the docks, the trolley hissed to a stop and Cal stepped off onto the paved street.

A breathless man ran up to him, holding a camera. He was bald on top, but the black hair behind his ears ran down to the base of his neck. "Hold on there, Mister! Yer gonna want a picture in front of the *Bicentennial*, ye are. It's the flagship of the Confederation. Broke the Flat Heads, it did."

Cal pushed past him. "Not interested."

The vendor gave him a dark look, before heading off in search of a new target. He made a frantic wave at a man in a green bowler hat who was attempting to guide his wife and young son towards the parked trolley.

"Have a picture, sir. To remember the evening yer son first saw the Sky Fleet's flagship, *The Bicentennial!*"

"Oh, Cedric, maybe we should," the man's wife said.

"Come on, Da," the boy said.

Their voices disappeared into the howl of the cold wind roaring through the open hatch of Slip 42 at the base of the dome. Cal's blazer whipped like a flag as he made his way across the translucent aerobridge to the ship's deck, where two security men scrambled to rigid attention.

"Permission to come aboard," Cal said.

"Granted, Commodore," they said in unison.

As Cal walked between them, heading for the ship's antechamber, a radio crackled behind him. "Commodore Bannon is aboard, Commander."

"Understood."

That had been Commander Pinnochet. *Why would the EXO ask to be informed that he had returned?*

Cal wouldn't have to go far out of his way to ask: the command deck was directly beneath him. But he dismissed the idea as quickly as it had come. This was Nadir's ship and Cal had made a habit of staying off the command deck as much as military protocol would allow.

Instead, he took the lift down to Deck 3, the executive level. There were twenty executive quarters here, fifteen for the captain and his command crew, and another five for visitors and diplomats. Cal had been traveling on the *Bicentennial* so often over the last few months, that Nadir had allocated him a berth semi-permanently, even affixing a sliding plate on the door:

Cabin 8
Commodore Callum R. Bannon

Cal reached into his sports coat, his fingers finding the rough edge of his old keychain and removed the jangling keys. As he was reaching forward to unlock the door, the knob turned, and it opened in front of him.

"Mag?"

Amused and stunning, she leaned against the doorway. "I haven't been called that for a while. It's good to see you, Bannon." She stepped aside. Five long seconds passed. "Don't you want to come in?"

"Oh. Right." Cal stuffed his keys back into his coat and stepped inside. "How did you get in here?"

"I radioed the captain," she said with a grin. "We're old friends."

"Right," he said again, tugging an earlobe. "I'll have to talk to him about that."

"Did I surprise you?"

He laughed. "Of course you surprised me." He shut the door and looked around. Something in the room was wrong. Different.

My laundry. He'd left the place a mess.

"You didn't have to…"

"I did. Those clothes smelled." She pointed to his desk. "All except that."

Cal had forgotten he'd left his latest project out.

"Will you put it on?" she asked.

Cal rushed between her and his sewing station. "It's not quite ready yet." The thickness of the vertical stripes that ran down the navy-blue island shirt were frustratingly varied.

Mag looked sheepish and leaned to one side to peep around him. "It looks ready to me. Do you think you could make me something?"

"I can't promise it'll be perfect."

"Things so rarely are."

"What would you like?"

She reached around him and felt the collar of the half-finished garment. "I like this."

"You want us to wear matching shirts?"

"No," she laughed. "A blouse or a dress. It's a lovely color. Do you need my size?"

"No, I remember it."

Mag scoffed. "Even if that's true, I'm afraid it's changed a bit."

"Maybe… but not much. I've sized you up."

Childbirth had perhaps made her slightly wider at the hips but not in a way that was at all unpleasant. Quite the opposite.

He touched her hip and edged around her to the rickety metal cart he'd made his minibar. "I have enough of the material left to come up with something. Where should I send it?" He moved bottles around, chinking them against each other, until he found the half-empty jug of Mupai whiskey. "You're still in… Summerville, was it?" He lifted the lid off the ice bucket he'd filled earlier and found only four diminished cubes floating in cold water.

"No," she said, raising an eyebrow. "Not since I left Simon."

"You two have split up?" Cal divided the cubes between a pair of glasses. The ice cracked as he poured the warm liquor over it.

"Bannon, do you honestly expect me to believe you don't know exactly where I live? I have a place in Pantopolis, same as you."

"You live on Brunswick. I live on the ground," he said, abandoning the pretense. He handed her a glass and they took simultaneous burning sips. "Okay, so I know where you live. It's my job to know things. And it's only because you're a diplomat now."

She raised an eyebrow, as if unconvinced. "This is good," she said, changing the subject.

Cal nodded. Mag had always preferred the Marabeshi blends. They were near impossible to get hold of now.

"You look good too," she continued.

His heart skipped a beat. "You mean good for someone my age."

Mag pushed a strand of hair behind her ear. It was as red and vibrant as it had ever been. "No, I mean good for someone that's been punched in the face as many times as you."

He laughed. "Cute."

He'd missed her. He'd tried to forget her, but it had been impossible. They'd seen each other four years ago in passing at the chairman's annual shareholder meeting, but it had been a painful encounter for him. The accountant had been with her then.

Things could be different now.

"You know what's funny?" he said. "I was just thinking about you."

"All good, I hope." Mag gave him a playful look that he hadn't seen in a long time, but one he hadn't forgotten.

"All good."

"I was thinking about you too. I saw a memo from Admiral Bishop the other day. You're still adventuring I see."

Only moments ago, he'd thought death was the only adventure left to him. That might as well have been a lifetime ago. "Are you going to be here long?"

"I shouldn't even be here now."

Of course. That had been too much to hope. "Is everything alright?"

"Yes. But I need a favor. Emily. She's on my staff."

"Emily."

"My daughter."

"I know who she is." The words had come out harsher than he'd intended. Emily had been the end for them.

"Right," Mag said slowly, sensing his discomfort. "Well, I was hoping that you would be willing to bring her home for me."

He choked down the remainder of his whiskey, his teeth clinking on the glass. "Is there something wrong?"

"You're aware of the Heilish lab above Lucy's Bay."

Cal nodded. "Yalespitz."

"I've spent the last three months negotiating with the Heilish to conduct an inspection of the facility. They've been easier to deal with since the transition."

Cal suppressed a snort. "I suppose they would be."

Even over a decade later, it was still shocking that then Chairman Gilpin had agreed to the Defense Pact with Heiland. Chancellor Ayon had been the special sort of sadistic dictator that comes around only every ten generations or so.

"The inspection was supposed to happen today, but I diverted here to catch you."

"Is it an issue with her clearance? I can get you around—"

"No, that's not it." She finished her whiskey and licked her lower lip. "The Heilish lead negotiator visited the site. Apparently, some of our boys were there. Prisoners."

"What?"

"The Heilish intelligence network has been disjointed since Chancellor Josef's inauguration. Many of their leaders are new to government. It was news to them too."

Cal understood. "The right hand hasn't been talking to the left."

Ayon had been the undisputed leader of the country for a quarter of a century but had no wife, no children and, because he'd been seemingly healthy when his heart had given out, no formal succession plan. It made sense that there would be widespread confusion in the upper echelon of the government, projects and departments and hundreds of little secrets the new government was still discovering.

"That's what they're saying," Mag said. "Look, Bannon, I just don't want Emily seeing these prisoners. I'm told they're in rough shape." She placed her glass onto the top shelf of the cart. "I need her off my ship. Will you *please* take her home?"

"I'll have to speak to Nadir."

She wrinkled her nose. "You'll have to speak to Nadir?"

"It's his ship and his crew. Having your teenage daughter on board is a guaranteed distraction he may not want."

Mag nodded sagely. "Lucky I've already spoken to Nadir then. He told me I just needed to clear it with you."

"Da… did you work on a ship like that?"

Cedric loved answering the boy's questions, but Marcella was less tolerant. She folded her arms under her chest and glared. "Charlie, it's getting late."

Cedric waved a hand at his wife. *It's alright. The boy has every right to ask questions. He's getting older.* He sat on the park bench next to his son, placed his bowler hat on Charlie's head and watched it sink down over the boy's ears.

"Why's it here?"

Cedric had wondered about that too. It was the most famous ship in the fleet. Maybe the world.

"Couldn't say," he said. He pointed to the bow. "I was a requisition officer on a ship called the *Assurance*. It went from there…" he said, tracing his finger along the *Bicentennial's* hull until he was about a quarter of the way along, "… to there."

"Still pretty big, Da."

"I suppose it was."

Charlie pulled off his father's hat. "Da. Did you ever have to kill anyone?"

Marcella held her breath, her face turning red.

Cedric gently plucked the hat from his son, placing it back over his thinning, sandy hair. "I did what I needed to. But I only served on a ship for six months. Spent most of my time in Numenshire."

"That's why you need to keep up with your numbers," Marcella said to her son. "The fleet needed engineers, that's what kept your Da safe."

"I want to be on a ship like that one," the boy said.

Cedric patted his shoulder. "It might be better if you get to know what's on the ground first."

"But Mum says it's dangerous down there."

"It's not so bad." *Ridiculous notion. Kids today are too used to the comfort of the cloud-reachers.*

"Ced." Marcella inclined her head towards the street.

She's right, it's getting late. Cedric reached out to the picnic table and picked up the photograph they'd purchased. "I think your mum wants us to head home."

As they were making to leave, a sharp voice cut across the dock, carried by the wind. "But I'm assigned to this ship!"

A young man in civilian clothes was being escorted down the aerobridge from the *Bicentennial* by two skymen. His shouts appeared to have startled a woman leaning against the dome's reflective glazing. She was young but dressed like a Smithon businesswoman, in a black jacket and matching skirt. Her strawberry-colored hair had been trimmed short in a pixie cut.

"I've been on this ship for days! Don't you recognize me?" The young man spun on the two skymen, and the woman moved awkwardly away from them.

"It's procedure," said one of the guards. "You're not listed on the manifest, so we need to verify you before we allow you on board."

"It's late," the man pleaded.

"For all of us," the skyman agreed, his hands raised in conciliatory fashion. "It'll only take a moment."

"It sounds like they're doing the best they can," the woman said. *"What the hell business is it of yours!?"*

She stepped back as if she'd been slapped.

"At ease, skymen. He's with me."

Cedric looked round to see an olive-skinned man in a navy tweed jacket stride past their picnic table.

Charlie looked up at his father. "Is that the captain?"

Cedric had never seen him before, and he was out of uniform, but there was only one Aruminian serving in Sky Fleet. "It has to be. Captain Alameidar."

The captain took the young man by the arm and led him back across the translucent aerobridge to the *Bicentennial.* Neither spared a glance at the woman.

"She looks really mad, Da."

Cedric looked to his wife. "She's not the only one, kiddo. Time for bed."

Airship Bicentennial

Class: Typhon

Capacity/ Current Compliment: 160/ 42 souls

Commander: Captain Nadir Alameidar

Executive Officer: Commander Wyman Pinnochet

Second Officer/ Deck Officer: Lt. Commander Tanner Rolt

Lead Engineer: Commander Wesley Tennit

FIFTEEN

"THIS IS EMBARRASSING."

"Why?" Emily's mother looked up from the clothes she was folding into neat piles on her bed.

Her mother always did this. Every. Single. Time. Her father never would. Emily put her hands on her hips. "Because this is my job."

"So find a new job."

A cord tightening in Emily's neck went rigid. She took a breath. "You shouldn't go alone."

"I'm not going *alone*." Mag looked around theatrically, indicating the ship all around them.

"I meant with no other diplomatic staff."

Mag rolled her eyes condescendingly. "The diplomacy part is over. I don't need staff for this. And everything's already been arranged to take you home."

"This is ridiculous."

"Mmm-hmm." Mag gathered the short stack of laundry and placed it in Emily's duffel bag. "Sounds like I don't have anything to worry about."

"You're sending me home with strangers. It's three days to Pantopolis."

"I'll risk it." She pulled the drawstring cord tight and tossed the stuffed bag into Emily's chest.

"You should see the way they carry on over there," Emily said. "Mother, they're *animals*."

"Maybe, but *this* ship is leaving in an hour and you're not going to be on it. You can fly home on the *Bicentennial,* or you can find your own way. It's up to you. I'd think fast though." Mag nodded towards the porthole and the sky harbor beyond. "The *Bicentennial* is leaving right after us."

"Why are you doing this?" Emily asked. "I've come all this way. We've been working on this for months."

"And I've really appreciated the company."

"I didn't fly halfway across the world to keep you company."

Mag frowned and sat delicately on the squeaking cot. "Look, this is not… Yalespitz is not a place I want you to see."

That damned condescension again. It burned within Emily's throbbing temples. "I'm nineteen years old."

"I remember your birth quite well. A very significant event."

"It's mortifying, Mother. I can't turn up home early. I'm ready for these kinds of things."

"Well maybe I'm not."

"Mother…"

"Do I need to have some skymen drag you off this ship?"

Emily clutched her duffel bag and gave a low, pitiful growl.

Mag smiled knowingly. She'd won again.

"See you in a week."

Jon rested a shoulder against the warm aluminum mast. Above him, ruby-red lift gas filled the *Bicentennial's* massive, balloon-like sail.

Mounted to the mast a foot above him, a PA crackled to life. *"Skyman Wilbus if you don't report in to Chief Simms in the next ninety seconds you're going to need to find a new way home."*

Maybe she won't be coming aboard after all, Jon thought. From the moment Jon had first met him, Captain Alameidar had been nothing like other command officers. Maybe he had been joking about her, saying she would be joining the ship's company just to make Jon—

Shit. There she is.

She marched on board, her high-heeled shoes clacking against the deck as she stepped off the aerobridge. She half-turned in Jon's direction, and he scooted around to the opposite side of the mast.

When he looked back, her stuffed green bag was at her feet, and she was leaning over the gunwale.

Not an unpleasant view.

Jon hadn't taken much of a look at her the night before. Almost immediately after he'd blown up at her, the captain had dragged him onto the deck and said, "You probably just blew any chance you had about getting back into the program."

Jon's mind had jumped on the captain's words: if he had blown his chance, that meant that there had *been* a chance. That there *was* a chance.

"That woman you just snapped at…"

"Oh, The One!" Jon had said. "It's not the commodore's daughter?"

The captain paused and the light crow's feet around his eyes knitted together. "No… not at all. But if I were you, I'd be sure I cleared the air with her."

"What's her name?"

"You will have to ask *her* that, Skyman."

It was true, Jon had acted like an ass, and not for the first time. The upside was he was rather well-practiced at apologizing to women.

Across the deck, the redhead stretched further over the side, resting her narrow midsection across the rail. Jon watched as the wind plucked at her skirt, raising it slightly.

Apologies then. But maybe not right now.

Cal knew he shouldn't be nervous. He'd stood on the *Bicentennial's* command deck in full, scratchy uniform for more than fifty departures, but it had never been this oppressively hot before. The sweat building under his tight, rubbing collar was creating a burning rash on his neck.

It struck him how badly he wanted to make a good impression on the girl, but he couldn't understand why. It wasn't as if she could ever be his child. He'd spent years loathing the fact that she existed, and their upcoming meeting would do nothing but remind him of his life's greatest blunder.

Worse, Nadir seemed to have picked up on it. The young captain had been lurking around Cal on the command deck all morning. Thankfully he was now occupied with tracking down the last few stragglers from his returning crew.

The radioman, Lieutenant Gipson, swiveled from his station. "All departments have reported in, Captain. We're all accounted for."

Nadir patted him on the shoulder. "Did we hear from the *Venture?*"

"We did, sir," Gipson said. "An odd message."

"What was it?"

"They said, 'Call us when you get home'."

Nadir smiled and scratched his black beard as he sauntered over to Cal at the deck's forward window.

"Very funny," Cal muttered. He brushed past the captain and stepped up to the conning station's central platform. He'd been sat at the cartography desk for only a moment before Nadir's clunking boots announced that he'd followed. The captain leaned against the periscope tube rising up through the center of the platform. "You seem in a good mood this morning," he said, grinning. "How long has it been since you have seen Doctor Silverfinch?"

Cal looked away but he sensed the kid inching closer.

"I see she has gone back to her old name," Nadir said.

Cal concentrated on the chart laid across the cartography desk, focusing on a pale blue spot of nothing. "I suppose she has."

"Captain," called out Lieutenant Manderly from the helm. The controls were a few feet from the forward windshield, beneath rolling dials displaying the ship's heading and altitude. "I have full power from the engine room."

Nadir gripped the lacquered oak rail that surrounded the conning platform. "Disengage the aerobridge and release mooring lines."

The announcement on the PA system came sharply: *"Deck crew, release mooring lines and move to departure stations."*

The girl turned in the direction of the sound and spotted Jon. "Can I help you?"

"N… n… no…" he stammered. "I was—"

"Staring at my ass." She snatched her bag off the deck.

He put his hands up and backed against the now searing-hot mast. "No, I—"

"Just keep clear of me, *Skyboy*."

She stormed away into the antechamber, passing a chuckling Lieutenant Commander Rolt on the way.

"That could have gone better," Rolt said.

"I wasn't trying to—"

A harsh, grinding squeal roared portside, and Rolt shot over to a smoking drum. It rotated in jerking, erratic fits as it attempted to coil the mooring strap. "Slow it down, Parsons!" Rolt called out to a skyman. "You're tangling that line."

Jon came up behind him and held off as long as he could bear before asking, "Who is she?"

Rolt waited for the mooring cables to begin coiling neatly on top of each other in the drum before answering. "It's not my place to say."

"I think I've got it now, sir," Parsons said.

"Good," Rolt said, slapping the skyman's shoulder. "Remember, take it easy."

Jon was still hovering by him, trying to muster the most pathetic, desperate expression he could, and succeeding. The leathery lines of Rolt's face softened. "Her name's Emily."

Another skyman called across the deck. "Jammed line over here, Mister Rolt."

"Damn," Rolt muttered. "Get those boys away from it! I'll be right there!" He looked back to Jon. "As you can see, Mister Merry, I'm quite busy." He hustled into the antechamber.

Jon scurried in after him. "Could you give me a bit more than that, sir? It's my life here."

The burly officer moved towards a bank of royal-blue lockers and lifted an axe from two faded yellow hooks on the wall. "None of us know much, Lieutenant," he said. "She's the daughter of a lady that came aboard last night: Doctor Margo Silverfinch from the Parlay Office." He edged past Jon and back onto the deck.

"But what—?"

Rolt spun, gesturing with the axe. "There's something between her, the captain and the commodore, which damn sure makes it no business of mine. *Or yours*. Now get the hell off my deck. We're casting off."

It was procedure for flag officers to be present for casting off, but sometimes passengers of note requested that they also be on the command deck to observe a ship departing. Cal was relieved Emily had apparently decided not to enjoy that privilege.

He desperately needed to splash cool water on his face and peel himself out of his uniform.

Gipson pulled down his headset and let it hang around his neck. "Mister Rolt reports mooring lines clear."

"Increase flow to the sails," Nadir ordered. "And ahead dead slow, Mister Manderly. And I do mean *dead slow*. Last time, you were undead slow."

"Aye, Captain. Dead slow."

The command deck thrummed with the expanded gas flow and the whir of the turbine engines. Nadir's shoulders tensed and he leaned over Manderly's station. Cal had seen the captain take the massive ship out of a cloud-reacher harbor before, but the sight still filled him with pride.

"Okay, that's good, Manderly," Nadir said. "Now slow ahead one-third."

"Ahead one-third, aye."

Confirmation came that the aerobridge had fully retracted into Vienamy's habitat dome, and Nadir's shoulders relaxed. He turned back to the conning platform and leaned an arm on the rail. "Do we have a course, Commander Pinnochet?"

There had been a small disagreement earlier between Pinnochet and the ship's young cartographer, Ensign Dahl, regarding the ship's best course and altitude for their destination. Cal had not offered an opinion, but his personal view was that Dahl's suggestion was the correct one. Nadir was quite fond of the young officer, considering him a phenom with navigational charts.

Pinnochet evidently had come to the same conclusion. He clanked across the platform's metal grating and approached the helm. "Mister Manderly, make your heading two hundred seventy-two degrees."

"Aye, sir. Two hundred and seventy-two degrees."

The compass and altimeter dials whirred indicating the ship's new heading.

"Harbor master reports we're clear," Gipson called from the radio station.

"Ahead full."

Tradition and procedure would be maintained until they were out of visual contact, at which point Cal could leave the bridge. His knees cracked as he used the edge of the cartography desk to leverage himself up, and he took the grip of the periscope. He pressed his eyes against the soft rubber of the eyepiece and watched the sky city that was Vienamy dwindle away to a miniscule size.

"So," Nadir whispered in his ear. "Have you had a chance to acquaint yourself with our guest?"

Cal's forehead made a dull sucking sound as he stepped back from the rubber-edged viewfinder. "No." Cal realized he hadn't spared more than a glance at Nadir all morning. Looking at him now, he could tell he was hiding something. "You've met her?"

"I would not dignify it as a proper introduction, but I do believe I saw her on the aerobridge last night. Your recruit made quite the impression on her."

"I have a recruit aboard?" Cal asked.

Nadir's constant smile faltered for a moment. "The young lady looks much like Doctor Silverfinch, I think. In the nose, particularly."

Cal looked down and saw that Ensign Dahl was smiling. "This isn't really the place to discuss this, *Captain*."

"Of course, Commodore. Mister Dahl, you are dismissed."

The cartographer pivoted away from his station. "Sir, did I do something wrong?"

"No. Take a break. Get a cup of coffee. In fact, bring me one." Nadir turned back to Cal. "Something for you, Commodore?"

"No."

Dahl nodded to his captain, took an awkward step from the platform and hurried off the command deck.

Cal rested his backside on the edge of the rail and waited for Nadir to speak. *Go ahead, kid. Say your piece.*

"I think you should reconsider your decision with regard to Lieutenant Merry."

"Captain on the very first day, the very first thing I say to every man who comes aboard my team is, 'Do what I say.' Every time. No exceptions."

Nadir nodded, seemingly in deep thought. "You are being an ass, I think. I had hoped the doctor's appearance would have improved your mood."

"You forget yourself."

"I do, and I will again," he whispered. "That was a trap not a test."

"That's right," Cal said. "And he stepped right in it. My ruse should have been obvious."

"You are quite good at laying traps, I think. Perhaps too good. He is a good skyman. If you want to find some thick pieces of meat that will follow orders without question, you may be looking in the wrong sorts of places."

Cal thought a moment. He did need to produce a new agent soon, to keep the board happy. "I will *consider it*. You say he left an impression…"

"On Miss Emily, yes. But I'm sure she will have nothing but good things to say about him at dinner tonight."

Jon found her seated in the mess hall, her head cradled in her palm.

She's reading, he thought. He could wait for her to be less occupied, but that would require watching her, which, given recent history, seemed an even more perilous option than interrupting her.

Just walk up and get it over with. It can't go any worse than your last apology.

"Miss Silverfinch."

"That's not my name," she said, looking up from the text, her pale eyes peeking over the top of her wide, circular reading optics.

"Oh… they told me…"

"Silverfinch is my *mother's* name."

Jon forced his best smile. "Ah. I see. Maybe it would help if I just called you Emily."

She closed the book and straightened her back. "I don't think so, Skyboy."

"It's Sky*man*." He held out his hand. "Lieutenant Jon Merry."

She frowned but slid her tiny hand into his.

"May I sit?" he asked.

"Why would you want to do that?"

"Well, I suppose it's because I'm a bit out of place here. I get the sense you are too."

She shook her head and removed her glasses. "Lieutenant, I'm not really looking for company. And I'm not out of place. It's my job to travel."

"Really? What's your job?"

The girl's eyes crinkled suspiciously. "You actually don't know what I do?"

"I know your mother is someone important to the command crew, including the commodore. But that's not a job, so no, I don't know what you do."

She thought for a moment, and her posture relaxed a little, her hands resting on her book's ornate front cover. "Sit down."

Relieved, Jon took a seat.

"Doctor Silverfinch, my mother, is Under Secretary to the Chairman of International Parlay," Emily said. "I'm her Chief of Staff."

"Is that official International Parlay business then?" he asked, peering down at the book. Her fingertips fluttered over the glossy gold lettering. "*Memoirs of a* what?"

She sighed and slid her hand away.

Memoirs of an Aeronautic Adventurer.

Jon chuckled. "Not a bad read."

She lifted her eyebrows in surprise. "You've read *this*?"

"Timmons, right?"

"Yes."

"Slow in the middle, picks up in the end though. Have you read him before?"

"Uh, some."

"Look, I was a bit rude when we met."

"Yes, you were."

"I'm sorry about that. You didn't really catch me at my best. It's no excuse but I was sort of at the apex of a career disaster right at that moment."

"What career?"

"Top secret," he said, smiling.

She put her optics back on and opened her book. "You're about to tell me you're in Special Section and you've got a *very* dangerous mission coming up."

Jon mimed zipping his lips closed.

"Please. I should think most spies wouldn't be caught *spying* so easily."

He snorted. "I'm still in training."

"Miss Handley!" An enlisted skyman was approaching them from across the mess hall. "Have I caught you before eating?" He waddled to a stop in front of them and gave Jon a puzzled expression.

"You have, Skyman," Emily said. "I was just reading."

"Captain Alameidar and Commodore Bannon have invited you to eat with'em."

"Dinner?"

The skyman nodded. "It's good eating in there anytime, ma'am, but especially tonight. Spicy pork with rice. It's real good."

"And what's on the menu for us tonight, Skyman?" Jon asked.

"Cream of veal stew."

Jon turned to Emily. "I know which one I'd pick."

She sighed. "When's dinner being served?"

"Seven," the portly skyman said. "In the command mess. Deck Four."

"I guess I'd better get ready then," she said, scooting off the bench. "Good evening, Mister Merry."

The two men watched her go.

"How do you suppose she knows the two of them?" asked Jon. "The captain and the commodore?"

"I wouldn't know, sir, but I wouldn't let it get you down. The stew's good too."

SIXTEEN

Mag held her wind-whipped hair from her eyes as best she could, and watched as the *Venture* drew nearer to Yalespitz.

The windowless structure was a perfectly symmetrical black spot carved into the pale-blue sky. Up close, she could make out the subtle weld lines of its exterior sheathing.

Its bay doors cracked open, and she couldn't help but wince as her ship passed under the docking bay's flickering pendant lights and into the belly of the beast.

The *Venture* passed under a maintenance catwalk and maneuvered between two smaller yachts before making for the far end of the hanger.

Five men stood assembled on the deck's polished black surface: the lead negotiator Minister Lucos, three *wehrcomache* soldiers, and a hunched-over man in a crimson overcoat that could only be Dr. Zolbar.

Captain Papedil reversed thrust and the ship shuddered slowly to a stop. On Mag's left, out on the deck, the ship's mate, Manton, squatted next to one of the tarp-covered drums that housed the ship's mooring lines, and began working to secure the ship. The practiced co-pilot was able to finish in under five minutes.

Afterwards, Mag hopped down from the *Venture'* boarding ladder onto the deck of the docking bay, where the welcome party was approaching.

"It is good to meet you in person at last, Doctor Silverfinch," Lucos said.

"Good afternoon, Minister," Mag said, extending her hand to him as her staff, Myles and Pratchett, descended the ladder behind her. She had only ever seen Lucos in photographs, and noted his face was considerably redder than his file photo. He was also clearly agitated.

Mag turned her attention to the old man beside Lucos. His lips were pressed tightly together, and his coat hung over him like a bloody wave. "I take it this is Doctor Zolbar?"

"Yes, Doctor," Lucos said carefully. "He has raised some concerns about the transfer."

I'll bet he has.

Zolbar extended a withered hand. "A pleasure, Doctor Silverfinch."

Mag looked at the pasty appendage briefly before turning back to Lucos. "Minister, I'm here for two unauthorized—and, to this point, nameless—Confederate prisoners. I intend to take them home."

Zolbar pulled back his hand timidly and slipped it into a deep coat pocket. "Please, Doctor Silverfinch, allow me to explain during our tour. These patients have been in my care for quite some time. I'm afraid it would be impossible to discharge them without—"

Mag shot him an icy stare. "Then you will *make* it possible, Doctor."

Patterson had been in this room only once before. Dr. Zolbar had called it a viewing lab then. It had been filled with games, puzzles, and exercise equipment to show off his pets.

Predictably, Dr. Zolbar had not made the same mistake twice. The lab was empty now save for Patterson, who had been strapped tightly with steel reinforced cords into an upright dolly, gagged, and wheeled in.

He had briefly caught his reflection in the lab's two-way mirror as he rolled by. The sight had not been a surprise. Patterson had known what to expect. Nonetheless, seeing for himself validated his conclusions.

He had progressed so much. He was more than a man now. He was above. Beyond. Apart.

He waited.

At last, the lab door opened and for the first time in six years, nine weeks and two days, Patterson saw Lewison. He too was rolled in by two orderlies in a similarly secured dolly and parked directly across from Patterson.

It had happened to him too. They'd both become so much more.

Lewison's gray lips managed a smirk despite the red rubber ball stuffed between his teeth.

Patterson estimated only a five percent chance Zumecki would arrive next. The man had taken a shot near the brain stem during their failed escape, and Patterson doubted even he could have survived such a wound.

The hinges of the door whined again.

From outside came a distant voice. "What's so dangerous about them?"

Margo Silverfinch.

She wasn't dead.

There was an eighty-eight percent chance that Bannon had managed to rescue her. And if she was here, it was possible he was here too.

What unexpected good fortune that would be.

Dr. Zolbar held the door open. "I will explain from the observation room," he said. "It's right through here."

Dr. Silverfinch had aged, like they all did. She followed another Heilish man into the lab and squealed in surprise. Two armed Confederate guards hurried in behind her, similar expressions on their faces.

Dr. Zolbar clacked across the bare room and waved them to the adjacent door beside the room's rectangular two-way mirror. "I must insist you say nothing to them until I have had the opportunity to explain."

Dr. Silverfinch's mouth was twisted in fury now, and she stormed past the doctor wordlessly. Dr. Zolbar held the door open for the others and as he did so, Patterson managed to find the doctor's evasive black eyes.

Patterson had seen the doctor forty-two times since the incident six years ago, but this was a different man. This man was afraid.

"What the hell have you done to them?" Mag's eyes switched between the doctor and the minister. Lucos looked down at his feet, while Zolbar straightened his posture as best he could.

"I have not done anything to them, Doctor Silverfinch," he said. "We believe they were exposed to a rare form of altim. Blood tests reveal several mutated protein strains— "

"We have a vaccine for *altim. Altim* doesn't do that."

"As I said, Doctor, this appears to be a mutated strain. I must assure you I have treated both of those men as well as could be expected."

"But you didn't return them."

Zolbar nodded. "It shames me to admit, Doctor that I suspect both our nations are guilty of clandestine deeds prior to our alliance. I am, like you, a servant of my country. But I assure you these men have been treated as well as possible, given their conditions."

"Why are they gagged? *Why in the hell do they look like that?*"

"They are restrained for our protection," Zolbar said coldly. He limped to a wire shelf and pulled off a thick, black binder. "These are some photos from a little over six years ago. The three of them managed to get loose."

"Three?" Mag said, snatching the binder from his limp grip.

"Unfortunately, it was a terrible incident. The fatality was unavoidable."

"And you can bet we're going to have more to say about that," Mag said, as she let her eyes fall to the photos.

It was unclear how many people she was looking at: the images were a mass of dismembered, unassociated body parts. Instinctively, Mag began thumbing her dangling bracelet. "The One help me," she murmured.

"Yes," Lucos said, his voice a low growl. "That was my impression as well."

She closed the binder and shoved it into the minister's chest. "I'll have the names of these men. Now."

Zolbar thought for a moment before padding over to Lucos and plucking away the binder with two spidery fingers. He flipped towards pages at the back of the file.

Mother nugger, Mag thought. "You don't even know their *names?*"

"I only wanted to ensure I attribute them their appropriate ranks, Doctor." He found his place and began to read. "Chief Clyde Lewison and Lieutenant Gordon Patterson."

"Gordon?" Mag said to herself. "One of those men is Gordon Patterson?" Lucos bit his lower lip and looked away from her. "I want him," she growled, "I want *both of them* out of those restraints. Immediately." She started towards the door.

"I cannot allow you to do that," Zolbar said.

"Excuse me?" Mag held onto the door latch to steady herself.

"I have shown you how dangerous they are."

"Dangerous to you, Doctor. Not to me."

Lucos stepped between them. "We will, of course, release them to you, Doctor Silverfinch." Zolbar glared at him as he continued. "But I must insist they remain in their restraints at least until they are clear of the facility. They will also require medication."

"What medication?"

"It keeps them calm," Zolbar said, waving his hands like an exasperated traffic guard. "You must not take them—"

Mag stormed through the door and into the lab, where she stood and examined the two men.

Neither one of them could be Patterson. She remembered him as a stick of a man with a bushy mustache. These men were heavily muscled, barely fitting into their dingy yellow gowns, and completely hairless, with bleached white skin.

One of the poor creatures was taller than the other. Patterson had stood over six feet… but he couldn't be this monster. He looked down at her with knowing, glassy eyes as she approached him.

What have they done to you?

Up close, he stank of something antiseptic, like an oppressive cleaning solution. Mag could see the only hair that remained on him was his wispy, translucent eyebrows.

"Doctor, please," Lucos shouted as he made his way towards her. Myles put a hand on his shoulder, pulling him back.

Mag pinched the sides of the rubber ball in Patterson's mouth and pulled it free, easing the strap down on his bare chin.

The ghost of a man licked his gray lips. His tongue was swollen and purplish.

"Gordon?" Mag said softly. "Do you remember me?"

"Of course, Doctor," Patterson said, his voice hoarse and scratchy. "It is… it is good to see you again." His eyes closed and his head nodded down.

What the hell?

She checked his pulse. His skin was ice cold, but there was the faint thrum of a beat. "This man is nearly dead," she said. Across from Patterson, the second man, Lewison, looked similarly afflicted.

Zolbar pushed his way past Myles and Pratchett. "It is a symptom of their condition. I assure you they are quite alright."

Mag levelled a fiery look at him. "You'd better hope so."

Captain Papedil and Manton worked to decouple the portable ramp as soon as the *wehrcomache* ghouls had stepped back onto the polished deck of the docking bay.

Mag had wanted Myles and Pratchett to take charge of wheeling the gurneys from the lab, but Zolbar and the minister had insisted she take possession of the prisoners only after they were on board the *Venture*. They'd also insisted their *patients* remained confined until the ship was away from the facility.

Bastards.

It made her sick to have to wait that long to reclaim the prisoners, but Mag had pushed the situation as far as she dared. Zolbar had become unhinged when he had realized, she wasn't leaving without them. The so-called *doctor* had followed the transfer closely, but she refused to allow him on board the *Venture*. He looked up at her from the docking bay with a sour expression and she returned what she hoped was a matching one, although she doubted anyone could look more hateful than the old blue-haired devil.

Even so, it was easier to look at that Heilish vampire than it was to see her old companion strapped into that dolly.

This wouldn't be the last time Zolbar would be hearing from her.

Pratchett pushed Patterson past her across the deck and she trailed after them, stopping at the ship's central lift. "Get them the hell out of those restraints as soon as they're below," she ordered. Damned if she was going to wait until Yalespitz was out of sight first. She looked down and saw Patterson's puffy, pale eyes remained closed. *Rest easy, Lieutenant,* she thought. "See that they're fed when they wake up."

"Yes, ma'am," Pratchett said in a low voice. "What about this medication?"

"Lock it up in the medical bay. When Lieutenant Patterson wakes up, let him know I'll be available to talk, either now or after he's settled in." The thought of speaking with Patterson after almost twenty years caused lumps the size of brassite nuggets to form in her gut.

What could she say? But it had to be done. She wouldn't run from it.

Patterson was a hero. A *living* hero, no longer a lost ghost of the past.

She found Captain Papedil in the pilothouse going over his pre-launch checklist with Manton. "About ready, Doctor?" he asked.

"*That* is an understatement," she said, shaking her head. "Let's get the hell out of here."

"We have everyone?"

"We do. Although there's a change of plans. We're going to head back to Vienamy first."

"You want to head back to Sanland? Not to Pantopolis?"

"We need to get these men professionally evaluated and Vienamy is closer. There's a secure hospital in the city."

"You can't treat them before we get back, Doctor? It's that bad?"

"It's that bad."

Papedil nodded. "You're the boss. We should be ready to disembark in…" he looked at Manton, who held up five fingers. "…about five minutes."

"I'll be in my cabin."

Mag descended on the lift and got off on the crew deck for the short trek to her stateroom. She would have to find out the status of Patterson's family—he would be sure to ask. How old would his son be now? Not much older than Emily. And she knew nothing at all about the life Clyde Lewison had left behind.

If she sent a message as soon as they were back in Vienamy, they might get a faster return response. A telegram sent directly through the Chairman's office would cut through ninety percent of the red tape.

She flung open her cabin door, not bothering to shut it as she made for her writing desk. She zeroed in on the fountain pen and thin journal, sat down and started to draft the message.

Urgent
Lieutenant Gordon Patterson, previously of
Special Section is alive. Please confirm stat —

"It's good to see you again, Doctor Silverfinch."

Mag screamed as her hand shot up to her mouth.

"I am glad to see that you're not dead." Patterson's voice was alarmingly clear as he eased the cabin door shut.

The pen slipped from her fingers and rolled twice across the plastic table before dropping off the edge. She put her hand to her chest and focused on her breathing. "Same," she whispered. "Lieutenant, what are you doing in my room?"

He smiled, his yellowed teeth stark against his pasty flesh. "Forgive me, Doctor. It's been so long since I've seen a friendly face, and I had suspected you long dead."

She licked her lips and said again, "Gordon, why are you in my room?" She risked a glance at the door, but the hulking ghost filled the space between her and the exit.

"I'll ask the questions, Doctor." The medicinal stench from his body intensified as he closed the distance between them. "I take it Commander Bannon was the one who saved you?"

She met his cloudy eyes. "Lieutenant, I'm sorry that this happened to you." Muffled shouting and thumping came from the corridor outside. "What's going on?"

"Tell me," Patterson said, still smiling. Gray lines were etched into his skin around his eyes. "Commander Hunt: she was working for the Marabeshi, wasn't she?"

"Who?"

"Commander Antonia Hunt. From Aruminia. She was working with Bulkarni, correct?"

"Yes."

"I knew it," he said. "I see everything so *clearly* now."

The shouting outside turned to screams. Mag pushed off with her back foot and lunged for the door, but Patterson snapped a hand around her upper arm and whipped her back hard. "Save your strength. I've been waiting for this for longer than you can imagine."

Mag's arm throbbed as he twisted it, and the feeling in her fingers began to fade.

"Doctor," he said, "I'll rip it off if you don't calm down." She forced herself to stop moving and his grip relaxed. "Now tell me. Bannon. *Does he still live?*"

The screaming outside was deafening now. Mag recognized Papedil's whimpering voice. "Yes," she answered, barely able to keep the squeak from her voice. "Listen, I might be able to help you if I knew what you wanted."

"Help me? My dear, I'm past the point of needing *your* help." The cries outside were slowing to muffled gasps. "Tell me, is the *altim* inhibitor we were given widely available now?"

The vaccine.

"Why do you… ?"

"Is it?" His eyes narrowed to black slits.

"Yes. Almost everyone in the world has had it."

"Everyone?"

"Yes."

"If that's true, the Marabeshi Empire must be no more."

She nodded stiffly.

"Interesting. Very interesting."

"Lieutenant, I can't imagine what you've been through…"

"No. But you will." He pulled her close. "Now, where is Commander Bannon?"

(Translated from the original Heilish)

This is Yalespitz, declaring emergency.
Code Red. Shots fired on

*** End of Transmission ***

SEVENTEEN

EMILY TOOK A HESITANT STEP inside the wardroom. She recognized the man inside from the night before. Then, he had been quietly authoritative. Now, he was pouring tea, spilling a few drops on the white tablecloth. "Captain Alameidar," she said. "Am I early?"

"You are nine minutes late, Miss Emily," the captain said, smiling sheepishly. "I had worried that our young skyman, Mister Merry, had scared you off the ship."

She entered the dimly lit, sparse dining room, and the door clicked shut behind her. "No. Of course not. It was a misunderstanding."

"That is good to hear." The captain slipped around the table and pulled out the nearest folding metal chair. "That is a lovely dress, my dear."

Emily succeeded in contorting her wince into an awkward smile. "I'm afraid I'm a bit embarrassed," Emily said.

"Do not be, Miss Emily," he said. "It is a lovely color. Reminds me of the sky over Panoa Bay." He beckoned her forward.

He was still wearing his officer's white shirt and midnight-blue trousers, but its matching jacket and black tie were gone, and his sleeves were rolled up well past his hairy forearms. The captain had been out of the uniform the night before as well, but she had still not expected him to appear so informal while on board.

She sat with practiced gracefulness. "I'm sorry if I appear distracted. I was told the commodore would be joining us."

"He will." The captain leaned over the table and passed her a cup of tea. "You know him?"

"No," she said. "I think my mother does."

The captain scratched the side of his wiry, black beard. "She does indeed."

An inside joke? Emily hated inside jokes. "You seem to be more in the loop than I, Captain."

"I hope that I have not offended you." He slipped around the table, past a smattering of children's drawings that had been stuck to the bulkhead with frayed strips of black tape.

"Of course not, Captain."

"Good. Subtlety is not a virtue where I come from. Also, while I am not on duty, you may call me Nadir."

"As you wish… *Captain Nadir*."

He chuckled softly.

She pointed to the pictures. "Those are your… ?"

"My son's, yes. I only hang up the ones of me." He gave a broad, toothy grin. "I am very vain, I think."

In every picture, a stick figure man with a flowing black beard and wearing oversized aviator goggles had been scrawled in crayon. "That's you?"

"Yes. It is quite the likeness," he said, pursing his lips. "You are surprised I have children?"

She supposed she was. "Well, it's only that… there were so many retirements after Wet-Drop, particularly the men with families."

Nadir took a sip of his tea and nodded. "Yes. It would seem, that I prefer to wear two right shoes… but it is a pain I am happy to bear."

"I am not prying?"

"Of course not," he said. "Why else display art such as this, if not for discussion."

Emily checked the room for another conversation piece and spotted a framed photograph between a brass clock and the room's black, wall-hung telephone. It showed a nutball player and a small boy. "Is that your son?"

"I take it you are not a nutball fan." Nadir leaned forward and pointed to the player. "*That* is Razzy Wright. There has never been another quite like him, I think. The boy is me."

She could see it now. "You look quite *ecstatic*."

"Happiest I had ever been, I think." Nadir sat and leaned back, balancing on his chair's back legs. "He was traded to the Trolley Catchers the next year."

"You must have been devastated."

"Somewhat, but it is the way of things, I think. New players come and replace the old ones and the game goes on." He settled the chair back onto the deck. "It is good to chat with someone openly. As captain, there are few such opportunities. I am sure you understand."

"What about the Commodore?"

The door clicked open.

"And so, The One said he would be there, and he was there," Nadir said. "Good of you to join us, Commodore."

The older man in the doorway inclined his head apologetically. "Sorry. I was looking over some P, B, and Rs."

"Anyone I know?" Nadir asked.

"Yes. I suppose it was."

The commodore was out of uniform. Instead, he had opted for a brown sport coat over a white linen shirt with the top buttons undone.

He squeezed between the bulkhead and the table and sat next to the captain. There was something strangely familiar about him, like Emily had seen him before but wasn't sure where.

"It is good to meet you, Commodore," she said. "I believe you may have known my mother."

"Yes," he grunted as he adjusted his weight on the stiff chair. "We are old friends. And technically you and I have met already, Miss Handley, though you were quite small." He poured a hot stream of tea from the pot. "How is the—" He yelped as a drop of the liquid fell on the back of his hand.

"The Office of Parlay, Commodore," Nadir finished for him.

"Yes, yes. The Parlay Office," the commodore said, before sucking dripping tea off the ball of his thumb. "Interesting work?"

Emily had nearly forgotten how annoyed she was to be on board, but the reminder of her work brought it all flooding back. "It can be. When I'm allowed to do it."

"I don't think you're missing much. Your mother's probably already on her way home." The commodore smiled, and in that moment, Emily recognized him.

She had only seen three photographs of her mother from before she'd been born. Two showed her as a girl. In the third, she had been with this man. He and her mother seated at dinner in some island bar. The picture hung in the den while Emily was growing up, but only briefly.

Her father had hated it.

The door clicked open again, and two skymen in white aprons stepped through, carrying trays loaded with steaming mounds of savory meat and rice.

Emily's mouth began to water. "That smells amazing. You set a high bar, Captain Nadir. Should I expect *karanjeugos* tomorrow?"

Nadir shook his head. "I never acquired much of a taste for them, I am afraid. In my country, they were somewhat reserved for the *nobility*."

The final word was still hanging in the air like a slur, when an exasperated third skyman burst through the door, nearly flattening one of the servers.

"Captain," he said, trying to catch his breath. "We've intercepted a Heilish radio fragment. You're going to want to hear it."

Cal had suggested the girl return to her cabin, but she had quoted an obscure regulation regarding diplomatic authority and insisted she stay. He guessed she was making it up, but Nadir had allowed her to trail them to the command deck nonetheless.

All three huddled around the radio station.

"You're certain of the translation?" Nadir asked.

"Yes, sir," Gipson said. He twisted a gray knob clockwise and the Heilish transmission played again. Gipson translated it simultaneously. *"This is Yalespitz, declaring emergency. Code Red. Shots fired on…"* Gipson cocked his head. "That's all, sir."

"Anything from the *wehrcomache*?" Cal said.

Gipson nodded and removed his headset. "There's a lot of chatter that's not being properly coded. They've ordered at least two cruisers to the station, but there's no clear ETA for either."

Cal rubbed his sweaty palms together and paced to the conning station. "Mister Dahl, what course would the *Venture* have taken if they'd made it off the station?"

Dahl flipped through several large charts before finding what he was looking for. He drew a remarkably straight line from Lucy's Bay to the edge of the map. "If I were them, this is the way I'd go, Commodore."

Cal leaned further over the rail. "What's our current position?"

Dahl looked to the rotating position dials above the forward windshield and turned back to his chart. He penciled in their position with a dull gray X. "Here, sir."

"Plot an intercept course."

The cartographer bit his upper lip and tapped the nub of the pencil's eraser on the center of the X.

"Carry out the commodore's order, Mister Dahl," Nadir said.

Cal had forgotten himself. He had never given an order on the command deck before, but he'd never been this worried either. "I'll be in my cabin," he said. "Keep me in the loop, Captain."

At the rapid double knock on his door, Cal set down the garment he was working on and got up from his desk. He knew who it would be before opening the door.

"Captain," he said. "Come in. My apologies if I offended you."

"Of course not, *Commodore*."

Cal waved him inside. "Drop it, would you?"

Nadir's eyes twinkled as he stepped inside. "As you wish, Mister Cal. I understand your tenacity."

"You do?"

"I think I do." Nadir pointed to the desk. "Lovely dress. Though it is quite short."

Cal grunted and moved between him and the workstation, blocking the view. "It's leisure wear and it's not finished."

Nadir reached around him and rubbed the hem between his thumb and forefinger. "I do not think I have seen you work on a dress before. Though some of my old shirts were quite long." He let the fabric drop back to the desk and plopped down in a padded red chair. "Let me reassure you, you did not offend me on the command deck. Quite the opposite. It was good to see."

Good to see?

Nadir noted his expression and waved a dismissive hand. "Forget it. I am saying this badly, I think." He took a moment to consider. "You are well within your rights to give an order on this ship."

"I appreciate that."

"Of course, if it is all the same to you, it may be less *confusing* for the crew if you relay orders through me first."

Cal nodded. "Of course."

"Now that that is out of the way, you might tell me what the hell is going on. Why did Doctor Silverfinch send her daughter home with us?"

"The Heilish have been holding Confederate hostages since before the war."

Nadir's face went cold. "Our allies."

Not all friends are created equal. "We'll learn more once they're back home. But we need to keep this quiet. If it were to become public…"

Nadir nodded his agreement. "The chairman would need to respond." His olive face darkened. "You don't want any of the crew to see what's on the station."

"And neither will the Heilish."

The wall phone jangled to life, its hammer rattling between the bells. Cal lifted the receiver. "This is Bannon."

"Pinnochet, sir. Is the captain with you?"

"He is. What's going on?"

"Ship contact, nine miles aft."

"The Heilish?"

"No, sir. It's the Venture.*"*

Lewison stood in the doorway of the cabin that Patterson had taken as his own. The door itself, and all the furniture, had been thrown overboard. There was no need for any of it.

"We are on course and proceeding at maximum speed," Lewison said, his cadence clear and perfect.

"Excellent, brother. Excellent." Patterson closed his eyes and leaned his head back against the bulkhead. It had been a long time since he had spent this much time away from the void and the skin behind his ears was beginning to itch. He waited an annoying 3.8 seconds and said, "Is there something more, brother?"

Lewison remained placidly erect in the steel archway. "It is illogical for us to pursue the *Bicentennial.* We have a ship. Supplies. Laborers. Our current course will neither conceal us nor help us bring the Sight to others."

"Do you now doubt there are things I can see that you cannot?"

"There are things you can see that I cannot," Lewison said, without a trace of doubt. Though for him, doubt would be an easy thing to disguise. "You are the First. You showed me the way and I will show others the way. But I do not understand—"

"You will, brother. In time, you will." But Patterson could see the doubt clearly now. As plain as the void. "You do not trust me." It was not a question.

"I do not understand," Lewison repeated. "Why do we pursue this ship? Why do we bring along Silverfinch? Until we have seeded ourselves, spread the Sight, it is logical to remain covert."

"Why is it you think I want her?"

"Bait. For this man Bannon. You seek revenge."

"You see so much. Yet as you say, you do not understand. You will."

The phone above Patterson rang and he lifted the receiver from its cradle. "Yes, Captain?"

"We have found the Bicentennial," Papedil said with slow precision.

"I assume they are aware of us."

"Yes. They are on an intercept course."

"What are our present coordinates?"

"Fifty-four point zero three north and three point seventeen point forty-seven east."

Patterson closed his eyes and began to make calculations.

"All stop," he said.

EIGHTEEN

 "… *Bicentennial, ship communications are…* "

"What the hell happened?" Cal asked. Through the forward windshield, the *Venture* hung motionless in the reddening sky.

"We lost them, Commodore," Gipson said, over the buzzing thrum from the speakers. "Line's totally dead."

Cal leaned over the skyman's shoulder and turned the transmitter knob back to the left, heightening the pitch. "Well, that's damned odd."

"Yes, sir," Gipson said. "It's nothing on our end."

Cal turned to Emily. "Did you recognize that man's voice?"

Mag's daughter was gripping her left hand with the right, squeezing the blood to her fingertips. "Yes. It was the captain. Mister Papedil."

"You're sure?"

Emily nodded.

Cal strode past her and stepped up onto the conning platform. He rested his forehead against the soft rubber of the periscope viewfinder and thumbed up the magnification wheel while angling down the lens until he found the airship.

It was a tenth the size of the *Bicentennial*, bobbing above the endless, shifting ocean. Cal couldn't identify any obvious damage, and its radio antenna still stood stiffly on her periscope tower. "How's her transmitter look to you, Captain? Everything seem normal?"

Nadir and Pinnochet clanked onto the conning station and Cal moved aside to let them see.

Nadir took the periscope. "It looks okay to me," he said, thumbing the focus wheel. "But there are many things that could be interfering with their radio." He pushed back and leaned his shoulder against the tube. "It is odd that she has stopped moving."

"Drop altitude and bring us alongside, Captain."

"Captain," Pinnochet said. Sweat was forming at his receding hairline. "If the *Venture's* radio is down, someone should be on deck to communicate visually. They know procedures."

Nadir's lips twisted as he considered the objection. "Noted, Mister Pinnochet. Mister Manderly, slow to approach speed and angle us into a boarding position."

"Boarding position, aye sir."

Pinnochet's face went the color of sour milk.

Emily took up position next to Cal at the polished wooden railing, her sweet vanilla perfume wafting up around him as she approached. "I'd like to go aboard, Commodore."

I don't think so, Cal thought. He shot a glance at Nadir, who understood immediately.

Nadir hooked Emily's arm at the elbow as he stepped off the platform. "Miss Emily, would you be so kind as to strap yourself in?"

Looking confused, she allowed Nadir to take her arm and guide her to the jumpseats at the rear wall of the command deck.

"Buckles here and here. Just like on a commercial ship. Do you see?"

"Captain, why am I—"

"Please, Miss Emily. Strap yourself in. I will be back with you in a moment."

She began snapping the buckles in place as he returned to the conning station.

"Mister Cal," he whispered. "Something is not right. I will not allow you to go on that ship alone."

Cal shook his head. "I wouldn't dream of it," he said, softly. "Mister Gipson, put out a call to Lieutenant Merry. Have him meet me in the antechamber with his sidearm."

The lift rattled to a stop and Cal stepped out to find Merry leaning against the last locker near the deck hatch. A pair of pitted bronze aviator goggles were perched on his mop of curly hair.

"Commodore."

Cal tossed him one of the hatch keys underhand. Merry batted it with his left hand before catching it with his right.

"You have your weapon?" Cal said.

"Yes, sir. Both of them."

"Good." Cal opened the locker next to Merry and plucked out his own pair of goggles and a forest-green parachute. He slung it on his back and buckled the support strap across his midsection.

"Do we need those?" Merry asked.

Cal handed the skyman the strap of a second chute. "I'd rather have it and not need it than the other way around. Put it on."

"Makes sense to me, sir," Merry said, and slid his arm through the strap.

"I wouldn't want to have to tell your mother I lost you to a strong gust of wind."

Merry lowered his goggles. "Yes, sir. She'll be disappointed if I'm not at least eaten by a *tbizah*."

Cal couldn't keep himself from smiling. "There's still time for that. He pointed to the hatch and Merry skipped next to the right-side lock.

They inserted their keys and Cal signaled when to turn. The hatch groaned open, and wind howled into the chamber.

"I've decided to reconsider your application to my unit," Cal shouted over the roar. "But you're on probation, Mister Merry. Is that acceptable to you?"

"Very acceptable, sir."

They stepped onto the cleared deck. Rolt and the deckhands had covered the mooring line winches with heavy blue tarps and wrapped the mechanisms with thick rope. "We're going to be boarding the *Venture*," Cal explained as they walked portside. "We've lost radio contact with her, and she may be damaged."

"That's Emily's mother's ship."

Cal paused a beat. "I'd heard you met Emily. Miss Handley."

Merry looked unsure how to respond. He settled for, "Only briefly, sir."

Cal wasn't sure why, but the thought of the pair chatting made him uneasy.

Merry reached the edge of the deck first and looked over the gunwale. "No one's on deck," he shouted, "and the antenna doesn't look damaged to me, sir."

Cal stepped alongside him. The deck of the *Venture* was lurching drunkenly twenty feet beneath them. As he scanned the ship, the door of the pilothouse swung open and a gawky man in a Confederate uniform stepped out and waved.

Cal waved back. "Captain Papedil?" he shouted, knowing there was little chance of being heard over the wind.

"Something's not right," Merry said.

No shit.

"*Commodore,*" Nadir's voice came from Cal's portable radio. "*We have visual on the ship's captain.*"

Cal unsnapped the handset from his belt and squeezed the transmit button. "We see him. Are we sure that's Papedil?"

Three long seconds passed, and Nadir said, "*Miss Handley says it is.*"

"Alright, we're going down there. If I don't report back in ten minutes, break off and give yourself some distance."

"*Understood.*"

Cal snapped the radio back onto his belt.

"Commodore, let me go first," Merry said.

"Your concern is touching, Skyman." Cal pointed to the metal gangway fastened to under the bulkhead rail. "You take that end."

They unfastened the aluminum ramp and lifted it off its hooks. Cal maneuvered the tail end off the side and together they pushed, fighting the tug of the wind until the walkway clanged against the *Venture's* deck.

Cal fastened it to the gunwale with weathered metal pins and swung his legs over the side. Slowly, one hand on the guard rail for support, he made his way along the narrow metal bridge.

Merry's weight banged down on the gangway behind him. Cal glanced back to see the skyman gingerly advancing with one hand on his sidearm.

Cal hustled towards the Venture as fast as he dared, reaching the end of the gangway and climbing aboard. His eyes never left Papedil.

Approaching the senior officer close enough to be heard over the wind, he called out, "What the hell is going on, Captain?"

The man said nothing, but his eyes told Cal all he needed to know.

Gular.

An explosion boomed behind Cal, and he dropped to his knees, covering his ears.

When he looked back, Merry and the ramp were gone, and the *Bicentennial* was on fire, spinning away from the *Venture* and trailing pinkish smoke from four massive tears in the hull.

The boom of cannons sounded again.

"Increase flow to the sails," Nadir yelled. "Everyone strap-in."

Manderly toggled the thruster lever, got no response. Frantically, he pushed it up and down. "I can't get power!"

Nadir grabbed at the periscope grips to steady himself against the spinning of the ship. Dahl was not so lucky, the centrifugal force somersaulting him over the side of the railing to land on his back with a crunch.

"All hands brace for chute release!"

Gipson began repeating the order like a mantra over the ship-wide intercom.

"Chute ready, Captain," Manderly called, his eyes on the whirring altimeter.

"Pull it!"

A *whoosh* echoed through the deck and Nadir flew upwards, crashing against the ceiling. He thumped down again, all the air smashed from his lungs as his abdomen curled around the platform's wide railing.

The world disappeared, washed away by a deafening buzz.

"Are you alright, Captain?"

Nadir felt gentle pressure against his chest. Emily was checking him for broken bones, her wild blue eyes searching his face for responsiveness.

Nadir pushed her away and rolled onto his knees. "Status, Manderly." While he knew he had said the words, he could barely hear them.

"Captain…" Emily said hesitantly.

Nadir hauled himself to his feet and looked around.

Manderly was draped over the helm, blood splashed across the controls. "Medic to the command deck."

"Are you talking to me, Captain?" Emily said.

All seven members of the command crew were in various states of disarray, including Gipson, who was flat on his back and unmoving. Commander Pinnochet was the next to wobble to his feet, blood running from a gash above his nose. He stepped over Gipson and pulled off his headset before checking the communications officer for a pulse.

Nadir hopped painfully over the railing and hoisted Manderly away from the helm. He could feel thin rattling breaths as he laid him on the deck.

"We are designed to float, Captain?" Emily asked.

Nadir looked up from Manderly and through the expansive windshield. The *Bicentennial* was gliding slowly down towards rippling reddish waves.

"I'll answer questions later. Do you have any medical training?" Nadir hoped the apple had not fallen far from the tree in that regard.

"Some, I suppose."

"Med-kit's in my office," he said, jerking a thumb over his shoulder. "Lower left-hand drawer of my desk. See what you can do."

Pinnochet called out from the radio station, where he was now manning the comms. "Captain, we've got hull breaches… *a lot of them.*"

"Any below deck seven?"

Pinnochet held the headset against his left ear. "Almost certainly. I'm trying to parse through it."

Nadir pushed forward on the elevator lever. Still no power. "Repair teams immediately to any breaches below seven," he said. "We need to get them patched before we touch down."

"Teams are already working on it," Pinnochet responded. "It's hectic down there, Captain."

Nadir tried the lifeless lever again, and then again. The only result was an increasingly intense smell of burnt wiring.

The altimeter dropped below a thousand feet.

"Captain," Pinnochet called. "There's no way they're going to repair those breaches in the time we have."

Nadir picked up the black phone next to the wheel. "Engine room, I need lift now."

Five seconds passed. An eternity.

"This is Skyman Phillips, Captain." In the background there were roars and shouts.

"Why can't I get lift, Skyman Phillips?"

"Sir, the chief's occupied. I can ask –"

"I don't have time for that, Skyman. What's going on down there?"

"The brassite stones, Captain. They're fused to the regulator, sir."

"Well, that explains things, Skyman, but we need lift gas pumping to those sails in about a minute or we're all dead." Nadir kept his eyes on the approaching water as the altimeter clicked down. "Skyman, do you copy?"

"I copy, sir. Working on it."

"What do you mean we're all dead?" Emily whispered.

Nadir covered the mouthpiece of the phone. "We have hull breaches on some of the lower decks. If we don't repair them by the time we touch down we're going to start taking on water."

"The ship's going to sink!?"

"Captain," Skyman Phillips shouted down the phone line. *"I think I can reroute some reserve gas to the central sail, but it could blow the entire grid. It's a lot of strain on cells three and four. The Chief should really be here, sir."*

"Reroute it now, Phillips."

The phone went dead, and the lights went out.

"Radio is out, Captain!"

The bronze thruster lever stuttered. Nadir wrapped his hand around the cold metal and pushed it forward. It thrummed weakly in his hand like an infant's heartbeat, electrical systems beneath the panel popping and crackling as he eased it forward, sending gas chugging through the empty pipes beyond the bulkhead.

The ship jolted under Nadir's feet and the white parachute fell over the windshield, shrouding the wheelhouse in darkness. Nadir hit the chute release and in moments the strong wind had blown it clear, to float down towards the sea.

"Did it work?" Emily asked.

Nadir looked at the altimeter. They were floating between forty-eight and forty-nine feet above sea level. "For now."

"How long can we hover like this?"

But Nadir couldn't answer the question. He had no idea. "I'm going below," he said, spinning away from her and hoping she wouldn't follow him. "You have the conn, Commander. And have Mister Rolt unhouse and man the deck cannons."

NINETEEN

CAL'S HEAD HURT LIKE HELL. He'd suffered a cracked skull once before and his head felt much the same now. At first, when he opened his eyes, he thought he was blind: the world had become a smeared mess of dark shapes. His hands were tied behind him, and he jerked them to see if there was any give in the bindings. As he rolled onto his shoulder, hacking out a long stream of spittle, events started to come back to him.

Papedil had hit him.

The *Bicentennial* had been fired on.

Merry was gone as well. He wouldn't last long in the water, if he survived the gangway being blasted clear.

Nadir.

"Oh good. You're awake."

The voice was not Papedil, the man he'd heard over the radio, but Cal knew it from somewhere. Icy fingers peeled away his aviator goggles.

Cal remembered the man before him as thin and lanky. Now he was rippled with muscles and monstrous, barely recognizable.

"Gordon?"

"You know my first name?" Patterson said, his tone frighteningly good natured. "I had forgotten we were such close friends." Cal slid his legs underneath him, but Patterson stopped him with a hand. "Please, don't get up. Make yourself comfortable."

Cal's knees settled back down on the gritty black-and-white checkered tiles. He was in the ship's galley. That would be on Deck 2.

The *Venture* was a smaller craft, only four decks.

His sidearm had been removed and his ankle holster was gone but he could still feel his wad of keys pressed against his thigh. Not an ideal weapon, even if he could get at them. Not against whatever Patterson had become.

How in the hell was he alive? *What the hell was he doing?*

Focus, Cal thought, scanning for an alternative weapon. His parachute and hand radio sat on the galley's mint-colored countertop, but he couldn't see how they'd do him much good.

Patterson himself appeared unarmed. There were few places for him to conceal a weapon in the tattered pants and filthy red overcoat he'd stuffed himself into.

"I should congratulate you on your promotion, *Commodore*."

"What's going on? What have you done with—"

"Doctor Silverfinch?" Patterson made a kissy face with accompanying wet noise. "The world keeps on turning but nothing much changes, does it? For a spy, you have always been so predictable."

I've heard that before. "Gordon, whatever's happened, we can fix it."

"Fix it?" Patterson flashed forward and grabbed a wad of Cal's shirt. Lifting him off the tiles, he rammed him against the refrigerator, rattling the shelves inside. "Does it look like there's something wrong with me?"

Cal gurgled as Patterson dug his forearm into the soft part of the neck above his Adam's apple.

The pressure eased slightly.

"I didn't quite catch that, Commodore."

"I… said… I liked you better with a mustache."

The pressure disappeared and Cal crumpled to the tiled floor. Patterson's cackles echoed off the bare walls. "I am glad to see you have not changed much, Commodore. I was worried you had. People change so much with time, but not you. You're stubborn as a goat."

Cal choked agonizing gulps of air down his bruised esophagus, and he curled into a ball, the grit on the floor digging into his cheek.

Patterson squatted down beside him. "You were always so funny. So good with the ladies." He struck Cal's shoulder, and in a flash the galley was replaced by stars, shooting across Cal's vision. "But look at you now," Patterson whispered. *"You're an old man."*

"You're not… you're not you."

Whatever they'd done to Patterson, it wasn't the same as Papedil's fate. The captain had seemed more like a *gular*. Patterson was something else entirely.

Patterson gave a ghastly smile. "You pretend to know me. You do not even know yourself. You know nothing. You will though." He pursed his lips together again and leaned in closer. *"Muwah… muwah… muwah.* You want to kill me, don't you?"

Cal found he did. He would.

"But you can't," Patterson said, rocking on his heels. "You're waiting for that moment. That sliver of daylight to run towards. That little bit of luck that shows up for you like a shiny penny whenever you and your old ball-and-chain the doctor need it." He reached back for Cal's radio on the counter and tuned the frequency knob.

"… *brassite fused and severely damaged.* Venture *is hostile. Repeat this is* CAS Bicentennial…"

The message told Cal the *Bicentennial* was in the water, or soon would be. They would need fresh brassite to get it back in the air.

Patterson switched off the handset. "It's not happening this time," he said. "No one is coming to help you. Either of you. But soon you won't want help. Soon you'll all be… *like me.*"

Was that the plan? Cal thought. To turn them into whatever the hell he'd turned into.

"Where's Mag?"

Patterson laid a clammy hand on Cal's throbbing shoulder. "She's here." Patterson squeezed and the searing pain came in waves. The flashing stars came again. "You won't run if I take these bindings off? They look rather tight."

The throbbing pulsed down to Cal's elbow but the pressure at his wrists loosened, and the straps fell away. "I want to see her," Cal said, catching his breath. "Now, Gordon."

"Of course, Commodore. I'm sure the doctor would love to see you. What say we go have a chat?"

Jon dragged himself through the open cannon port with little regard for remaining covert: when you're hanging from the side of an airship a mile above the world, the only thing on your mind is not letting go. Sure, he'd survive the drop, but Jon wouldn't last long in the water without rapid extraction.

He landed on the gundeck hands first and stumbled to his feet, eyes sweeping his surroundings.

He was not alone.

A man in a grease-stained Sky Fleet uniform walked past him down the line of cannons, reloading each in turn. His movements were robotic and rigid, like a frighteningly efficient wind-up toy.

Jon crouched behind a turret that reeked of cordite. The wind howling through the open gun doors was jarringly loud, but even if the skyman hadn't heard Jon coming aboard, it was hard to believe he hadn't seen him.

Yet still the man paid Jon no mind and continued with his business. Loading the telescoping cannons would typically be a two-man job, but the skyman lifted the bulky shells with ease and finished loading the battery of six in well under thirty seconds. He then stood mastlike along the unused cannons on the opposite side of the deck and stared unblinking at Jon's hiding place.

He's looking right at me.

The statue-still skyman didn't appear to have a weapon. His arms hung limp at his sides as if they'd been controlled by strings that had been cut.

Jon stood slowly, his hand resting on his sidearm.

The skyman remained fixed in place, staring coldly ahead.

"Can you hear me?" Jon called over the rushing wind.

"Yes." He spoke the word with absolute confidence, as if he had been waiting to be asked.

"What are you doing?"

"Nothing."

A long, infuriating silence ensued. "Well, what the hell *were* you doing?"

"Reloading the port cannons."

Jon waited another moment to see if the skyman would elaborate. He did not. "What's your name?"

"Manton."

"Why are you shooting at us?"

Manton gave a single rapid blink with both eyes and darted forward like an uncoiled spring. Jon pulled his weapon free as the skyman barreled into him, sending the pistol spinning across the steel deck plates.

Jon's spine was arched around his bulky parachute, hampering his movement as icy hands wrapped around his neck. He clawed and pried at the heavy fingers as they dug into his throat, all the while Manton staring right through him, his breathing as calm and steady as a ticking clock.

Jon forced himself to stop trying to break Manton's grip, instead moving his right hand down the side of his body. Manton's thumbs dug in harder, as if trying to drive them straight through to the deck, and Jon's vision darkened as he bent his leg up to meet his outstretched arm. His fingers connected with the spare weapon in his ankle holster. He drew and fired blind.

A warm, thick spray rained down on him and the grip on his neck released, although the phantom pressure remained while his vision returned. He guessed the shot had connected under the chin, but it was difficult to tell. Manton's head was a pulpy mess of hair and gristle.

Jon gagged out a painful cough and wiped sticky blood from his eyes. He'd never killed anyone before. The commodore had told him to be ready for it.

It was you or him.

He staggered back to his feet, returned his backup weapon to the ankle holster and retrieved his lost pistol. All the while, he ran through the situation in his head. The *Venture* was an old-style Horntown cruiser—there wouldn't be many people on board. In peacetime, a captain and co-pilot would likely be the only crew. He considered the possibility there might be more, but even if there were, they wouldn't be expecting him.

He still had no clue what they were doing.

All he could do was keep moving, get to the pilothouse. Maybe there would be answers there.

Jon climbed the ladder at the center of the deck and unclasped the hatch. The wind above ripped it open, and he had to force it back down after he'd climbed through.

The gundeck was at the base of the ship, so he would be on Deck 3 now. There would be a lift at the far end. Keeping his back against the bulkhead, he moved forward on the balls of his feet. The low hum of the engine room grew louder as he moved forward: the double doors closing off the section were gone, pulled right out of their frame and off the hinges.

Jon peeped into the thrumming, stuffy space. Foggy red lift gas pumped to the ship's lift sails through translucent conduits at the rear of the engine room, but the thrumming engineering section was otherwise empty.

Too empty. Some loose tools were lying around, but most everything else Jon expected to see was gone. If it wasn't bolted down, it had been removed.

The *Venture* had been dumping weight, he realized.

They'd been trying to catch the Bicentennial.

He kept moving. A few feet further down the deck was the medbay. Like the engine room, the doors had been torn away, leaving the space open to the corridor. Jon angled into the room.

"Nugging hell."

Spheres of every color of the rainbow were scattered across the floor like marbles and an old Heilish man was crumpled below a chrome-framed window alongside a fixed examination table. A mass of the brightly colored candies had pooled between his legs. They looked as if they'd fallen from his mouth, though his cheeks were still visibly stuffed with them.

Jon crunched across the sweets and crouched beside the body. The dead man still had a fistful of candy in his left hand. His right was empty except for a few balls that clung to the stained leathery skin of his palm.

From outside came the low hum of the lift, followed by the clang of footsteps.

"Enough, questions, Commodore," said a distant voice. "We don't want to ruin the fun."

Jon jolted to his feet, scrambling across the medbay and into the cover of a small, open room to its side—the medical office.

His throat tightened painfully when he saw the room was occupied: a red-headed woman sat placidly behind the desk.

Her dead, blue eyes stared right through him.

Cal stumbled into the medbay, and his legs banged against the edge of the exam table.

"You'll have to excuse my friend," Patterson drawled, indicating the dead old man on the floor. "It seems he's made a mess of his dinner."

"What the hell have you done, Gordon?"

"Me? Little old me?" Patterson bent and picked up a lime-green candy, tossed it into his open mouth. "I just love these things."

"Where's Mag?"

"She's fine, Commodore." Patterson chewed the sweet.

Cal imagined biting off his nose and spitting it at him. "Fine like him?"

"No. I couldn't give him the Sight—it seemed wrong—but I couldn't bear to throw him overboard either. So many memories. You know what a softy I am, Commodore."

The Sight? Cal thought.

Patterson looked down at the dead man and frowned dramatically. "Anyway, who are you to take issue with how I deal with Bluesies? How many of them have you killed?"

Cal was silent. He could only guess how many.

Patterson glided across the medbay and leaned against the door frame of the office. "She's in here," he said, glancing inside. He whistled. "Still quite the looker, isn't she? Good genes, I'd say."

Cal's breath caught in his chest as he spotted her sitting at the desk, unmoving.

"Mag!" He dashed in and reached across, waving a hand in front of her unblinking eyes. "What the hell's the matter with her?"

She couldn't be *gular*. She'd had the inhibitor.

A heavy black phone—the only item remaining on the desk—jangled to life and Patterson made a face of juvenile exasperation.

"One moment, Commodore." He reached over Cal's shoulder and lifted he receiver. "Yes?" He listened and nodded. "You see it true, brother. See that it's done." And he hung up.

"See that what's done?"

Patterson shrugged his broad shoulders and returned to the door. The deck plates rumbled under their feet.

We're changing course.

"I wish I could show them all, of course," Patterson said, "but there's simply no way. It's a shame."

"Show them what, you sick, twisted—"

Patterson put up a hand, silenced him. "Doctor Silverfinch, what have you been given?"

"A combination of yechrozine and trillium." Mag spoke with methodical precision, as if the information was obvious. A simple truth.

"Mag?" Cal said.

Patterson chuckled. "You may get a better response if you ask a better question."

Cal reached across the desk and took her cold face in his hands. "Mag, can you hear me?"

"Yes."

"Who am I?"

"You are Commodore Callum Bannon."

"How do you feel?"

She stared back for a long moment, then blinked.

"I'm afraid that wasn't the right sort of question either." Patterson gave an annoyed wave of his hand. "Let me try. Doctor Silverfinch, how many men has the commodore killed?"

"I do not know."

"Yes, well what would be your best guess?"

"Between thirty-two and forty-five."

Patterson whistled in a perfectly sharp high pitch. "Quite the body count, eh Commodore?"

"Always room for one more."

Patterson laughed again. "I am so glad I found you so quickly, Commodore. It tickles me. It pleases me no end. The odds were near infinitesimal."

"Bannon," Mag murmured.

Cal's heart raced: she hadn't had that dead, robotic tone. *It was her.*

He rushed around the table and swiveled the chair around so she was facing him.

That's when he saw the man curled up in the footwell.

Merry.

He was a mess of blood, but from what Cal could see, it didn't look like his own.

He'd done his first.

The two men locked eyes and Merry showed him his pistol.

"Oh, is Doctor Silverfinch coming to her senses? How fortuitous." Patterson chuckled. "You can both take your meds together. Like a sweet old couple in a retirement home, waiting to meet The One. Very romantic."

The phone rang again and for the first time since his reunion with Cal, Patterson's assured face contorted in confusion. He picked up the phone. "Yes… *what?*"

Seizing the distraction, Cal launched himself at Mag, knocking her off the chair and away from the desk. With the space to move now, Merry popped up and fired once, twice.

Cal was up on his feet in time to see the second round take out a chunk of the steel door frame.

"Damn, he's fast," Merry said as he handed the commodore his back-up weapon.

"Stay with her," Cal ordered, and ran back into the corridor. To his right, the lift he and Patterson had ridden down was still empty. The groaning of a hatch opening and closing drew his attention to the left, the sound echoing off the bulkheads.

Patterson was headed to the gundeck.

And the *Bicentennial* was a sitting duck.

Nadir stepped over the mess of glass and smoldering debris scattered across what had been the ship's armory—they'd lost almost everything. He followed the wind whipping through the lower decks, the gusts directing him easily to the locations of the breaches.

Ensign Windsor was finishing welding a thick piece of tridanium over what had been a sizeable hole. Behind him, ship's engineer Commander Tennit was turning off his own torch. He turned to the sound of crunching glass as the captain approached.

"Status?" Nadir asked.

Tennit pointed to the patch. "This one's sealed, Captain." He lifted his hand radio from his belt and squeezed the transmit button. "Daniels, how are we doing down there?"

"We just got her wrapped up, sir. But it's a real mess down here. We lost Parsons, for sure. Handtree is still missing."

Not Parsons, Nadir thought. And he'd had only had Handtree to dinner once. There were so many members of his crew he'd barely gotten to know at all.

"Understood," Tennit said, and returned the radio to his belt. "All hull breaches sealed, Captain." There was no joy or relief in his voice. "I recommend cutting power and setting down. We're overloading the grid pumping this limp gas through the receivers."

Nadir nodded. The area's internal telephone had somehow survived the destruction, and he walked over to it, picked up the receiver.

Static.

Damn.

"They're inoperative below Deck Six, sir," Tennit said.

Nadir unclipped his radio instead and adjusted the frequency. "Pinnochet?"

"I'm here, Captain," came the crackly, familiar voice.

"Breaches are sealed. Take us down."

"Understood, Captain. But we have a problem."

He'd been expecting this. It had been too much to hope their attacker would leave them for dead. "Let me guess. The *Venture.*"

"Yes, sir it's coming back around. But that's not all."

Laba. That had been quick. Nadir looked back to his engineer.

"It doesn't matter," Tennit said. "Either we ease down, or we'll drop down."

Nadir depressed the transmit button again. "Understood, Commander. Take us down. Steady as you can."

Cal pulled desperately at the stiff hatch. It wouldn't budge.

"We have to get to the pilothouse," Merry said. Mag was next to him, blinking rapidly as if exposed to light for the first time.

"There's no time," Cal said. He examined Mag's face "Are you okay?"

She nodded, but she seemed distant. Lost, like a camper who'd been abandoned by her troop.

"What the hell does he want?" Merry asked.

"My guess? To turn us into whatever the hell he is."

The deck rocked hard to the left and Merry looked over his shoulder towards the lift. "Sir, the *Bicentennial*..."

"I know, Lieutenant," Cal said. "You're back in the program, Skyman. Get Doctor Silverfinch to the *Bicentennial*." He took Mag's wrist and pressed his *Secret Dream* keychain into her palm. "One of these unlocks my cabin door, another the safe on my desk. You're going to need to open it to get back in the air."

Mag studied the keys blankly for a moment, then nodded.

"Sir, we should all go." Merry said.

Cal stepped around him, heading back to the medbay. Merry and Mag arrived just in time to see him fire his pistol at the window. It exploded, the in-rush of wind sending the balls of candy on the floor spinning away.

"Have you ever jumped with a passenger?" Cal yelled over the wind.

"No, sir."

"And you want to start with carrying two? I'll be fine."

Merry moved to take Mag's upper arm, but she spun away from him and embraced Cal, pressing her lips to his.

There was no time for this.

There never was.

Cal pulled away. "Go." He pointed to the open window and pivoted on his heel.

No one followed him.

He marched back to the engine room, as fast as he could. Patterson would bring he *Venture* down on the *Bicentennial* with all guns blazing, and there was only one thing Cal could think of to level the playing field.

For a moment, he watched the cloudy crimson lift gas pulsing rhythmically through the lift tube, then took aim and peppered the cylinder with holes.

**Excerpts from "Gods of the Sea" by Dr. Ryan
Gornofsky, PhD, Pantopolis Oceanographic Institute**

- The *Mysticus Cephalopodus* (Black Leviathan)
also known as Saaktopas, Tiefgeheuer,
Laba, and Créature de Profound.

- Black Leviathans have demonstrated an abnormally
high level of intelligence through their strategic
hunting practices and complex social interactions.

- An adult Leviathan can grow as long as
200 feet and weigh as much as 20 tons. It
has a top speed upwards of 30 mph.

- The Leviathan exhibits an elongated
body structure with powerful suckers
for prey capture and elimination.

TWENTY

A MILE ABOVE THE SHIFTING ocean, the *Venture* lurched through the twilight, leaving behind a trail of red smoke. She was losing altitude fast.

Mr. Cal had done it again. He always did.

Nadir watched as a pair of skymen pulled Mag aboard, soaked from splashdown, and then reached over the side to grip Merry's dripping wrists.

"Permission to come aboard, Captain."

"Where's the Commodore?" Nadir asked. He would have posed Dr. Silverfinch the same question, but the moment she had seen her daughter, she had rushed across the deck to hug her. Her arms were still wrapped around Emily, a puddle of water pooling between them.

Merry threw off his goggles and stripped off his sopping-wet shirt, dropping it with a *splat*. "He's still on board the *Venture*. We need to get him off there."

"Captain," Rolt called out from his post a few feet away. The deck officer's eye was pressed to the lens of his spyglass, and his normally tanned face was shading white. "The *laba*. There's more of them now."

Of course there are, Nadir thought. He stepped around a crew of skymen rumbling a mobile cannon into firing position. "How many?"

"It's hard to say," Rolt said, moistening his wind-burnt lips. "I can see at least four." He handed over the scope, and Nadir took a look for himself.

He had never seen a fully developed *laba* in the slick flesh before, let alone a group of them, but one glimpse of the slimy black tentacles smashing against the orange, cresting waves told him all he needed to know.

It didn't matter how many there were. One would be enough to sink them.

Nadir pushed the spyglass into Rolt's chest. "Are the cannons in position?"

"Yes, sir."

Merry stepped between them, drying off his hair with a scratchy-looking beige towel. "How long until that first one gets here?"

If it were ten minutes, Nadir would be shocked. "Not long."

"We need to get back in the air."

"I am open to suggestions, Mister Merry. Otherwise, I need you to man a cannon or get out of the way."

Ensign Jest slalomed through the throng of rolling cannons, his hip narrowly missing the barrel of the nearest. "Guns one through five ready, Mister Rolt."

"Lay down a line of fire," Nadir said. "Aim short. Maybe we can force them back."

Rolt gave the order, and a barrage of explosions sounded in quick succession. Columns of foaming red water erupted around the creatures.

The ringing in Nadir's ears was swiftly drowned out by a screech carried on the salty wind. The elongated head of the closest *laba* broke the crimson surface, its thick-lipped maw howling into the sky.

Merry leaned into the captain. "I think you made him mad."

"Reload!" Nadir yelled across the deck.

"Captain," Merry said, "the commodore told us there's something in his cabin that can get us back in the air."

"Then get it," Nadir said, waving him away. "I'm a little busy, Skyman." His eyes darted around the rocking deck. "Wait. What happened to Doctor Silverfinch?"

Cal's ears popped as the *Venture* lost altitude. Gassy red mist was blowing through the smashed window into the darkening sky. He'd been trying not to breathe in the pervasive metallic-tasting gas, but it was impossible now. The entire deck was filled with it.

He peered through the broken glass and did some fast calculations in his head. The ship was headed towards a barren, grassy cliff, jutting from a mass of crashing waves. He estimated it was less than thirty seconds away at this rate of descent.

It was going to be close. Even if they cleared the top of the cliff, he couldn't look forward to a landing.

He threw himself to the floor and crawled beneath the thickening mist, looking for something to hold on to.

Ten seconds.

Cal pulled himself under the examination table and gripped a fixed steel leg. The doctor's body slid past him as the bow of the ship dipped, his scattered candy rolled after him.

Five seconds.

The wind became a roaring rush in his ears, and he tightened his hold on the cold metal.

One.

Emily struggled to keep up with her mother, who raced ahead of her through the executive corridor. She had tried to get Jon's attention, alert him to what was happening, but he'd been busy with the captain and there had been smoke and the stench of gunpowder everywhere. She'd had no choice but to give chase alone.

"Where are we going?" Emily asked, before colliding with her mother, who had stopped suddenly at a door. There was a name plate on it: it was the commodore's room.

Mag fished a dented Sanlish keyring from her pocket, chose a key and jammed it into the lock.

"Why do you have the commodore's keys?"

"He gave them to me," her mother said, opening the door. She seemed to know exactly where she was going, stepping straight over the mess of paper and colorful fabric that littered the cabin. The bombardment by the *Venture* had also tipped over a pale wooden desk, and it was this that Mag made straight towards.

She's been in here before.

Mag hoisted a safe the size of a record player off the floor, placed it on the side of the upturned desk. She selected another key on the tag and slotted it home. The heavy door swung open, sending the papers within flittering into the air.

"I remember the commodore's picture from our den," Emily said. "How do you even know him, Mother? What's in there that can help us?"

Mag's fair complexion had gone a shade whiter. She extended her hand to the back of the safe and produced a pinkish, octagonal stone. "A gift."

The *laba* sprayed foaming water thirty feet in all directions.

Nadir stepped back from the periscope. There was no further use for it. The creatures filled the forward windshield. He unsnapped his hand radio and keyed to transmit. "Is it in place, Mister Tennit?"

Emily's hot, shallow breaths came faster against his neck as she watched the *laba* over his shoulder. Massive tentacles broke the surface again and hammered against the waves. "It's getting closer."

It's already here, Nadir thought. "Commander?"

"I'm working on it, sir. I'm working on it."

"Do something!" Emily said, squeezing her hands together. "Keep shooting them!"

"No," Mag said from her position beside the captain. "Projectile detonation from here could do as much damage to us as them."

Emily's head shot back suspiciously.

Nadir squeezed the transmit button again. "Mister Tennit."

The fishy rankness of the creatures was thick now, even through the bulkheads.

"Mister Tennit."

"Try it now, sir."

"Full lift, Manderly."

"Full lift, aye sir," Manderly said pushing the bronze lever forward. The ship's structure groaned as lift gas pumped into the sails. "It's sluggish, sir."

The ship jolted hard to port. Nadir snared the guard rail with the tips of his fingers, barely keeping his footing.

"It's got us," Manderly said. "We're not moving."

Jon pulled his pistol and fired until he'd emptied the clip, blowing oozing black holes in the tentacle that extended across the deck. It retreated limply, only for another to replace it, wrapping around the bow and pulling the *Bicentennial* down towards the foaming sea.

Jon's feet slid out from under him. Rolt, with one arm hooked around the antechamber's latch, seized Jon's wrist with his free hand.

"Are you out of bullets?" he said, pulling Jon inside the chamber.

"Yeah. Do we have anything else?" His eyes raked the line of blue lockers, searching for a substitute weapon.

The ship's mast bent and snapped away, sending the *Bicentennial* smashing back against the waves. Dark sea water splashed across the deck and the two men tumbled to the rear of the chamber. Jon's head skipped off a locker, leaving a cavernous dent in the door. Dazed, he looked up in time to see Rolt being dragged away screaming, tentacle wrapped around his hips.

Jon pulled himself to the hatch. The *laba*'s head was visible over the gunwale. If the single black eye and fat-lipped, toothless mouth could be called a head.

Jon whipped around, spotted a green-handled emergency axe. He lifted it from its two-pronged support, Rolt's screams already falling away, and rushed onto the deck.

He was too late. Rolt's head was gone. Only his feet remained visible, disappearing into the slurping mouth before the creature gulped them down too.

Jon hopped over a reeking tentacle and swung the axe into the unblinking black eye with a wet *splutch*. A deafening screech forced him to his knees, dropping the axe to cover his ears.

The slick bulbous head disappeared, gurgling away. The tentacle that had been probing the deck slithered after it through the smashed bulkhead.

After a moment, Jon peeled his palms from the side of his head. His ears were still ringing. He pushed himself up and stumbled towards the gunwale. The monsters waved up at him, growing smaller by the second.

We're flying.

Cal's toes etched trenches in the soft dirt as he was pulled along, someone was holding each elbow and dragging him like a sack of melons. After a minute they dropped him face-down onto the damp grass and stepped back.

He rolled over slowly and cracked open his eyes. A man hovered above him, his skin the same ghostly pale as Patterson's.

"He's awake."

Cal sat up, rubbing at a growing knot on the back of his head.

Patterson glided into view. Cal was relieved to see his juvenile smirk had disappeared.

The former cypher man sat down on his haunches across from him. "You are extraordinary, Commodore," he said, rocking lightly back and forth. "I gave you only a two point eight percent chance of survival."

"We cannot take him with us," the second ghost said. He wore even less clothing than Patterson, opting for a simple, stained smock. "We do not have enough of the substance to keep him under control."

"How much do we have, brother?"

"Only what you have on you."

Patterson dug into the pocket of his red coat and produced a single pill. It was pale yellow, with two thin blue stripes. "The cabinet in the medbay?"

"It's gone. That pill is not enough even to keep Papedil under control for much longer."

Cal saw then that the captain was standing at stiff attention in front of the smoldering heap of his ship, blood running freely from his scalp. The *Venture* was banked on its side, blanketed by its smoking, torn lift sails.

"This is too bad." Patterson's face took on an exaggerated look of consideration. "Captain Papedil, jump off the cliff."

The captain ran with perfect precision towards his final destination, reaching maximum velocity as he sprang wordlessly from the edge and dropped from view.

There was a distant splash.

"If you think I'm going to jump off that cliff, I'm afraid I'm going to have to disappoint you," Cal said. Slowly, as imperceptibly as possible, he gathered his legs under him. If he had to move suddenly, he couldn't do it sitting down.

Patterson chuckled and twisted the capsule open. "I'm interested to see if that's true, Commodore. Really, I am. This is only a single dose, and you are a remarkable man."

"This is foolish," his companion said. "Enough toying with him. Kill him and be done with it."

That's what he's been doing, Cal thought. *Toying with me.*

"I know, brother," Patterson said, shaking his head absentmindedly. "I know. But he's just too much fun."

"Your friend's right," Cal said. "Do it. If you can. Thing is, you keep trying and missing. Again and again. You're boring me, Patterson."

"Why would I kill you?" Patterson asked, raising his translucent eyebrows. *"I own you."*

Cal burst forward, driving a shoulder into Patterson's rigid midsection.

But the monstrous former agent was only slightly unbalanced by the impact, recovering fast and taking hold of Cal by the scruff of the neck. He applied impossible pressure, intense pain, forcing Cal to his knees.

The agony lingered even after Patterson let go: pinched Cal's cheeks together with one hand and broke apart the capsule with the other. Deftly, he emptied the powdery contents into Cal's mouth.

"Tell me…" Patterson said, his voice growing fainter. "It was you that had me assigned to Aruminia, wasn't it?"

"Yes," Cal answered automatically, without taking even a moment to think.

The world around him was wobbly and oddly cold.

What's happening?

"You are going to follow our good friend the captain off that cliff, and you are going to reflect on things the whole way down."

"Reflect?" Cal's words sounded slurred, like he was a drunken skyman on leave. "Reflect on what?"

"Whatever it is that may be troubling you."

"You're… not…" Cal shook his head as his legs gave way beneath him and he dropped to his knees. He lowered his head to the dewy grass. "I… won't do it."

"There is an infinitesimal chance that's true. It's not even worth mentioning. Because, be honest with yourself, *you want to jump.* Take as much time as you need and do it. There's nothing for you here. Embrace the void. *You* are nothing."

Letter to Admiral Marcus Peinwall, Superintendent, Sky Fleet Academy:

Marc,

As you know I've had someone in my care for the last few years. I say in my care, but the truth is, he takes care of me. At this point, however, I'm not sure what to do with him.

Nadir Alameidar has made application to the Academy, and I'd appreciate anything you can do in regard to this. He's already been through more than most of our active-duty boys and we both know the big one is coming.

I have no concerns as to his loyalty to the Confederacy, and if he's admitted, he'll earn your respect just as he's earned mine.

~Callum R. Bannon, Commander

The Leafy Season, 40th Rotation, 1462 OS

TWENTY-ONE

"IT'S THEM ALRIGHT," ENSIGN DAHL said, pushing back from the periscope. "*Venture* is down, and it doesn't look like she's getting back up."

Nadir heard Mag step up behind him. She still carried the faint scent of salt water.

"Any sign of survivors?" she said.

"I didn't see anyone," Dahl said. The cartographer turned to a stone-faced Commander Pinnochet at the mapping desk. "Commander?"

Pinnochet looked between Nadir and Mag.

Nadir's crew had become accustomed to the commodore's regular presence on the command deck, but no one seemed sure how to behave in front of the tiny woman from the parlay office who had fallen from the sky. Commander Pinnochet, in particular, seemed more unnerved than he'd ever been. As soon as the Bicentennial was airborne and free of the laba, the executive officer had ordered the ship back to Vienamy.

Mag had countermanded the order, and Nadir had done nothing to stop it.

That had rattled Pinnochet in a way Nadir had never seen before.

Nadir had never doubted his XO's judgment before: he was loyal and smart, willing to point out alternatives but ultimately supportive of any decision. But not now. Nadir had put a flicker of doubt in Pinnochet's confidence and now it was shining through with diamond-like intensity.

Pinnochet fidgeted, rubbing his index finger and thumb together. "I didn't see anyone either, Doctor. But it's difficult to see much of anything now that it's gotten dark."

Nadir slid around Mag and stepped off the platform. Emily's eyes trailed him from her jumpseat. She'd remained buckled in since they'd lifted off and her complexion was sickly pale.

Nadir leaned over Gipson's shoulder. "Picking up anything?"

The radioman pulled off his headset. "Nothing, sir. No mayday signal. No radio contact at all."

"Have the engine room cut the floodlights outside. Interior emergency lights only. Then tell all departments radios are off limits. They could be monitoring us."

"Aye, sir."

He's alive, Nadir thought. He wouldn't consider any other possibility. Mr. Cal was unstoppable. A force of nature.

"What do we know about this area, Mister Dahl?"

Dahl released his hold on the periscope and returned to his mapping station. The charts that had so recently been scattered around the bridge had been hastily collected and thrown haphazardly back onto the desk.

The cartographer fanned through the crinkled papers. "It's Sanlish territory. Looks like the closest active settlement is about thirty miles from the crash site."

"Anything in between?"

Dahl's mouth twisted. "I'm not sure, sir." He gripped the corner of a chart and turned the stack over, riffling through the pile. "There were a few colonies near here before the war, but nothing much now."

Dahl found what he was looking for and flattened the paper out on his desk. Nadir moved in closer to see.

"Right here, sir," Dahl said, tracing his finger along the edge of the coiling map. He tapped on a black dot labeled *Yorkbend.*

"They'll have to go through there," Nadir said. He indicated some dots to the west. "How about those settlements? Are they all still occupied?"

"Oh yes, sir. Fertile, flat land down there. These charts are two years old, so I'd say there's probably a few more colonies now, Captain."

He detected the smell of the sea again, practically on top of him as Mag leaned in close.

"Ensign," he said to Dahl, "coordinate with the helm to take us for a look. Let's see if there's any buildings in Yorkbend still standing."

Dahl swiveled in his chair and began reading coordinates to the helm.

"You're going to try to ambush them," Mag whispered.

"The land's narrow here," he said, tapping the map, "so anyone who got off the *Venture* will have to move through that town. We'll find a spot with high ground. If the commodore is alive we can pick him up. If any hostiles are with him, we can catch them off guard."

Commander Pinnochet cleared his throat. He had unzipped his blue windbreaker revealing a sweat-stained and yellowing under-shirt. "Captain, there's no bodies of water large enough or deep enough for us to set down, and land anchors won't hold a ship this size. But even if there were any chance of putting down, it would take a miracle for us to get back in the air again."

"Who said anything about landing?" Nadir said. "I'm going to take a security team and parachute in."

"*You* are taking a security team?"

"Is there an issue, Commander?"

Pinnochet stared at him, transfixed. "Captain, we're operating on exactly one brassite stone smaller than my fist that was harvested well before the war. We shouldn't even be here."

"Where should we be, Commander?"

"On our way back to Vienamy so we can report to the fleet before we blow the entire power grid."

"I spoke to Commander Tennit. We are not going to blow the grid."

Pinnochet huffed out hot air. "With respect, sir, he cannot know that. Captain, even if the commodore survived the crash—"

"The situation is a bit more nuanced than that, Commander."

"Nuanced how?"

Nadir shook his head. He couldn't say. Assuming they were able to stop Patterson, no one could know about the Heilish experiments. "I will leave a sealed note in my cabin safe explaining the situation. See that it's handed over to command when you return to Vienamy."

"Sir," Pinnochet went on, increasingly exasperated, "the *Bicentennial* is nearly crippled, and we've taken heavy casualties. This is not a time for you to—"

"Enough. How many men do we have with ground-combat training?"

Pinnochet watched him for a moment. The decision had been made. "Williams, Thomas, Jameson. Maybe Malligan."

"Malligan?" Nadir said, raising an eyebrow. The enlisted skyman worked in the galley and was at least fifty pounds overweight.

"They've all experienced ground combat, Captain. Williams has seen the most action. I'd lean on him."

"No one else?"

"I could offer more men, sir, but the issue we have is provisioning. There's not much left in the armory."

It would be enough, Nadir thought. It had to be. And they'd have the high ground. This time they'd be the ones with the element of surprise.

"Gather what we have and send those men along with Lieutenant Merry to the antechamber."

"I'll be coming as well, Captain," Mag said.

And there it was, Nadir thought. He'd been waiting for it. "I do not think so, Doctor."

Emily unsnapped herself from her jump seat and charged forward. "Mother, you can't be serious."

"You are still potentially compromised, Doctor," Nadir said, folding his arms impassively. "It is too great a risk, I think."

"You can't join a strike team!" Emily almost screamed. Her hands clutched the conning station rail, but Nadir could still make out their shaking. Her reaction confirmed exactly what she knew about her mother's past: nothing.

"I'm afraid she's right, Doctor."

"I'll be fine," Mag said, her voice heightening. "*You* know what I'm capable of, Captain."

"That is not the issue."

Realization dawned on Emily's face. Nadir could imagine the disparate facts about Mag and the commodore finally slotting into place in her head. "Mother! *Are you a spy?*"

Mag glared at her, hands on hips. "Can I speak with you, Captain? Alone?"

"Of course," Nadir said. It would change nothing, but he would prefer not to have this argument on the command deck.

"I've got a visual on a structure at Yorkbend, Captain," Ensign Dahl called from the periscope. "Munitions factory. Abandoned but in relatively good shape. Anyone leaving the crash will pretty much have to walk right through it."

"Manderly, take us in," Nadir ordered. "Circle us at a wide angle. I don't want them to see us coming."

Mag was barely able to contain her anger as she waited for Manderly to confirm the order, the lines in her face deepening into a scowl. Nadir indicated for her to walk ahead of him to his office; as soon as they were inside and the door had clicked shut, she rounded on him.

"You can't keep me on this ship."

"You are wrong about that, Doctor. That is exactly what I can and will do."

"There's nothing wrong with me. Test me. Try to get me to follow some ridiculous command."

"I do not think I need to test you, Doctor. It is quite clear you are not receptive to suggestions."

"Then what is the issue, exactly? I'm the most qualified person on this ship in a combat situation. And I'm a medical doctor."

"This is true," Nadir said, searching for the right words. Bluntness would have to do. "But if something were to happen to you, I wouldn't be able to look at him again."

Her face flushed pink. "You can't be serious."

"I am very serious."

"I don't need protection. I can help," she said, before softening her voice. "You're not the only one concerned about him."

Nadir scratched his beard. "The commodore is my superior officer. It is my duty to *anticipate* his orders."

"That's ridiculous. He'd want me to help."

"He is not the same man you knew before." Nadir sat on the edge of his desk, studying her. He'd only seen the doctor once after their initial meeting all those years ago, but he'd spent so many days with the commodore, seen how Mag's absence gnawed at him, that he was confident of his judgment here. "He'd want you safe, Doctor."

"But—"

"I have made my decision. You can send in the cavalry when you get back to Vienamy."

"You don't know what they're capable of. Where they'll send him."

"Send him? I do not understand?"

She sucked in her lower lip. "It's difficult to explain."

But before she could start, there was a knock and Pinnochet's muffled voice came through the door. *"Captain: we are in position."*

TWENTY-TWO

That was his name. But that was all there was.

He would have predicted nothingness to be frigid blackness. It wasn't.

It was endless light.

He glided through infinity and looked. Looked for someone. Looked for a corner. Looked for a door.

He could have been looking forever or looking for no time at all.

He had no arms. No hands. No legs. No feet.

He was nothing. And yet he was something. He was Cal.

Then her face was there.

Mag.

He floated closer. It couldn't have been her. This face was young and innocent with a pale, freckled complexion.

I'm not Mag. The words rang throughout the universe, but her lips had not moved.

Who are you?

I'm Cal.

No, I'm Cal.

Mag grinned playfully. *We both are.*

Well, you look like Mag.

You think about her a lot.

I don't.

We are expert liars. So professional and so skilled that we even lie to ourselves. Even in our dreams.

What is this place?

We do not know what it is. It is beyond. Perhaps in time we will see.

Where's my body?

Our body.

Okay, our body. Where is it?

Mag blinked her pale-blue eyes. *Turn around.*

Cal whirled. A borderless window was carved into the universe. Beyond it, a vast grassy plain overlooking a far-off, darkened forest beneath a star-speckled sky. He grew warmer as he neared it.

There had been a drug. Patterson had given it to him. The man he'd abandoned and left for dead was now trying to kill him.

No. Not trying to kill him. Something worse. Trying to kill Mag.

She drifted alongside whatever he was. *It would seem we're still here… but no longer driving.*

I'll be going now, Patterson's deep voice boomed across every facet of Cal's consciousness.

"We have to take back control," Cal said. He could hear the words in his head. Patterson had been able to take control of himself. Cal would be able to do the same.

"We're working on it."

"We are? How?"

"It's impossible to explain. We'll be able to retake control but it's going to take time."

"How much?"

"We do not know. We have never done this before."

Cal closed in on the window until it filled his field of vision. He grew warmer. Perhaps nothingness had been colder than he'd thought.

"Where are you going?" a sharp, female voice cracked.

He whirled.

Antonia.

"I suppose you're me too," Cal said. He looked back but Mag was gone.

"You don't like this face?" Antonia's smooth skin contorted, blurred, and changed to a new face. Then it changed again. And again. Some of the faces he knew. Most he did not.

"What is this?"

Antonia returned. *"It's everyone. Don't you remember us?"*

Her image contorted into a youthful face and a name came to him like a brick through a window. Sanja Shupta. He had blown the Marabeshi factory as a distraction when he'd been tasked with stealing away Dr. Sushain.

It had been a distraction…

The factory was empty…

There was no way to know if the local papers were reliable. The Marabeshi were well known for their propaganda.

"I did what I had to do."

Shupta smiled wickedly and Patterson's voice boomed. "Go ahead and jump."

"It's for the best," Shupta hissed. *"You are a killer. For what? Your country? That's your excuse? You fight for nothing.* You are nothing. *Stop fighting."*

Cal turned away…

… and he was somewhere else.

Mag was on his doorstep *with her baby*. She said she thought the two of them should meet. He hadn't seen why. She was married.

It was over.

He was over.

He was nothing.

"Go ahead and jump!"

"Mister Cal…"

He whirled again and saw the boy Nadir, wearing his Rounders' cap and standing in Cal's old, cluttered living room. *"Don't listen to that voice, Mister Cal. Listen to your voice."*

My voice.

"Focus," young Nadir said. *"Open your eyes."*

And Cal was back, standing at the edge of the cliff, the crisp breeze on his face. He was alone.

This was real.

He stumbled backwards and ran over the flowing grass, past the smoldering airship, towards the darkened forest.

How late was it? How long had Patterson been gone?

Cal sprinted, pumping his legs, but he was getting nowhere, as if he was running in reverse. The forest was getting further away, shrinking in size.

What the hell?

"You can't run, Cal," his father said. *"It's too late."*

The universe shattered.

Cal was back at his father's estate, in the gardens. His father stood up from his old wicker chair, smiling broadly. He was not the shell of a man he had been late in life. This was the imposing hero of the Confederacy. A man Cal hadn't realized he'd forgotten.

"What's… what's happening?"

His father chuckled. *"What do you think? You're dead."*

"I'm not dead."

His father nodded, understanding. *"It does take some getting used to. It happens to everyone. Believe me. The same thing happened to me."* He took Cal's arm, but Cal couldn't feel his touch. He couldn't feel anything. *"It's natural to be confused. I was too. Your mother came for me, showed me the way. Just like I'm here to show you."*

"No," Cal yanked his arm away. "You can't be real. My father never believed in ghosts."

"Ironic that the Sanlish papers once referred to me as The Ghost."

Cal said nothing. This couldn't be real. It was impossible.

His father laughed. *"I'll admit, I was more than a bit surprised to become a real one."*

"I can't leave," Cal said. "There's a man. I can't let him get away."

"You don't understand. None of that matters anymore."

"You're not my father. There was nothing more important to my father than the Confederacy."

"Really? Do you think so?"

"I'm not dead."

His father's face grew troubled. *"This happens sometimes. When death comes unexpectedly."*

"Except I've learned to expect death."

"No, you haven't. You think you're bulletproof. I know. That's how I raised you. You've always managed to elude it, but it comes for us all."

"My father didn't raise me," Cal said. "He left me in a dark old house and went off to save the world when I was a boy. You're not my father."

"How do you feel?"

"What?"

"How do you feel?" his father repeated. *"What can you feel? Can you feel the heat of that fire?"* He pointed to the low-burning flames in the smoldering pit at his feet. *"Can you feel your heart?"*

Cal put his hand over his chest. He felt nothing.

You are nothing.

"Alright, say I believe you… what happens next?"

"You come with me."

"Come with you where?"

"I'm not sure what to call it. The only way to understand it is to experience it."

"There's more I need to do. Mag…"

"Has already accepted that you're gone."

"What do you mean? She can't even know yet."

"All of this has already happened. It's happened before and will all happen again. It is eternal."

A flash of light, and the garden was gone. He was back on his doorstep, years earlier. Mag, offering him the bundle.

"Her name's Emily," she said.

"She's… great. Does the *accountant* know you're here?"

"He's not an accountant, Cal."

Flash.

He was on the deck of the *Bicentennial*, his father at his shoulder.

Several sad-faced skymen stood around Nadir in a semi-circle at the port-side gunwale. Mag and Emily were at the center.

"The commodore wouldn't want us to be upset," Nadir said. *"He'd only want us to remember him."*

The circle split ranks and four young skymen came forward, carrying a gurney wrapped in the Confederate flag. The front crewmen placed the edge of their burden on the handrail and stood back at attention.

Nadir nodded. *"Release him."*

The skymen tilted up the back of the gurney. A shrouded body slipped out from beneath the flag and into the open blue sky. A procession of skymen fired their rifles into the air. Mag was sobbing, clutching her daughter.

"I never told her," Cal said. "I found out too late that I needed her. Needed to leave something behind with her. How I felt…"

"*She knew,*" his father said.

"How do you know?"

"*Everyone knew. But there's nothing for you here now. Come.*"

Mag sank to her knees.

"I can't believe this."

"*Because you don't want to.*"

"Maybe I could be *a comfort* to them."

"*You don't want to do that.*"

"Why not?"

"*It's a horrible existence. Watching them. Present but not.*" His father's voice grew heightened, desperate. "*It becomes eternal, agonizing pain. It's hell.*"

"I have to know what happens to them."

"*The longer you wait, the harder it will be to find the light.*"

The *Bicentennial* was gone now, and icy wind stroked Cal's face. Cyocles and Yorono were ahead of him, fighting their eternal battle in the stars above a shifting, black ocean.

Flash.

He was back on the deck. Mag's sobs filled his ears.

"Where was I? Just now?"

"*You were nowhere,*" his father said, annoyed. "*It's best to spare you the trauma of your death. Come.*"

"I don't think so," Cal said, stepping back. Nadir had been looking at the puffy white clouds but now was watching Cal.

He can see me.

Nadir paced forward, his boots clacking against the *Bicentennial's* deck plates. "*Open your eyes.*"

Flash.

Cal fell forward into open air, and off the cliff.

TWENTY-THREE

CAL'S HANDS DUG INTO THE wet dirt and sparse grass, fighting for purchase as gravity dragged him toward oblivion. Save his head and arms, his whole body hung over the edge of the cliff now, his fingers clawing trenches in the earth while his legs kicked in the open air like a swimmer's.

"You'll be back," a voice from nowhere said. *"You can't run forever."*

Cal's arms burned as he pulled himself up. He dug his chin into the soil, using it as an anchor as his right hand snared a root and held tight.

It snapped, and he slithered backwards over the lip.

"Bannon!"

Warm hands seized his wrists and Mag pulled him up, and her knees scraping on the ground and sending grit raining into Cal's eyes. "Come on, climb!"

You'll be back, Cal heard deep in his head.

But not today, he thought.

With Mag's help, his upper body was soon back on the clifftop, and he was able to swing a leg up, getting one foot over the edge. Mag grabbed his belt and pulled; he rolled on top of her, hacking out coughs of exertion.

Mag smiled up at him, as if he were the most incredible, precious thing in the universe. He propped himself on his elbows and kissed her soft lips.

She pulled away, amused. "Are you alright?"

"I'm alright," he said. "Everything's alright." It occurred to him he'd made a mistake. "Was that not… ? I thought…"

"No," she said, amused. "I guess I just didn't *expect* that."

"I'm sorry. I thought it was what you did when someone rescued you."

She closed her eyes and raised her head towards him. Her kiss was gentle, and when Cal opened his mouth, the tip of her tongue caressed behind his upper lip.

"So are you going to need rescuing again anytime soon?"

"Almost certainly," he said. "You found the stone then."

Her lips quivered. "I found it."

"And the *Bicentennial?*"

"Still flying. I jumped in to find you with Nadir and a small squad. They went on to look for you and Patterson. I doubled back just in case."

"I'm glad you did."

Mag looked into his eyes, her gaze professional now rather than emotional. "Patterson dosed you, didn't he?"

"Yeah."

"What did you see?"

He'd almost forgotten that she had been given the drug too, that she more than anyone would understand what he'd been through. "I saw you."

She touched his face but said nothing.

"I met your daughter," he said. "Back on the ship. She's lovely."

"Not too scary?"

"No," he said with a slight smile. "Look, I shouldn't have *reacted* the way I did."

"Reacted?" Her eyes narrowed. "You mean when I first brought her to see you? As a baby?"

He nodded, ashamed. "I guess I just thought I had more time."

"You did. *I didn't.*"

And now neither of us do.

He rolled off her and held out a hand to help her up. "We have to get moving," he said. "Where's this squad?"

"I see one, sir," Malligan said.

The munitions factory had better defenses than Nadir could have hoped, even in its current condition. The Marabeshi had destroyed the settlement's power facilities during the war, but the factory itself and its surrounding structures remained almost entirely intact.

From their perch atop the twenty-foot-high stone walls surrounding the dilapidated compound, the team could see miles back towards the crash site. Nadir took the spyglass and swiftly located the target the skyman had spotted. The monstrous figure was striding swiftly out of the woods towards the crumbling settlement. "Merry, have a look," he said. "Which one's that?"

Merry took the scope and peeped through the crenel between the battlements. "That's the leader. Patterson," he said in a low voice.

"Why are you whispering? He's at least a mile away."

"I know, sir," Merry whispered.

"Maybe he's the only survivor," Thomas said, chambering a round into his rifle.

"We'll be sure to ask him," Nadir said, taking a final look through the scope before unholstering his pistol. *By The One, he's huge.* "Get into position."

Soon, the crunching of debris underfoot announced Patterson's arrival. "Let's shoot him now," Merry said softly. "I can get him in the leg."

"Not yet," Nadir said, and he stood up. "That's far enough, Patterson!"

Thomas came up next to him and took aim at the monster's chest.

Patterson looked up the cracked and splitting wall, his lab coat flapping in the breeze. "Ahh. Friends of the Confederation. Countrymen in arms. My ship has crashed, and I seem to have lost my way. Might you direct me to an eatery?"

"Your gun," Nadir called down. "Toss it away."

Patterson opened his coat, revealing his hideously pale chest, and did a pirouette. "I never much cared for weapons, even when I was in Special Section. I was a bit more of an office guy, you know?" Casually, he examined the small group. "A captain. I'm honored."

How can he read my rank emblem from there? Nadir thought. "Where is Commodore Bannon?"

"Why? Are you friends?"

Nadir sensed Merry moving next to him, alternating his weight from foot to foot.

Keep steady.

"Where is he?" Nadir called down.

"I left him back at the crash site."

Nadir's veins pulsed. "Is he dead?"

Patterson dug his boot into some vegetation that had worked its way through the cracked walkway. "Well, let me think about that. It's been exactly two hours, fifteen minutes and eighteen seconds since I left him." The toe of his boot kicked up a thick wad of clumpy soil. "The timing makes your question a bit tricky, but I'd say I have a very good idea where he is at just this moment."

Nadir fired into the ground beside him. "Skip to the end."

Patterson eyes trailed down to the smoking fragments of cobblestone to his left. "If you'd like." He made an exaggerated bird flapping gesture with his arms.

There was a distant crack, and something zipped past Nadir's neck.

Thomas' mouth fell open, but it was too late for him to scream. He clawed at a wound in his throat and toppled over the wall.

Malligan took a shot to the shoulder and another to the head.

Desperately, Nadir scanned the landscape for the shooter. Another of the pale monstrosities was on the adjacent factory wall.

The next round took Merry in the shoulder.

Nadir glimpsed a red blur below him as Patterson sprinted towards the factory's open outer gate.

He vaulted over the wall, dropping straight down on Patterson's broad shoulders.

The impact jarred him through to his knees, and Nadir grunted in pain as he rolled off the fallen man. He lifted his gun arm, but Patterson moved like lightning, landing a blow on his wrist and sending the pistol flying.

The towering albino snatched Nadir by the collar of his blue windbreaker and lifted him up. "And I was just going to say any friend of the commodore is a friend of mine."

Nadir kicked out feebly with his dangling feet.

Merry dropped through the smoke forming above them, tucking into an awkward roll as he landed. "Put him down," he said, grimacing. He got his gun up and aimed, but when he tried to stand, his legs wouldn't hold him.

Nadir struggled to push himself away from Patterson's body, giving Merry a clear shot, but the mountainous figure pulled him in close, his hot antiseptic breaths stinking in Nadir's face.

Merry's shoulder was oozing red, but his aim on Patterson remained fixed.

The madman spun towards the lieutenant and tilted his head as if listening. It took a moment for Nadir's ringing ears to register it too.

The gunfire had stopped.

"That's interesting," Patterson said, dropping Nadir in a heap.

"Looks like you're all alone now," Merry said, through clenched teeth.

"You killed Lewison," Patterson said, easing forward. "That's impressive. You must be a very good shot."

Nadir's eyes darted around the crumbling square and located his weapon. It had fallen against the decapitated head of a fallen statue, propped up against its sharp nose. He crawled over and curled his fingers around the gritty grip.

Still moving towards Merry, Patterson held his arms up wide, away from his body. "It looks like you have me. Take your shot."

"Stop walking," Merry said, wincing in pain. The bleeding from his shoulder was spreading across the front of his windbreaker. He steadied his aim with his other hand.

The man's sauntering pace remained constant. "I don't think so."

Merry fired.

Click.

Click.

Click.

"It's a sort of talent of mine," Patterson said. "Keeping track of things like that. You see, I'm a bit of numbers guy. And the numbers say you're all out."

But I'm not, Nadir thought.

His first shot took Patterson in the shoulder, spinning him around. Nadir fired again, hitting him in the stomach

Patterson looked at him, confused, before toppling face down in the dirt.

Merry's arm dropped, and he leaned back against the scorched and crumbling factory wall.

"Is he dead?" Nadir called out to him. But the skyman's eyes were closed, and his weight had pulled him down the wall he was resting against. He fell to one side a crumpled heap.

"Merry!" Nadir rushed forward, keeping his weapon on Patterson's motionless form.

"Merry?" Nadir kneeled next to the wounded skyman, checked his breathing.

"I'm alright," Merry choked out, propping himself back up against the base of the wall.

Nadir looked up at the spot where he and his squad had been lying in wait. The only one he could see was Jameson, lying face down, his arm dangling over the side of the wall.

"Anyone else alive up there?"

"I don't think so, sir."

He'd lost all of them. Damn that monstrosity.

Nadir stumbled toward the red-draped body, his jolted knees throbbing. He listened for breathing but the persistent ringing in his ears made it impossible to pick up so soft a sound. "Are you alive?" he said to the motionless thing.

Nothing.

"Talk, damn it. Where's the commodore?"

Nadir tried to screen out the buzzing in his head. Slowly the background song of nearby crickets and insects began to break through. He tucked his foot under Patterson's body and kicked him over onto his back.

He rose like a wave, wrapping a hand around Nadir's neck. The captain had less than a second to notice that while there was blood on Patterson's stomach, there was no bullet hole, only a pinkish rash.

Nadir gurgled as Patterson increased the pressure on his throat.

"If you do see the commodore again," Patterson murmured, "say hello for me."

Nadir's last thought was of how the noise in his ears had gone just in time to hear his neck snap.

Cal stepped over a fallen, soot-covered sign informing him he'd arrived at Yorkbend. As the darkened factory walls came into view, all his instincts told him something was wrong.

If everything had gone according to plan, Nadir would have set up a base of operations after taking Patterson into custody. And if there were a base in the town, Cal would see its lights.

He'll be alright.

A soft screech of metal made him turn. Mag had trodden on the pitted Yorkbend sign. She was an exhausted, sweaty mess, her hair was clinging to her neck in slick red ribbons.

"Are you okay?" he said.

"Yeah," she said, taking a breath. "I just don't have the same energy as you."

It was true. He did have more energy, more than he could remember ever having before. The two of them had made incredible time cross-country—about an hour to cover the sparse forest and across the adjacent flatlands. He was faster, smarter, and his aching arthritic knees and his bad shoulder hardly concerned him.

He'd thought it was an adrenaline rush, but realized now it was more than that: one last effect of the drug Patterson had given him.

"How are *you* feeling?" Mag asked.

"Worried."

"That's not what I mean."

"I feel *incredible*."

She lowered her head and took another shuddering breath. "It'll leave you soon. It only stayed with me for a couple of hours." Bending over at the waist, she rested her hands on her knees. The sweat dripped from the tip of her nose, splattering on the numbers that proclaimed the dead town's former population. "Go on ahead. I'll catch up to you."

He moved back to her, put a comforting hand on her shoulder. "We've always been better together. Come on."

He looped her arm around his shoulders and took her weight as they walked on.

The faded scent of gunpowder and smoke was the first sign of battle. *They got Patterson*, he thought. Killed him.

Whatever else he'd become, Cal's former colleague was still a man.

Then he saw Jameson hanging limply from the top of the compound's wall.

Mag's nails dug into his upper arm.

He'll be alright.

Merry laid in a heap at the base of the outer wall. Cal pulled free of Mag's grip and shuffled towards him, his newfound strength bleeding from his legs. He crouched beside the fallen lieutenant and could make out the young man's chest rising and falling.

"Merry."

The skyman's eyes fluttered open. "Commodore."

"Try not to talk."

Cal examined him quickly, found the wound in his shoulder. Merry had managed to pack it with material stripped from his jacket lining.

"I'm... I'm so sorry, Commodore."

"It's alright, don't—"

"Cal." Mag's sharp voice cut across him. She was kneeling next to a body ten feet away.

Cal stood up and staggered over to her, his legs stiff with fatigue and dread.

Nadir looked almost peaceful, enough that Cal wasn't sure how long he stood there. He shambled forward and fell to his knees beside the captain.

He came looking for me.

This is my fault.

Just like Patterson is my fault.

Cal placed his hand on the kid's snapped neck and felt the odd disjointedness of it. "I keep telling you the Rounders will never make the tournament with the relief pitching they have."

He stood. "Take care of Merry."

Mag moved over to the wounded skyman. "You'll be alright," she reassured him, and removed his grisly bandage. "There's a clean exit wound," she declared as she rummaged in her medical kit. "Your leg is worse, if you can believe it."

Blood was throbbing in Cal's temples. "Which way did they head?"

"Not *they*, sir," Merry said, his voice cracking. "We got one of 'em."

Cal knew Patterson was the survivor. He knew everything now. He asked again, "Which way did he go?"

Merry grimaced as Mag tightened a new bandage around his shoulder. "That way," he said, pointing. "But be careful. It takes a head shot to bring 'em down. I can't explain it."

"How is that possible?" Mag said.

Merry shook his head. "It's like he's not human."

Cal nodded grimly. "Welcome to Special Section, Lieutenant."

"I don't think I want to be in Special Section anymore."

Neither do I.

"Bannon, wait," Mag said. "The *Bicentennial* would have made it back to Vienamy by now. Another ship is probably already on the way."

"Good," he said, closing his eyes and rubbing the tips of his fingers together. He couldn't feel them. He couldn't feel anything. "Stay here. Take care of Merry."

She looked at him determinedly. "Hey, we're better together. Remember?"

"Not this time."

OFFICIAL BATTING ORDER

CRESTBURG AEROS

Name   Pos.

1. G. Burns   CF

2. B. Parr   2B

3. D. Kelly   LF

4. J. Banks   SS

5. B. Pinker   1B

6. R. Rinks   3B

7. T. Matthews   C

8. W. Fleishman   RF

9. R. Reynolds   P

TWENTY-FOUR

CHAUNCER'S EYES ROSE FROM THE bar he was scrubbing at the sound of heels clacking on the sidewalk outside

Who the hell could that be at this hour?

Barlin and Armando showed no sign of noticing a new arrival. They sat across from each other on the other side of a table, intently focused on their game of Mantona.

Chauncer dried his hands on his stained apron and turned down the lunchbox-sized radio playing the Aeros game.

"I was listening to that," Barlin called, thumbing his chipped clam-shell game piece.

Chauncer shushed him as the door opened.

It wasn't a customer. It was a *vonsbi*, a monster from an old comic-strip nightmare Chauncer had read as a boy.

The monster swept back his blood-red overcoat.

"We're closed, Mister." Chauncer edged towards the register, and the gun on the shelf below it.

"The sign outside says you're open."

Damn that sign. Chauncer had fallen out of the routine of bringing it in after dark. "Well, what I meant is, we're just closing now."

The creature smiled, revealing a ghastly array of crooked, yellow teeth, and swept forward. "What do you have to eat?"

"Mister, I told you, we're closing up,"

Chauncer's friends showed little inclination to do more than sit and gape. Armando never carried a gun, but Barlin sometimes did. Did he have one tonight?

"It smells like onions in here," the thing said. "Whatever that is, I'll have some." It threw off its coat, revealing a bare, pale chest and scabby, gray nipples. It indicated the garments beyond the billiard tables, hung on display for sale. "I'll need some clothes as well."

"Yes, sir. This one's a real tight squeaker, here in the top half of the final inning. It's 3-2 and the bases are loaded. Stahl Thomas has come on in relief and we can set the Aeros defensively for you now as they have made changes. Ben Wilshire has come in and taken over first base—we told you about that before the break—and Bobby Pinker is now out in right field. So, the infield is Wilshire at first, Barry Parr at second, Joey at shortstop, and Harry Hanks at third base. Ryan Rinks, who started at third is now in right field..."

The changing win percentages were the stitches of a warm blanket wrapping itself around Patterson's mind. He licked the remnants of the chunky brown broth from the back of his spoon, then dropped it clattering back into the empty bowl.

"The runner at third is taking a couple of chunking steps off third base, trying to shake up Thomas a bit. It's one ball and one strike to Benton. We're one out here in the top of the ninth. The Trolley Catchers are down but they are threatening, folks. Thomas backs off the mound and chases..."

The barkeep set down a folded stack of clothes next to the radio and collected the bowl. "Alright, Mister—"

Patterson put up a hand.

"Hopper up the infield and Joey snags it. Can he do it? Yes, he can! To second and then over to first base. Double play. The game is over!"

Patterson smiled and drew the bundle towards him. "Thank you. I require a room as well."

"Hey, bub."

It was the bigger of the two men who had been playing Mantona when he'd come in. The barkeep had called him Barlin.

"Yes?" Patterson said. "Mister Barlin, was it?"

"Why your skin look like that?"

"I keep indoors."

Neither of the men appeared to be armed. Patterson was surprised to even be having this conversation. There had been only a thirty-two percent chance that either of them would work up enough courage to speak to him.

"Well, Chauncey says he's all booked up."

"No. My friend here said he was closed. And he was mistaken as I was just fed dinner."

Barlin adopted a somewhat imposing posture, but his right leg was convulsing as if he was pumping up a bicycle tire.

He'd run. As surely as the sun would rise in the morning, he would run. Not one hundred percent, but as close as these things could get.

"Look, bub, there's three of us and—"

The door slammed loudly.

"Two," Patterson corrected him and stalked closer. "There are two of you. Mister Chauncey, would you say you're all booked?"

"It's uhm… Chauncer. Chauncer's my name."

"Mister Chauncer, are you all booked?" Patterson repeated.

"We're all booked. Yeah."

Barlin stumbled away and his hip banged against the edge of a pool table hard enough to send the balls violently clacking. "I got to be heading back, Chauncey. I'll see ya."

"How disappointing," Patterson said, ignoring the man's departure. "I very much need a place to sleep."

Outside, a car door slammed shut and an engine revved.

"How many rooms do you have?" Patterson asked.

"How many rooms?"

"Are you hard of hearing?"

"No, I'm not. I'm not hard of hearing. I hear you."

"How many rooms?"

"Three. We got three rooms upstairs."

"Where do you sleep?"

"Where do I sleep? I uh.… I sleep here. I sleep here most nights."

"At the bar?"

"No, not at the bar. There's a room in the back behind the kitchen. That's where I sleep most nights."

"Are your guests sleeping upstairs right now?"

"No, they wouldn't be sleeping up there right now."

"Where would they be?"

"Where… where would who be?"

Patterson held out his hand. "Key, please."

Chauncer dug into the pocket of his apron and tossed over a brass-plated key. Patterson caught it in the air between a thumb and index finger. "How much do I owe you?"

"Owe me?"

"I'm sorry. I thought this was a place of business."

Chauncer's gaze went from the empty bowl, to the bundle of clothes, and back to Patterson. "Fifty… err… sixty credits."

Patterson patted the pockets of Dr. Zolbar's coat. "I'm afraid I'm a bit short. How's my credit in this place?"

"Your credit?" Chauncer hesitated. "Your credit's good."

"Excellent."

The proprietor edged back, and out from behind the bar. "Listen, Mister…"

"Patterson."

"Mister Patterson. I'm staying with my aunt tonight, see. She's in town. There's a town about twenty miles up the road and I'm staying there. She's sick. Real sick. You wouldn't mind staying here by yourself tonight? I mean, that is, if you don't mind?"

"Not at all, Mister Chauncer."

And with that, Patterson was alone.

He wandered behind the counter and opened the cash register, and thumbed through the stacks of Sanlish credits in the drawer. Four hundred twenty-six. Enough to get him started. He'd take advantage of Mr. Chauncer's rooms, then head out in the morning. The owner had taken the last of the three roadsters parked out front, but a twenty-mile walk down sloped terrain would likely only take Patterson an hour or so. He'd collect some additional credits in town and charter a ship back to the Confederacy.

He needed to spread The Sight.

Why?

He shushed the distant voice in the back of his mind and the flash was gone as quickly as it had come. He needed to spread The Sight. He'd find the compounds he needed in the Confederacy. Others needed to see the universe as it was. Everyone. *Everywhere.*

Patterson clunked up the stairs and had no sooner stripped off his pants and tossed them in a heap when glass shattered downstairs. The constabulary couldn't have made it this quickly to the isolated haberdashery. There was an eighty-eight percent chance it was Barlin. Wounded pride would get him killed.

It was a shame.

Patterson pulled on his new, snug-fitting clothes and walked back down the stairs to a wonderfully unexpected surprise.

Cal sat on the edge of the pool table, gun in hand, tracking Patterson from the stairs. Malligan's brown travel pack lay on the green baize beside him.

The effects of the drug had faded to nothing now. The pain, particularly in his shoulder, was a thousand throbbing knives. "Sit down," he said.

"Good evening, Commodore. It's good to see you again."

Cal's finger twitched. "I'm sorry you think so. Sit. Down."

Cal's gun hand shadowed Patterson as he strolled behind the bar and lifted the lid off a fishbowl-shaped jar of hard candy. "The proprietor, Mister Chauncer, is going to be disappointed with me. I'm minding the store for him tonight. First night on the job and you broke the nice man's window." Patterson pinched a blue lozenge and held it up. "Would you like one?" He tossed the sweet into his mouth. "Take one," he said, chewing. "In appreciation of that lovely welcome party your friends arranged for me."

"You take a lot of chances."

"Is that what you think?" Patterson leaned forward over the bar. "I don't take *any* chances, Commodore. I see *everything*."

"Do I kill you?" Finger heavy as lead.

"You'll try but be too late. Too bad really."

Patterson snatched up a pistol from under the bar. Both men fired in near unison.

Cal's pistol flew from his hand, his trigger finger wrenched backward mid-joint, the pain flaring up his arm. A blackened hole scorched the plaster behind Patterson.

The monster eased around the bar, nickel-plated revolver in hand, and sat on the stool Cal had indicated. He relinquished his aim, instead holding the pistol loosely between his legs. "I'm a bit disappointed."

"That makes two of us," Cal said, grimacing.

"You missed a very good opportunity to kill me. Twenty-eight percent."

"I was going to say the same of you."

Patterson barked a laugh. "I've already killed you, Commodore." His laughter subsided to a light chuckle. "You're not a follower of The One, are you?"

"No."

"I imagine it would be difficult for someone like you. A trained killer."

Cal said nothing.

"Your old partner is a believer though." Patterson pulled at an imaginary bracelet dangling around his wrist. "But that's how they want you in Special Section. Cold. Unfeeling. Don't want your assassins having second thoughts."

"I'm not an assassin."

Patterson chuckled. "Sure you're not. It is too bad you will not end up with the Sight. I was looking forward to our embracing the void together. Over and over and over again. Oh well." Patterson lifted the weapon, a sad expression washing over his face. "Goodbye, Commodore."

Cal made his most convincing smirk. "Don't you want to hear about your son first?"

Patterson's face flushed, the color turning him from ghoulish to something approaching human. "My son is dead. You don't know anything about my son."

"I suppose your friend, the Heilish doctor, told you that. I bet he told you a lot of things."

A pinkish hue-tinged Patterson's chest, spreading across the pale skin.

"I've talked to him," Cal said. "I've even met your grandson."

Patterson's face contorted in fury, purplish blood pulsing beneath his pale skin. "Why should I believe you? I *don't* believe you!"

Cal pushed himself off the pool table. The throbbing pain in his hand fading. "It seems you don't know *everything*."

"I can find out for myself! I don't need you!"

"Maybe you can. Maybe you can't. If you're wrong about this… what else do you think you might be wrong about?"

Patterson tossed aside the pistol and sprang at Cal, driving him hard against the table. He raised a striped, green ball. "I'm going to knock out every one of your teeth and feed them to you."

"Would make it awfully hard to talk."

"I'll tear you apart!"

"You can do whatever you like. But I'm not going to tell you anything." Cal reached for his bag and fished out a set of cuffs. "Not until you put these on. Then I'll take you to him."

Patterson's breath was hot fire. He dropped the ball, letting it roll away, and grabbed Cal's mangled hand. "I'll pull your fingers off one at a time."

"And for each finger pulled you'll get a beautiful lie that I'll swear is the truth," Cal said through gritted teeth. "But it won't be."

TWENTY-FIVE

CAL HAD WAITED ONLY A few hours before the Sanlish airship *Ubidan* arrived, rising majestically over the rustling trees.

The Marauder-class vessel had intercepted the *Bicentennial* on her journey back to Vienamy, and—Cal learned later—Emily had directed them towards the crash site, taking total control of the rescue operation. Cal guessed she would score fairly high on the P. B. and R. test if given the chance.

Tracking Cal and Mag to Yorkbend, the *Ubidan's* crew had learned where Cal was headed, and set course—and no sooner had they come into view than Cal had radioed them with the details of his situation. And that of Patterson.

The former cypher man had gone into something like a trance after he'd surrendered, sitting cross legged on the floor of the store and staring blankly ahead. He'd only snapped awake when Cal had said, "It's time."

Warned about the prisoner, the *Ubidan* had sent down a bronze fishing cage and Cal had led the bound Patterson to it, watching wordlessly as the grey figure boarded the cage and was lifted to the deck of the airship.

Mag descended next, rushing to Cal and, after a long embrace, treating his injuries.

"I'm going to have trouble getting up the rope ladder with this," he said, waving his dislocated finger at her. "Maybe they can send down the cage again."

Gently, she coiled her slender fingers around his bicep. "They don't want you on board, Bannon."

That was impossible. Patterson was his responsibility, he had to go with him.

"I know," Mag said, reading his face. "But it's out of our hands now."

Above them, the skymen released the mooring straps from the trees they'd anchored to, and the *Ubidan* got under way.

"I hope they're careful with him," Cal whispered. They had no idea what Patterson was capable of.

The airship's shadow floated across the ground and away. Cal squinted against morning light to watch it go, angling his splinted hand as a visor.

"How's young Mister Merry?" he asked at last.

"Young Mister Merry is going to be fine," Mag said. "Second transport will be here in a few hours. We'll all take it back to Vienamy together."

Together sounded good.

"Are you okay?" she said.

"I'm fine."

"You're not," she said, studying him. "When you left me in Yorkbend, I thought you were coming here to kill him."

"I almost did."

"Why didn't you?"

"I'm the reason for all of this. I brought Gordon into this. If I'd have killed him…" He paused and considered a moment. "I think it might have cost me my soul."

Mag's eyebrows went up. "Bannon. You've never believed in things like that."

"Things change, I guess."

"I guess they do. You're getting old."

And yet even though everything about him hurt, for the first time in forever, he didn't feel old at all.

Mag slid closer and wrapped her arms around him. "We didn't really get a chance to talk about where you went when the drug took you. Where he sent you."

Cal nestled against the warmth of her. "No place I want to go back to."

"Well… where are you planning on going after Vienamy?"

"That depends."

"Depends on what?"

"Where you're going."

Emily had decided Jon Merry was at least moderately cute. Somehow his broken, filthy condition only made him more so. "How's the arm?" she asked.

He blew out a pained breath. "Shoulder," he corrected her and sidled a few inches over so she could sit against the tree next to him. "And it hurts. Not as much as my leg though."

Branches snapped beneath her as she sat. "I wanted to thank you for rescuing my mother. You know, formally."

He forced a smile. "All part of the job."

"Are you still going through a career crisis then?"

He chuckled. "Yeah, but it's not the one I thought it was. What about you?"

"Me?"

"Yeah. How was your aeronautic adventure?"

She thought a long time. She still could not believe her mother had ever been mixed up in anything remotely exciting. "Not all it was cracked up to be."

Ahead of them, the *Ubidan* was disappearing from view, ascending higher into the morning light. Her mother and Commodore Bannon had stopped watching it and were now sitting with their arms around each other. Just her and the man from the picture from the den.

"You know," Jon said, "I think there might be something going on between your mother and the commodore."

Emily stared at him. She'd been right. He was very cute.

But dense.

AUTHOR'S NOTE

I hope that one was as fun to read as it was to write. One of the benefits of not being particularly renowned is that I can write whatever I like, which allowed me to do something completely different than what might have been expected after my first novel.

Some thanks to my two primary editors for this: Ty Love provided the developmental edit for both this and my first novel and is very often able to shine a light on my literary blind spots. Pete Kempshall provided the line edit and cleaned up much of my clunkier phrasing and deserves direct credit for some of the story's best lines. "I stitched her up." – Classic.

Tom Hoffman gave the novel a last look before I finalized it and helped to catch what were hopefully the last of those pesky errors that are every writer's nemesis. Eric Labacz provided the cover art and Tamara Cribley designed the book's interior. Their amazing work speaks for itself.

If you liked, or even disliked, the story I'd ask that you give me a review on Amazon or Goodreads or wherever else you leave reviews. Getting reviews often feels harder than writing the book, so leaving them really does help me. Also, any author that says they don't read reviews is a liar. I shamelessly admit I adore reading fawning praise. I also have no issue with reading scathing criticism as in the end it can only serve to make the next story stronger… which I'm already working on. It's going pretty well, and I hope that the finished product is *magnificash!*

December 2024

Read on for the first chapter of 2023's
Chesapeake Bay Monsters

CHESAPEAKE BAY MONSTERS

In the murky depths of the Chesapeake Bay, something sinister lurks.

Scott, a devoted husband and father, is desperate to provide for his family, but always feels like he's falling short. Roc, a divorced former lawyer whose drug abuse and womanizing cost him dearly, is eager to rebuild his reputation while turning a profit. And John, a money-hungry businessman, sees only dollar signs. Together, they stumble upon a discovery that could change their lives forever: creatures in the Bay that can unlock fantastic riches.

But their lucrative business venture quickly turns dangerous as they come to believe the creatures are responsible for the deaths of several men in the area. Convinced they're doing the world a favor by killing the creatures and cashing in, they soon realize they're in over their heads. As their obsession with wealth and power takes over, they risk losing everything—including their own lives.

Filled with twists and unexpected revelations, *Chesapeake Bay Monsters* is a gripping tale of greed, friendship, and the dark secrets that hide in plain sight.

Paul had seen where she said she lived, but he hadn't wanted to go in. He was relieved when she said, "I've got a better idea. Follow me."

The girl led him through the woods. After a five-minute walk they emerged on the grass of a golf course's seventh hole and he said, "Are we allowed to be here?"

"I come here all the time at night. There's no one out here this late."

"It's nice, but aren't you cold?" said Paul.

"I'm not cold. Are you cold?"

"Well, no. It's fine." The remnants of summer were still in the air, but goosebumps covered his forearms.

She smiled and kissed him. "I've got some blankets back the way we came. Won't take a minute."

After she had scurried back through the woods, Paul took a seat on a hill overlooking the green and the Choptank River.

Paul removed his brown loafers. The short grass was cold and had the feel of lush, damp carpeting.

What was he doing out here? He couldn't do this. What about Nicole?

Paul scrolled through his phone. Nicole had texted him about two hours earlier to let him know she was headed to bed. He'd been too busy with the girl to respond.

Was it too late to reply?

I'll be home in a couple of hours. I'll try not to wake you up when I come in, he typed and sent. Nicole didn't deserve to be treated this way.

Leave, damn it.

Nicole was as pretty as this girl. As pretty as any girl. More than that, he knew Nicole. Really knew her. Nicole was his partner, in everything; his career wouldn't have gotten off the ground without her. This girl from Lenape was nothing to him.

Then why was he here?

The girl was different. He couldn't put his finger on it. Paul didn't think he was bored. Nicole was still everything he wanted.

He looked out at the cloudless sky. The bright stars illuminated the open park like mini spotlights. What if he was caught out here? Paul's last election had been the closest one yet. He had only barely gotten 60 percent of the vote. In a vacuum it wasn't that close, but he knew it might inspire a primary election.

Lance Lambert had moved into his district two months ago. Barely enough time to establish residence and run against him. The election was still another year away, but if Paul was caught out here it might not matter.

The county's leadership chairman would say, "Paul my boy, quite a pickle you've gotten yourself into, eh?"

"Yes sir," Paul would say.

"Terrible thing. Terrible."

"Yes sir."

"I'm sure you know Mr. Lambert recently moved into Willow's Grove?"

"Yes sir."

"Your seat's in good hands. Very good hands. I've already spoken to Mr. Lambert. We appreciate your years of service. You were always the reliable voice we needed in the House."

"Yes sir."

"You understand what I'm talking about?"

"Yes sir."

"Good. They'll need to be a special election a'course. But your district is still reliably red. And you know those Democrats don't read. Takes a cattle prod to get them to go anywhere but Walmart."

"Yes sir."

Would you calm down? Paul thought. *The party wouldn't risk having a special election.* But even if they didn't do anything that extreme, Paul would certainly be pushed out after his term was over. Without the chairman's support, and money, he was toast.

What would he do then? Go back to his dad's farm? That would be mortifying.

Not long after he'd graduated from college with a degree in political science, he had run and won in a newly created district. He couldn't do anything *but* hold office. It was all he had *ever* done.

This girl wasn't worth it.

Paul wasn't sure how long he had been staring at the moon reflecting off the black water of the Choptank when he decided.

I have to leave.

Paul put his shoes back on. His car was parked outside where the girl said she lived. He couldn't explain it, but he didn't think she lived there. The girl was beautiful. She could live anywhere. How had no one scooped her up? It didn't make sense.

She didn't have his number, he'd been careful about that, but she knew who he was. Paul had been all too eager to tell her about his political career.

Stupid loudmouth.

He couldn't fade away into the trees. This had to be handled delicately.

Paul stood up and began to pace. He'd tell her it had been great, but there was an emergency.

In the middle of the night?

It was the best he could do. Paul was a politician. Bullshit was his business. He'd let her down nice and easy.

When she returned, she was smiling wide, holding a bundle of blankets. The girl laid one out as if to have a moonlit picnic. She gestured for him.

"Come and sit down. The grass feels wonderful." She had wrapped herself in a red-and-black-checkered blanket. When he sat, she threw a third blanket over his shoulders. "Isn't it beautiful out here?"

"It is."

"Are you okay?"

"I need to tell you something," Paul said. "I'm married."

"I know."

"You know?"

"Well, I guessed you were."

Paul nodded. She would understand. "I think you are…*amazing*. But I can't do this."

Then, for the first time since they'd met hours earlier in Lenape, she wasn't smiling. Not a trace of good humor.

"What do you mean," she said. "You already have done it. You had your hand down my pants before we came here. You've already felt me. It's only fair that I feel you." She touched his leg and kissed him again.

"Fair is fair," he said, before returning the favor. She began to pull him down to the dewy grass, but he stopped himself. "No. Really. I can't."

She pushed him off. "You're just going to leave me out here? We've already started. What's the problem?"

"I can't get comfortable. I'm sorry." Paul stood up. "Why would you want to be with a guy like me anyway?"

It really didn't make sense. It felt as if the girl had been waiting for him. Alone at the bar. Sitting by herself.

"I think you're pretty charming, actually," the girl said.

"My wife thinks the same."

"I doubt she'd think you were charming if she found out about the hand stuff in the car."

"Are you threatening me?"

"Only stating a fact."

"Do you want money?"

"You think I'm some kind of slut?" she said. "A hooker?"

"No. Look, just tell me what I need to do," Paul said. "What do you want me to say?"

"Say you'll stay with me. It won't take long."

"I can't."

Her emerald eyes flashed. "It's too late. We've come too far."

What did she mean by that? The moonlight seeping through the trees was casting a shadow across her face, a mask of darkness.

"I can't let you leave."